“Dancing isn’t all that hard. I could teach you the basics.”

“You mean here? Now?” Laura asked.

“Why not?”

Caleb swept her into his arms. The hand that caught the small of her back was firm and strong. He held her close, following the subtle cues of her legs and body until he felt sure enough to take the lead.

Laura could feel the light brush of his arousal through her skirt, and the sweet, wet burning of her own response. She closed her eyes as his lips brushed her hairline and nuzzled her forehead. They stood holding each other, both of them trembling in the darkness.

His mouth skimmed hers. She responded hungrily, her body arching upward to press against his. He lifted her off her feet, and she hung suspended against him.

Abruptly, he groaned. “Laura, you need to go back to the dance now.”

“Why?”

“Because if you st ... le
for what I do to yo

The Stranger

Harlequin® Historical #856—July 2007

Author Note

As a descendant of pioneers who settled the American West, I live in awe of the women who survived frontier life. The thought of how it must have been for them, facing danger, illness and unthinkable hardship every day for the sake of their families, fills me with admiration and gratitude.

Most amazing of all were the women who survived alone—raising children, plowing fields, herding livestock, planting and harvesting. These women had to be teachers, doctors, farmers—even warriors, when danger threatened their loved ones.

Having been a single mother myself, I know that even with a good job and modern conveniences, raising a family alone can be tough, sometimes heartbreaking. This book is my tribute to all of you, single and married, who give of yourselves to make a better world for your own children and children everywhere. Enjoy.

ELIZABETH
LANE

The Stranger

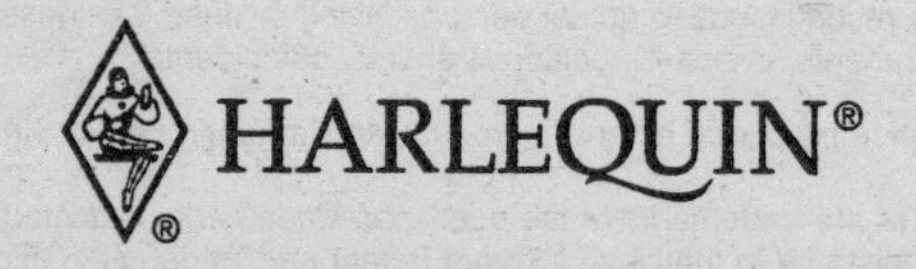

TORONTO • NEW YORK • LONDON
AMSTERDAM • PARIS • SYDNEY • HAMBURG
STOCKHOLM • ATHENS • TOKYO • MILAN • MADRID
PRAGUE • WARSAW • BUDAPEST • AUCKLAND

ISBN-13: 978-0-373-29456-5
ISBN-10: 0-373-29456-5

THE STRANGER

This edition published by arrangement with Harlequin Books S.A.

www.eHarlequin.com

Printed in U.S.A.

For my sister, my friends, and strong women everywhere.

Available from Harlequin® Historical and ELIZABETH LANE

Wind River #28
Birds of Passage #92
Moonfire #150
MacKenna's Promise #216
Lydia #302
Apache Fire #436
Shawnee Bride #492
Bride on the Run #546
My Lord Savage #569
Christmas Gold #627
"Jubal's Gift"
Wyoming Widow #657
Wyoming Wildcat #676
Wyoming Woman #728
Her Dearest Enemy #754
Wyoming Wildfire #792
Stay for Christmas #819
"Angels in the Snow"
The Stranger #856

Other works include:

The Guardian

Silhouette Romance

Hometown Wedding #1194
The Tycoon and the Townie #1250

Silhouette Special Edition

Wild Wings, Wild Heart #936

Prologue

New Mexico Territory, May, 1876

Caleb McCurdy saw the girl as he rode through the ranch gate with his two brothers. She was standing outside the modest adobe house, her arms reaching up to hang a pair of faded long johns over a sagging clothesline. Her figure, clad in a blue gingham frock beneath a spotless white apron, was small and neat. The loose ends of a yellow ribbon fluttered from her taffy-hued curls.

She looked to be about seventeen—Caleb's own age. The sight of her after the long desert crossing was like a drink of sweet, cool water.

"Quit your gawkin', boy," Caleb's eldest brother, Noah, growled. "Pretty thing like that, hangin' up a man's underwear, I'd wager she's already taken."

"What the hell!" Caleb's second brother, Zeke, grinned and licked his chapped lips. "Ain't no law against a fellow fillin' his eyes is there? Lawse, what a little sweetheart! Gets me hard just lookin' at her!"

Caleb shot him a look of disgust. Their father had always claimed Zeke was born crazy. As a child Zeke had enjoyed tormenting small animals. Then he'd hit his teens and discovered women.

"Shut up, Zeke," Caleb muttered. "What if she hears you talkin' like that?"

Zeke's only reply was a derisive snort.

The girl had seen them. Clothespins dropped to the dust as they pulled their mounts to a halt. She hesitated, gazing at the trio with wide, startled eyes like a doe about to bolt.

"Howdy, ma'am." Noah touched the brim of his grease-stained Stetson. "Didn't mean to spook you. My brothers and me, we come all the way from Texas, and it's been a long, dusty ride. We was hopin' you'd be kind enough to let us water our horses and fill our canteens. Then we'll be on our way."

She gazed uncertainly at the three riders. Caleb knew she didn't like what she saw. They looked like filthy saddle tramps, which they pretty much were. Noah was slit-eyed and lantern-jawed, with a scruffy beard that had been gray for as long as Caleb could remember. Zeke had pockmarked skin, prominent yellowish eyes and full red lips that curved in a humorless smile.

When the girl's gray eyes found him, Caleb knew that she saw little more than a shadow, dark and wiry and silent beneath his low-brimmed hat—a gangly youth who looked more like his Comanche mother than he did like his fully white half brothers. She gave him the barest glance before she spoke.

"Wait here, please." Her throaty voice carried an ill-hidden note of anxiety. "I'll go and get my husband."

Zeke chuckled as she fled around the corner of the house. "What a little honey," he murmured. "Lawse, what I wouldn't give for a go at what's under them petticoats!"

"That's enough, Zeke." Noah shifted in the saddle, pulling his long jacket over the hefty Colt .45 that hung at his hip. "Last thing we need out here is you makin' trouble with the squatters. You can damn well keep your pants buttoned till we pull off that big job and get to California. After that, you can hump all the women you want!"

Caleb glanced from one man to the other. He'd known all along that his brothers were wild. Still, he'd been elated when they'd agreed to let him tag along to California after their father's death. For a boy who'd never been out of the county where he was born, the trip had loomed as a great adventure.

So far, however, the journey had been disappointing. The endless days in the saddle, eating dust and listening to Zeke and Noah snap at each other, were beginning to wear on him. And what was this talk about pulling a job? Something didn't sound right, Caleb thought. Maybe it was time he thought about cutting off on his own.

But now that both his parents were dead, Noah

and Zeke were all the family he had. How could he just ride off and leave them? Blood had to count for something, didn't it?

Caleb's thoughts dissolved as the girl came back around the corner of the house. With her was a tall young man with fair hair, blue eyes and a long-barreled Winchester rifle in his hands. To Caleb he looked like a hero from the cover of a dime novel.

He took a moment to look the three riders up and down before he smiled and lowered the gun. "Mark Shafton," he said. "And this is my wife, Laura. You're welcome to the water, gentlemen. In fact, we'd be pleased to have you stay for a meal. Laura makes a right tasty pot of bean stew, and today she's cooked enough for an army."

The young wife kept her face lowered. Her fingertips pressed her husband's arm in what Caleb guessed to be a silent plea to get rid of the strangers. But Mark Shafton paid her no attention. The man was either a saint or a fool, maybe both. The smell of seasoned beans that drifted from the house made Caleb's mouth water, but he couldn't help hoping—for pretty Laura's sake—that Noah would decline the offer.

"That's right hospitable of you, Mr. Shafton." Noah swung wearily out of the saddle. "We been hankerin' for a home-cooked meal ever since we left Texas. I'm Luke Johnson, and these are my brothers Sam and Will."

Caleb shrank into his jacket as the two shook hands. It wasn't the first time he'd heard Noah give false names. Clearly he meant to cover their tracks. But why? That was the question that chewed on Caleb's nerves.

Maybe after they left this place he'd confront his brothers and demand to know what was going on. After all, he was practically a man now. He had a right to know.

"You can water your horses at the trough over there," Mark Shafton said. "By the time you've washed up at the pump and filled your canteens, dinner should be on the table."

"I'll get more butter out of the springhouse and set some extra places." Laura darted off like a little hummingbird—so beautiful, Caleb thought. Just looking at her gave him pleasure, like the sight of a cactus in bloom or the deepening glow of a sunset.

Inside, the sparsely furnished house was well kept and cheerful. Strings of garlic and Mexican chiles hung from the open rafters of the whitewashed kitchen. Sprouting herbs in little pots lined the windowsills. The plain plank table had been scrubbed and oiled till it glistened. In its center, a small pottery vase held fresh yellow buttercups and blue columbines.

Laura ladled the beans into bowls from the big iron pot on the stove, then joined the four men at the table. She sat directly across from Caleb, her eyes focused on her food. Caleb watched the careful motion of her spoon as it traveled from the bowl to her pretty rosebud mouth. She took tiny bites, as if she were only pretending to eat.

"We came west last fall, right after we were married," Mark Shafton was saying. "My wife had inherited a little money back in St. Louis, and I invested it in this prime land. We've got five hundred acres, with a good stream running down from the Sangre de Cristo Mountains. You may have noticed the dam I built—I'm right proud of it. It channels water through the springhouse, just a few steps from the back door, so Laura doesn't have far to walk. That's important these days." His eyes lingered on his pretty wife. A smile tugged at one corner of his chiseled mouth.

"Well, you'd best keep a sharp eye out for floods," Noah muttered around a mouthful of beans. "Strikes me that a big storm could bring enough water down that channel to do some real damage."

"So I was told." Mark Shafton buttered a piece of crusty bread. "But when I build something, I build it to last, so I'm not greatly worried. In a few years I plan to have one of the finest cattle ranches in the territory." He leaned back in his chair and regarded the visitors with a smile. "That's enough about us. Tell me about your trip, gentlemen. I always enjoy talking with travelers. A man can learn a lot about the country that way."

While his brothers chatted with Mark Shafton, Caleb stole glances at Laura. Once she looked up, and her dove-gray eyes met his before they flashed downward. After that he was more careful. He loved watching her, but she was already ill at ease. He had no desire to worsen her discomfort.

All too soon, the meal was over. Noah rose from his chair, stifled a belch and announced that it was time to leave. "We're right grateful for your hospitality, ma'am," he said, lifting his Stetson from the back of the chair. "It's been a long spell since we had such tasty vittles."

He strode outside, followed by Mark Shafton, with Zeke trailing behind. Laura had risen and was gathering up the bowl of butter and the pitcher of milk to take to the springhouse.

"Can—Can I carry that for you?" Caleb's voice squeaked, forcing him to clear his throat before he could finish the question.

She shook her head. "You'd better catch up with your brothers, Will. You don't want them leaving you behind."

The name threw him for an instant. Then he remembered it was the one Noah had given him. She had actually remembered it. As for being left behind by his brothers, there was nothing he'd like better, Caleb thought. Maybe the Shaftons would hire him to stay on and help with the ranch. He was a good worker and there was nothing he didn't know about horses and cattle.

But Caleb knew better than to dream. When Noah and Zeke rode out the ranch gate, he would be riding with them, and he would never see Laura again.

As Laura hurried out the back door with the butter and milk, he turned away and headed outside. Noah was standing by the horses, talking to Mark Shafton. Zeke was nowhere to be seen.

As he walked toward the corral, Caleb felt a sudden, embarrassing urge, likely brought on by having eaten so many beans. "Beg your pardon, Mr. Shafton, but would you mind if I used your privy?" he asked.

"Go ahead," the young man replied. "It's out in the trees, past the springhouse. But you might have to wait for your brother. He went that way a minute ago."

Caleb found the privy empty, with no sign of Zeke. He did his business and was bending to wash his hands in the creek when he heard voices coming from behind the closed door of the springhouse.

"Just hold still, girlie, while I get a hand under them petticoats." Zeke's voice was rough and ugly. "Behave yourself, now, and you'll be fine. Hell, you might even enjoy it."

"Please don't..." Caleb could barely make out Laura's strained whisper. "Please, I'm going to have a baby. You might hurt—" Her words ended in a gasp.

Caleb pounded against the wooden door. "Zeke! You crazy fool, let her go!" he shouted.

The door resisted as if it might be latched or braced. Frantic, Caleb backed off and flung his full weight against the rough-sawn planks. This time the door gave way so suddenly that he hurtled through the opening and crashed full force against the opposite wall. Something snapped in his shoulder. Dizzy with pain, he careened backward to crumple on the earthen floor.

His eyes caught the flash of a blade in a dark corner of the springhouse. Zeke, he realized, was holding his big Bowie knife against Laura's throat with one hand while the other hand fumbled beneath her skirt. Dazed and hurting, Caleb scrambled to his knees. His left arm dangled uselessly at his side.

"Get out of here, you stinkin' little half-breed," Zeke snarled. "And don't you go runnin' to Noah, or I'll carve you up like a—"

His words ended in a shriek as Laura sank her teeth into his forearm. "You hellcat!" he howled. "I'll show you—"

They were grappling now, the blade catching glints of the light from the open doorway. Caleb flung himself toward them but he was weak with shock and pain. A kick from Zeke's heavy boot sent him crashing back against the wall.

Laura screamed like a wounded animal. Caleb's stomach contracted as he saw the crimson slash where the knife had cut her face from temple to chin, barely missing her eye. He lunged forward, only to stumble into the shadow cast by the tall figure in the doorway.

"You...bastards!" Mark Shafton's hands gripped the rifle. His voice cracked with fury. "Is this how you repay decent people? By God Almighty, I'll kill you both!"

Laura had twisted free. She reeled against Caleb as her husband raised his rifle and aimed it at Zeke's chest. Shafton's finger was tightening on the trigger when an ear-shattering report rang out from behind him. He dropped the rifle, crumpled forward onto the ground and lay still. A dark red bloodstain began to spread across the back of his clean chambray shirt. Laura fell across his body, wailing like a child.

In the doorway, Noah lowered his smoking pistol. His face was a mask of icy rage. "Get to the horses, damn you!" he snapped at Zeke. "You, too, boy, unless you want to watch me kill a woman!"

"No!" Caleb staggered to his feet and planted himself in front of his brother. "Let her alone! Haven't we done enough to these people?"

Noah shook his head. "Show some sense, you young fool. If we leave her alive she'll go straight to the law. We'll have a posse on our trail before nightfall."

"She's going to have a baby," Caleb said. "If you want to kill them both, you'll have to shoot me first!"

Noah swore and spat in the dirt. "Damnfool boy! All right, come on, then. We'll lock her in the springhouse and make tracks. By the time she gets out we'll be long gone."

"No. I'm staying here."

"In a mule's ass you are!"

"She's hurt and needs help. I can keep her quiet long enough for you to get a head start and—"

Caleb gasped as he glimpsed Noah's raised arm. Then the butt of the pistol cracked against his skull and the world crashed into blackness.

It was the last thing he would remember about that day.

Chapter One

July 1881

On the crest of a long ridge, where the eastern slope of the Sangre de Cristo Mountains fell to high desert, Caleb McCurdy paused to rest his horse. Below him a sea of summer-gold grama grass, dotted with clumps of sage and juniper, rippled over the foothills. Willow and cottonwood formed a winding ribbon of green along the creek that meandered into the valley. If he followed that ribbon, Caleb knew it would lead him to an adobe ranch house with sheds and a corral out front and a springhouse just beyond the back door.

He had never wanted to come here again. But the memory of the place had haunted him for the five years he'd spent in Yuma Territorial Prison. Now that he was free, Caleb knew he had to return and face what had happened here. He had to find out what had become of Laura.

His being arrested had nothing to do with the crime against the Shaftons. It was later that same spring that his brothers had gone into a Tombstone bank and left him outside to watch the horses. By the time Caleb had realized there was a robbery in progress the deputy was already snapping the handcuffs around his wrists. Zeke and Noah had made their getaway out the back of the bank. That was the last he'd seen of them.

Caleb had been tried as an accessory and sentenced to six years behind bars. The torrid Arizona nights had given him plenty of time to ponder his mistakes. Staying with Noah and Zeke had been his worst choice. They were family, he'd rationalized at the time. Besides, it wasn't as if Noah had killed Mark Shafton in cold blood. Noah had fired to save his brothers. As for Zeke, he couldn't help being the creature he was. For all his flaws, he, too, was blood kin.

Caleb's fist tightened around the saddle horn. Lord, what a fool he'd been, tagging along with his brothers like a puppy trotting after a pair of wolves. He should have known his trust would lead him straight down the road to hell.

If the tragedy at the Shafton Ranch had cracked the shell of Caleb's innocence, the weeks that followed had shattered it. Liquor, gambling, women—he'd sampled them all. He would have done anything to blot out the sight of Laura's bloodied face and the sound of her screams.

His brothers had roared their approval and declared him a man. Then they'd staked him out like bait in front of that Tombstone bank to draw the lawmen while they got away with the loot.

Good behavior had gotten him out of prison a year early. But the hot hell of Yuma had toughened, aged and embittered him. He was twenty-two years old. He felt fifty.

Nudging the sturdy bay to a walk, he wound his way down the brushy slope. The day he'd walked out of prison, he'd taken work with a road-building crew that hired ex-convicts. Two months of backbreaking labor had earned him enough to buy a horse, a beat-up saddle, a gun and knife, a blanket and a change of clothes. With twenty dollars in his pocket, he'd headed east, toward New Mexico and the Sangre de Cristo Mountains. Now, on this day of blinding beauty, the long ride was coming to an end.

The afternoon sky was a searing turquoise blue. Where the horse walked, clouds of white butterflies floated out of the grass. A red-tailed hawk circled against the sun.

Caleb's throat tightened as he watched it. How many days like this had he missed, locked away in that sweltering heap of rock and adobe where the cells were ovens and the earth was hot enough to blister bare skin? How many days without fresh air, clean water and decent human companionship?

Annoyed with himself, he shoved the question aside. Self-pity was a waste. Rotten luck was a fact of life, and he'd long since learned not to whine when he got whipped. Besides, Caleb reminded himself, his time in prison hadn't all been wasted. He'd made one friend there, a dying man who'd helped him turn his life around. If his beaten soul held a glimmer of hope and truth, he owed it to Ebenezer Stokes.

Maybe that was why he'd come back here. For Ebenezer—and for Laura.

Without willing it, he began to whistle a soulful melody—a song whose words had long since burned themselves into his brain.

Eyes like the morning star, cheeks like the rose.

Laura was a pretty girl, everybody knows.

Weep, oh, you little rains, wail, winds, wail...

Those cursed lyrics hadn't left him alone in five long years. They had tormented his days and nights, conjuring up the image of Laura as he'd last seen her, slumped over her husband's body with blood streaming down the side of her face. Maybe after today that image would finally begin to fade.

Stopping at the creek, he watered his horse, splashed his face and slicked back his sweaty hair. The place he'd known as the Shafton Ranch couldn't be more than a couple of miles downstream, he calculated. What would he find there? Strangers, most likely. Noah had sworn that he'd left Laura alive. But even if that were true, Caleb couldn't imagine her remaining alone on the ranch. The best he could hope for was that she'd sold out and moved on, and that someone would know where she'd gone.

If the worst had happened, maybe he could at least beg forgiveness at her grave.

The creek was overgrown with brush and willows. Moving back into the open, he followed the tangled border out of the foothills and onto the grassy flatland. His gut clenched as he spotted the ranch in the distance. The memories that swept over him were so black and bitter that he was tempted to turn the horse and gallop off in a different direction. Setting his teeth, he forced himself to keep moving ahead.

He could see the gate now, and the corral where he and his brothers had tied their mounts while they ate the meal Laura had prepared. Mark Shafton's dam was still intact, as was the springhouse, spared over the years from the danger of flooding. But the whole place had a forlorn look to it. The windmill was missing two slats and the corral gate hung crooked on one broken hinge. Two dun horses and a milk cow drowsed in the corral.

The small adobe house was closed and quiet. The only sign of human life about the place was the batch of washing that fluttered from the clothesline in the side yard. Caleb rode in through the gate, dismounted and looped the bay's reins over the corral fence. He could see now that the clothes on the line consisted of little shirts and overalls, stockings, underwear and nightgowns. He could see the swing hanging from the limb of the big cottonwood that shaded the springhouse. Caleb didn't want to think about the springhouse and what had happened there. But the idea of children living here, running and playing in the bright sunlight gave a small lift to his spirits.

Taking a deep breath, he strode up the path, crossed the shaded porch and rapped lightly on the door.

"Go into your bedroom, Robbie," Laura whispered to her son. "Latch the door. Don't open it until I knock three times and say the password."

Robbie, who'd been headed outside to play, obeyed without question. He knew better than to argue with his mother when a stranger came to the house.

Laura waited until she heard the metallic click of the latch. Only then did she take the double-barreled shotgun from its rack above the bookshelf and thumb back both hammers.

The rap on the door came again, more insistently this time. Laura's heart, already racing, broke into a gallop. "Who's there?" she called.

"Caleb McCurdy's the name. I didn't mean to scare you, ma'am. Just wanted to ask a question or two, then, if you want me to leave, I'll be on my way."

McCurdy. Laura groped for some memory of the name and came up empty. There was something familiar about the voice that filtered through the heavy wooden door, but without a face to go with it…

Bracing the gun stock against her hip, she opened the door a few cautious inches. "What do you want?" she demanded.

The man who filled the narrow opening was tall and lean, with straight, black hair and a battered face. A closer look revealed jutting cheekbones, obsidian eyes and skin that was burnished to the hue and texture of saddle leather. He was dressed for the trail in unfaded clothes that looked recently bought, but what struck Laura at once was his expression. He was staring at her as if he'd seen a ghost.

His throat moved. Then he closed his mouth tightly, as if he'd thought the better of what he'd been about to say. For an instant his gaze lingered on the ugly scar that zigzagged down the left side of her face. Then he averted his eyes, as most people did when they met her.

Laura jabbed the shotgun's twin barrels toward him. "Well, then, speak your piece, Mr. McCurdy, or be on your way. Strangers aren't welcome around here."

Caleb filled his eyes with her defiant face. Lord, she hadn't recognized him. Otherwise, by now, he'd have a belly full of buckshot. After what had happened five years ago, he could understand why she greeted callers with a gun. She was likely terrified. What he couldn't understand was why she'd stayed in a place with so many tragic memories. Surely she had kinfolk back east who would have welcomed her home.

Her large gray eyes studied him cautiously. It made sense, now, that she wouldn't know him. His real name would mean nothing to her. And he was no longer the bashful teenager who'd adored her across the kitchen table. Five years had put height and muscle on him, and prison had altered his features. A fight with the prison bully had broken his nose. An accident with falling rocks had split his lip and laid a puckered scar across his left eyebrow. Even his eyes had long since lost their look of innocence.

Laura had changed, too. The knife wound on her face had healed badly, leaving a jagged white streak from her temple to the corner of her mouth. Her hair was pulled harshly back and twisted into a tight knot. But it was her dove-colored eyes that struck him to the heart. They were an animal's eyes, wounded and mistrustful.

They had done this to her, he and his brothers. And Caleb knew that, in his own blundering way, he was as much to blame as Zeke and Noah. He had tried to rescue her and failed. Worse, his interference had opened the way to Mark Shafton's death.

"I'm waiting," she said. "You've got ten seconds to tell me what you want before I blast you off my porch!"

Caleb scrambled for words, saying the first thing that came to mind. "Your corral gate needs mending. I'll do it in exchange for a meal."

She hesitated, her eyes coming to rest on the pistol that hung at his hip. Impulsively, he unfastened the gun belt and held it toward her. "Take this for safekeeping if you're worried about me," he said. "Believe me, I'd never hurt you or take anything I hadn't earned."

She recoiled slightly, more from him than from the pistol, Caleb suspected. "Lay the gun on the porch," she said. "You'll find some tools in the shed.

When you finish mending the gate, your food and your weapon will be waiting on the front step. You can take them and go."

Caleb nodded and turned away, aching for her. Even with the scar, Laura was a beautiful woman. With the ranch as a dowry, she could have had dozens of suitors fighting for her hand. But fear, it seemed, had made her a recluse. He could not imagine such a woman letting any man near her.

The fluttering clothes on the line caught his eye again. He remembered now that she'd told Zeke she was pregnant. Her child would be a little more than four years old, a boy, judging from the pint-sized shirts and overalls. Laura would have her hands full, raising a son alone.

Was there any way he could help her? Not likely, Caleb told himself as he walked toward the shed. He'd be a fool to stay within shotgun range for long. A look, a word, anything could trigger Laura's memory and her finger. Worse, if she recognized him and sent word to the sheriff, he could end up in prison again, this time as an accessory to murder.

And if he did stay, what could he do for her? Tell her lies? Hurt her again? Caleb sighed as he unlatched the door of the toolshed. He had learned all he'd set out to learn. Laura's life was far from perfect, but she was surviving as best she could. The wisest thing he could do now was ride away and leave her alone. And he would—as soon as he mended the corral gate.

* * *

Laura peered past the frame of the window, watching as the man named McCurdy rehung the sagging gate. He moved with a quiet sureness, one shoulder bracing the timbers while he hammered the nail that held the iron hinge in place. She had tried to do the job herself a few weeks ago but had lacked the strength to hold up the heavy gate while she worked with her hands. Caleb McCurdy made the task look easy.

Her fingers brushed the scar that trailed like spilled tallow down the side of her face. Who was Caleb McCurdy, she wondered, and why had he come this way? Laura was curious, but starting a conversation would only encourage him to stay longer. She'd agreed to his offer out of the necessity to get the gate repaired. But all she really wanted was to be left alone.

He was well spoken and decently dressed. But aside from that he was a rough-looking sort with the face of a brawler. There was no telling what a man like that might do to a helpless woman with a child. Until he was out of sight, she would be wise to watch his every move.

"Who's that man, Mama?" Laura had let Robbie out of his room a few minutes earlier. Now he was standing on tiptoe beside her, peering over the sill.

"Nobody," she said. "Just a saddle tramp who needs a meal. At least this one's willing to work for it."

"Can I go outside and swing now?" the boy asked. "You said I could if I cleaned up my room."

Laura hesitated, torn, as always, between the need to protect her son and the awareness that even a small boy needed some freedom. Every time Robbie left her sight she was sick with worry. But the last thing she wanted was to raise him to be a timid, fearful man.

"Please," Robbie begged. "Just for a little while."

Laura sighed. "All right. But stay close to the swing. Don't go near the creek, and leave that man alone, do you hear?"

"Yes, Mama." He skipped across the kitchen and out the back door, letting the screen slam behind him. Laura watched him through the window as he ran toward the swing. Such a beautiful, open, trusting little boy. So like his father.

But her husband had been too trusting, she reminded herself. In the end, Mark's faith in the goodness of his fellowmen had killed him and very nearly destroyed her.

In those black days after his murder, only the thought of their unborn child had kept her alive and fighting. Now Robbie was her life—her whole life. She would die, or kill, to keep him safe.

The sight of Caleb McCurdy's gun belt, coiled like a rattlesnake on the seat of the rocking chair, reminded Laura of the bargain she'd made. Slicing off four slabs of brown bread, she made sandwiches, layering them with meat from the grouse she'd shot in the foothills and with lettuce from her garden. When she was finished, she wrapped the sandwiches in a clean piece of flour sack, knotted the corners and left them on the porch next to the gun belt. As an afterthought, she filled a tin cup with cold water from the kitchen pump. He'd been working hard, and the early summer sun was hot.

Locking the front door behind her, she went back to the kitchen window and looked outside. Caleb McCurdy had the hinges in place and was testing the gate, moving it back and forth to make sure it swung smoothly. Soon he'd be returning to the porch for his meal. It was time she got Robbie back into the house.

She hurried through the kitchen, out the screen door and onto the stoop to call him.

Her heart froze.

The swing dangled empty on its long ropes. Her son was nowhere in sight.

Caleb was gathering up the leftover nails when Laura burst around the corner of the house. Her face was white. "Robbie—my boy!" she gasped. "Where is he?"

"He was on the swing the last time I looked over that way. He can't be far." Caleb dropped the nails and the hammer next to the gatepost. It was the nature of little boys to run off and explore. They did it all the time. But the expression of stark fear in Laura's eyes went beyond motherly concern. Did she suspect *him* of doing something to her child? Was she afraid he'd snatched the boy to lure her outside?

But why brood about it? After what his family had done to her, Laura had every reason to be fearful and suspicious.

"Come on," he said. "I'll help you look for him."

They sprinted back toward the tree, where the boy had last been seen. Laura called her son's name while Caleb checked the creek, which flowed high with runoff from the melting snow in the mountains. There was no sign of the boy in the water, nor were there any fresh tracks along the bank.

"Have you looked in the springhouse?" he asked her. Laura shook her head. "I always keep it locked. He wouldn't be able to get in."

A glance toward the springhouse confirmed her words. The door hasp wore a forbidding steel padlock. Caleb understood Laura's need to keep her son away from the horror of that place. But there was nothing he could say about it. Even in his silence, he had already begun to lie to her.

The sooner he rode away from here, the better it would be for them both.

While Laura searched the willows, Caleb studied the bare earth around the huge, gnarled cottonwood that supported the swing. His Comanche mother, who'd died when he was twelve, had taught him all there was to know about tracking. But he could see no small, fresh footprints leading away from the base of the tree. Where could a little boy go without leaving a trail?

And then, suddenly, he knew.

Speaking softly, he beckoned to Laura. "Come and stand right here. Wait till I'm out of sight. Then look up into the tree and call to him."

With wondering eyes, she stepped onto the spot

where he'd stood. Caleb moved back under the eave of the springhouse. He wanted to make sure the boy wasn't too frightened to show himself.

"Robbie?" Laura looked up into the branches above her head. Relief, shadowed with exasperation, swept across her face. "Robert Mark Shafton, what on earth are you doing up there?"

A joyous giggle rang out from ten feet above her head. "I climbed up here, Mama. All by myself!"

Laura's voice shook. "You had me scared half to death! I've been calling and calling. Why on earth didn't you answer me?"

"I was playing hide-and-seek! You were supposed to find me!"

"Well, pardon me, Master Shafton, I didn't know this was supposed to be a game." Laura stood glaring up at her son, her hands on her hips. Caleb watched her from the corner of the springhouse. Five years ago, Laura Shafton had been a shy, enchanting young bride. Tragedy and motherhood had brought out her inner strength. She was magnificent, he thought.

Too bad he couldn't risk telling her so.

"You get down from there, Robbie," she said. "Carefully, now, so you won't fall."

"Are you going to spank me?" Robbie straddled a sloping limb, clinging to his perch like a treed cat. He was a beautiful child, with his mother's eyes and his father's golden coloring.

"No, I'm not going to spank you," Laura said firmly. "But you'll be spending some time in your room, young man. We'll talk about it when you get down."

The boy inched backward down the limb, but he couldn't see where he was going. His small feet groped for purchase. He was clearly in trouble.

Laura gasped. "Wait, Robbie! Don't try to move!" But the child was already slipping off the limb.

Caleb sprinted out from the shelter of the springhouse and started up the tree. "Hang on, I'll get you!" he shouted, scrambling up the knotted trunk. But he was already too late.

He heard Laura's scream as Robbie lost his grip and plummeted downward in a shower of twigs and leaves. She sprang for him, trying to break his fall, but as she reached out, she lost her balance and stumbled. The boy fell through her fingertips, struck the ground with a sickening thud and lay still.

Chapter Two

"Robbie! No!" Laura crumpled to her knees beside her son's body. He was lying facedown on the grassy earth, one arm bent outward at a nightmarish angle. She could see no sign that he was breathing.

"No—" She reached for him, frantic to snatch him up and cradle him in her arms, but a steely hand gripped her shoulder, pulling her back.

"Don't try to move him," Caleb McCurdy said. "That could hurt him worse. Give me some room. I'm no doctor, but I'll do what I can."

Struck by the urgency in his voice, Laura shifted to one side. She felt a cold numbness sinking into her bones, as if she were being frozen in a block of ice. The birds had fallen silent and she could no longer hear the gurgling creek. The only sound to reach her brain was the pounding of her own heart.

McCurdy knelt beside her. She held her breath as his long, brown fingers probed the length of Robbie's spine, pressing gently against his ribs. Seconds crawled past. This was all her fault. If she hadn't scolded the boy, insisting that he come down at once, he would have waited for help. He would have been safe. Now he could be dying or so badly hurt that he would never run, swing or climb a tree again.

Laura prayed harder than she'd ever prayed in her life. Five years ago she'd almost given up on prayer, but the words came now in a rush of silent pleading. *Please…please let him be all right, I'll do anything, give anything…*

More seconds passed in frozen agony. Then Robbie coughed, gulped air and began to struggle. His legs kicked freely, but when he tried to move his arm, he flinched and broke into a wail of pain.

"There now, your mother's right here." McCurdy eased the sobbing boy onto his back and lifted him off the ground. Supporting the broken arm, he laid him tenderly across Laura's lap.

Laura pressed her face against Robbie's dusty hair, kissing his ears and his dirt-streaked face, murmuring incoherent little phrases of love and relief.

McCurdy exhaled and sank back onto his heels. The bright sunlight cast his eyes into shadowed pits. "My guess is he just got the wind knocked out of him. But you'll need to watch him for a few days. Get him to a doctor if there's any sign that something's wrong. And that arm's got to be set and splinted."

"There's no doctor within twenty miles of here," she said. "Can you help me with the arm?"

He hesitated, then slowly nodded. "I've seen it done—had it done when I broke my own arm as a boy. There's not much to it, but it'll hurt." He looked down at Robbie. "How brave are you, boy?"

Robbie's eyes opened wide in his tear-stained face. "I'm not scared of anything. Not bugs or snakes or even our big red rooster. Not even trees," he added with a wan little grin.

The ghost of a smile tugged at the corner of Caleb McCurdy's mouth. He looked younger when he smiled, Laura thought. She had judged him to be in his thirties. Now she realized he might be closer to her own age. But he had clearly seen some hard living. Like her he was scarred. Inside, she suspected, as well as outside.

Reason told her he was the last man she should trust. But right now her son needed help, and Caleb McCurdy was all the help she had.

"Are you brave enough to let me straighten your arm?" he asked Robbie. "It's going to hurt."

"It hurts now," Robbie said, grimacing. "I'll be brave."

"Good boy." McCurdy brushed a knuckle against the boy's flushed cheek. For Laura, the awkward caress was one more reminder of what Robbie had missed growing up without a father. She was doing her best with the boy. But there was only so much a lonely, frightened widow could do to raise a son to manhood. Every day the task became more daunting. The killer who'd gunned down Mark Shafton had shattered three lives—Mark's, hers and Robbie's.

Caleb McCurdy rose to his feet. "The sooner we get this over with the better," he said. "I'll need some thin, straight wood for the splint and something to wrap around it."

"Try the woodpile," Laura told him. "I've got an old nightgown I can tear into strips. That should do for wrapping."

"Fine. Take your boy inside. Lay him down and get him as calm as you can. I'll be in as soon as I get the wood ready."

Cradling her son in her arms, Laura carried him through the back door and into the house. Through the window, she caught a glimpse of McCurdy rummaging through the woodpile. Less than an hour ago the man had been a complete stranger. Now he'd be coming into her home. She would be trusting him with her life and the life of her precious son.

The last time she'd opened her door to strangers was the day of her husband's murder. The thought of doing it again sent a leaden wave of fear through her body. Not all men were evil, she reminded herself. So far, Caleb McCurdy had treated her with courtesy and kindness. But she couldn't afford to lower her guard. Robbie's life and her own could depend on her vigilance.

Robbie was whimpering with the pain of his broken arm. Laura laid him on her own bed, propped him with pillows and arranged the arm gently across his chest. She could see where the bone angled halfway between the wrist and elbow. The sight of it made her stomach clench.

Soaking a cloth with cold water from the pump, she laid it over the swelling flesh. Then she brought him some fresh cider to drink out of his special blue china cup. "My brave little man," she whispered, kissing his damp forehead. "Close your eyes and rest. Everything's going to be all right."

She waited until his whimpering eased. Then she found the threadbare flannel nightgown, sat down on the foot of the bed and began tearing the fabric into strips.

Caleb chose a straight chunk of pine and split off two thin slabs with the hatchet. Then he sat down on the chopping block and began smoothing the pieces with his knife, rounding off the rough edges and shaping them to the contour of a child's arm. Laura's son would need to wear the splint for at least six weeks. He wanted it to be comfortable.

As he worked, his mind pictured Laura, seeing the terror in her eyes as she plunged toward her fallen child. What if the boy had been killed? Laura was so deeply scarred by the past that one more loss would have shattered her.

And the boy was not out of the woods yet. He could have internal injuries that might not show up right away. Days from now, he could start vomiting blood. Caleb had seen a man die that way in prison after a vicious kick to the gut. The same thing could happen to a child.

Caleb sighed as he shaved the last rough edge off the makeshift splint. How could he ride off and leave

Laura alone at a time like this? Unless she ran him off her property with the shotgun, it would be a kindness to stay for a few more days, at least until her son was out of danger. There appeared to be plenty of work to do around the place. He could use that as an excuse, to avoid worrying her.

Brushing the wood shavings off his denims, he sheathed the knife and went around the house to the front door. Laura still viewed him as a stranger. She'd even left his food and gun belt on the porch so he wouldn't have to come inside. Now he was about to invade her home. One misstep on his part could plunge her into panic. He would have to weigh his every move and measure his every word.

Cautiously he rapped on the door. He heard her light, quick footsteps coming from the back of the house. Then the door swung inward and she stood on the threshold, wide-eyed and trembling.

"Robbie's resting on my bed," she said. "I'll hold him while you set the arm. Will it hurt a lot?"

"I'll be as gentle as I can. But yes, it'll hurt. He'll likely scream, but it's got to be done." He followed her through the parlor. Except for the little wooden train cars scattered over the braided rug, the room was much as he remembered it. "If you've got some whiskey, we could use it to make him drowsy," he said.

"No." She didn't look back at him. "I don't keep whiskey in the house."

She led him into her bedroom, where the boy lay in a nest of pillows. Clearly, Laura was more concerned about her son than she was about having a strange man in this, the most intimate room in her house.

Caleb knew he should keep his eyes on the boy, but he couldn't help noticing the store-bought mahogany bed with its quilted muslin coverlet and the matching wardrobe and dresser. The wall behind the dresser, where a mirror would have hung, was bare. In fact, there didn't seem to be any mirrors in the house at all.

A silver-framed photograph of Mark Shafton sat on the nightstand. At the sight of that clean-chiseled face, Caleb's stomach contracted so violently that for an instant he feared he was going to be sick.

"That's my papa," the boy said. "He got killed by some bad men."

"Lie still, Robbie," Laura said. "Don't try to talk."

"His name was Mark Robert Shafton," the child persisted. "Like my name, only backwards. My name's Robert Mark. My mama's name is Laura. What's your name?"

"Caleb."

"My mama says I should call men mister. Can I call you Mr. Caleb?"

"Fine. Now let's take care of that arm." Changing the subject, he showed the boy the two pieces of the splint. "Your mother's going to hold you while I pull your arm and straighten out the bone. Then we'll put these sticks around your arm and wrap them so it'll heal straight. All right?"

"You said it would hurt."

"It will. But only for a few seconds."

"I won't cry."

"It might help if you do." Caleb glanced at Laura. "Hold him."

Laura gathered her son close, burying his face against her breast. He squirmed and twisted his head away, wanting to see. She let him, even though she doubted the wisdom of it.

"Brace his shoulder," Caleb McCurdy said, leaning above them. "Ready?"

Laura gripped the small body, feeling the thin bones strain beneath her fingers. A tear trickled down her cheek. He was so small and so brave. "Ready," she whispered.

Caleb gripped Robbie's wrist with one scarred brown hand. The other hand rested on the spot where the boy's forearm was bent like a badly hammered nail. Gently at first he began to apply pressure, stretching the arm and pushing the break into position. Laura had read that the bones of small children were like green willows, more apt to bend and splinter than to snap. From the look of Robbie's arm, the bone was still in one piece. Still, the pain had to be excruciating. She bit back her own sobs as her son began to whimper, then to scream.

"Done." Caleb eased back on the straightened arm. Sweat was streaming down his face. "Good boy, Robbie. You're as brave as any man I know. Now, if your mother will wrap your arm to cushion it and hand me the splints…"

Robbie's screams had subsided to jerking sobs.

Easing him back onto the pillows, Laura wrapped the first layer of flannel lightly around his arm, then handed Caleb the splints. He held them in place while she wound the wrappings. Working so closely together, it was difficult to avoid contact. The male aromas of sage, wood smoke and fresh perspiration crept into Laura's senses until she felt strangely warm. Each accidental brush of his fingers against hers sent a jolt of awareness shooting up her arms and prickling through her body. She focused her attention on Robbie, diverting her thoughts from the rough-looking stranger who'd invaded her life. Soon he'd be gone. Then she could get back to the safe, private world she'd created for herself and her son.

He stepped away from the bed as Laura finished the wrapping and knotted the end of the flannel strip. Robbie lay back on the pillows, quiet now.

"Keep the arm raised as much as you can," Caleb said. "That will ease the swelling."

Laura rearranged the pillows to support the splinted arm. "I'm going to make you some chamomile tea, Robbie. You can get up later, after you've rested awhile." She glanced back at Caleb, who was moving toward the bedroom door. "I'm beholden to you, Caleb McCurdy. Why don't you bring your food into the kitchen and eat at the table. I'll get you some cold cider and a slice of apple pie to go with the sandwich. That's the least I can do."

He hesitated for the space of a breath, as if pondering her offer. Then he thanked her and left the room. Laura covered Robbie with the soft merino blanket that had comforted him since babyhood. Bending, she brushed a kiss across his forehead. "Your father would have been so proud of you, my little love," she murmured. He gave her a teary smile. She kissed him again and hurried out to the kitchen.

Caleb unwrapped his sandwich and laid it on the chipped bone china plate Laura had placed in front of him. He had sat at the same table five years ago. This time he occupied the place at the end, where Mark Shafton had sat on that day of horror.

Caleb was hungry and the food was well prepared. But his dry mouth had lost its ability to taste. Why had he come back here, to this place, these memories and this beautiful, damaged woman? He should have headed west to California or south to Mexico, where he could put the past behind him. Instead he'd chosen to open old wounds, and he was already bleeding.

Laura stood at the stove, measuring dried chamomile into a porcelain pot. He noticed the way she kept the left side of her face turned away from him, hiding the scar. "We don't get many travelers out here since they finished the railroad," she said, making polite conversation. "Where are you headed?"

"Texas. San Antone, most likely. Thought I'd take my time and see some new country on the way." Another lie, as was everything he'd told her except his name. "I don't see any hired help around," he said, changing the subject. "How do you manage out here, a woman alone with a youngster? Wouldn't you be better off selling the place and moving to a town?"

"I might." She poured boiling water into the teapot. The flowery aroma of chamomile drifted into the room. "But I stay here to keep the land for Robbie. That's what his father would have wanted—a legacy for him, his children, his grandchildren..." Her voice broke slightly as she spooned some honey out of a jar and dribbled a little of it into the tea. "I sold off the beef cattle and the spare horses after Mark died," she said. "I wasn't up to taking care of them, and I needed the money to live on. Steers and mustangs can be replaced. Land can't. I'll wear rags and go barefoot before I sell a single acre."

Struck by the passion in her voice, Caleb studied the proud angle of her head and the determined thrust of her jaw. He had thought of Laura as fragile. But underneath her porcelain doll exterior was a core of tempered steel. He had glimpsed that steel when she'd turned on Zeke, sunk her teeth into his arm and grappled for the knife that would slash her face. Now he was seeing it again.

He should have guessed he would find her here, holding on to what was hers. So why hadn't he turned around and left as soon as she opened the front door? Why was he still here, risking the chance that he might be recognized?

"But it doesn't make sense to sit on the land while your money runs out," he heard himself saying. "A ranch like this one could make you a right handsome living. You could run a herd of cattle, fatten them up on this good grass and ship them east by rail, or sell them to the army. Sheep would do all right in this country, too."

She toyed briefly with her thin gold wedding ring. "You sound like my husband. He always said that one day we'd have the finest ranch in New Mexico."

Caleb's throat constricted around the piece of bread he'd just swallowed. He willed himself not to choke.

"I became a widow six months before Robbie was born," she said. "I didn't know the first thing about running a ranch. It was all I could do to survive and take care of my baby. When my nearest neighbor offered to buy the stock, I agreed to his offer, even though I knew he was getting a bargain. I needed the money."

Caleb took a sip of cold cider and managed to swallow it. If he had any brains he'd get up from the table, thank Laura for the meal and ride away before he dug himself any deeper. But there was the matter of a small, broken boy who might yet need a trip to the nearest doctor. And there was the matter of this scarred, beautiful woman to whom he owed a monstrous debt.

Caleb's mother had told him that among her people, if someone died because of another's actions, the bereaved family had the right of adoption. They could claim the offender to take the place of their lost loved one and help provide for their family. It was a wise custom, one that served both justice and practicality.

Not that Caleb could ever replace Mark Shafton

as husband, father and provider. That notion was unthinkable. But if he could teach Laura how to run the ranch, get her started with some cattle and hire some reliable help before he moved on, it might at least ease his conscience.

"You've got the makings of a good ranch here," he said. "But the place needs some work. The windmill, the fences, the sheds…"

"Yes, I know." She poured the tea into a small blue cup, set it on a saucer and added a splash of milk. "When Robbie's a little older, I'll have more time to spend keeping the place up. I'm not as helpless as I look. I can hammer nails and slap on whitewash with the best of them. But right now, I don't dare turn my back on the little mischief. You saw what happened today."

"I could help you," Caleb said, feeling as if he'd just stepped over the edge of a cliff. "For a few good meals and a spot to lay my bedroll, I could have the place looking like new."

She looked hesitant, and for an instant he felt his heart stop.

"You understand it wouldn't be a regular job," she said. "It would only be for a week or so, and I can't spare the money to pay you. If you'd be satisfied with a bed in the toolshed and three square meals a day—"

Caleb forced himself to grin. "Lady, for pie like this, I'd mend fences all the way from here to California!"

She picked up the cup and saucer in her work-worn hands. Again, as she moved toward the bedroom, Caleb sensed her hesitation. He was a stranger. And even if you were kind to them, strangers could turn into monsters.

"Give me time to think about it," she said. "I'll let you know."

"Fine." Caleb laid down his fork and rose from his chair. "While you're thinking, I'll go outside and start on that broken windmill."

Without giving her a chance to protest, he walked out the front door and closed it behind him. By the time he reached the bottom step, his knees were shaking. What in hell's name did he think he was doing? If Laura recognized him, he could be a dead man or, worse, on his way back to prison for life. Mount up and ride away, that would be the smart thing to do. Laura was a strong woman. She could manage fine without his help.

But the force that had drawn him to this place was pulling him deeper into Laura's life. Whether it was guilt, duty or destiny's unseen hand, Caleb sensed that he'd come here for a reason. Whatever the cost, he could not leave until he understood what that reason was.

Picking up the hammer and nails where he'd dropped them by the corral gate, he strode to the base of the windmill and began to climb.

Chapter Three

Laura had taken extra pains with supper, mixing up a batch of sourdough biscuits, churning fresh butter and adding a pinch of precious ground seasonings to the rabbit stew. Caleb McCurdy had put in a long, hard afternoon, she reasoned. Not only was the corral gate mended, but he'd replaced the missing vanes on the windmill and patched the holes in the roof of the chicken coop, to say nothing of setting Robbie's arm. Since she had no money to pay him, the least she could do was serve him a decent meal.

Glancing out through the kitchen window, she could see him washing at the pump. He'd tossed his brown flannel shirt on a sapling and unbuttoned the top of his long johns to hang around his waist. He was bending forward, letting the water stream through his raven hair. Now, slowly, he straightened, raking his fingers through his dripping locks. Water flowed over his bare shoulders to trickle down along the muscled furrow of his spine and vanish beneath the damp waistband of his denims. He was as lean and sinewy as a tom cougar with no trace of fat on his lanky frame. Where the setting sun shone on his wet skin, he blazed with liquid fire.

Turning, he cupped his hands and sluiced water over his chest and under his armpits. The nicks and scars that marred his coppery body spoke of violent times and rough living. Laura's fingers tightened on the frame of the window. Caleb McCurdy had appeared out of nowhere, like an angel in her time of need. But he was clearly no angel. His dark eyes were too feral, his reflexes too quick. He had all the marks of a wild animal, ready to strike out at the first unguarded moment. She could not afford to trust him—or any other man in this godforsaken, bullet-riddled country.

So why did she stay? Laura had long since stopped asking herself that question. She knew the answer all too well.

Another letter had arrived last week, this one from her sister Jeannie, urging her to leave the ranch and come home to St. Louis. There would be a room for her in the family home, Jeannie had said, and a room for Robbie, where he could grow up safe and happy, surrounded by people who cared for him.

For the space of a breath Laura had been tempted. But who would she be in St. Louis? The scarred sister, hiding from curious eyes in some upstairs room, a prisoner of her own ugliness. And Robbie—he would be the son of a dead father and an unseen mother, dependent on others for a leg up in the world. Here the boy was heir to five hundred acres of fine ranch land. Here he would have his own piece of the earth. He would grow up to be a strong, independent man. For Robbie's sake she had to stay—to bear the hardship of grinding work and the lonely terror of black nights. Her own life had ended with the flash of a knife and the roar of a pistol. Now she lived for her child and the man he would become.

Caleb McCurdy glanced toward the house. Laura shrank back from the window. Heaven forbid he catch her watching him. The last thing she wanted was to put wrong ideas into the man's head—ideas that might be there already, she reminded herself. She would be wise to keep the shotgun handy.

He was reaching for his shirt now, thrusting his glistening arms into the sleeves. Soon he'd be coming inside to eat. It was time she fetched the milk from the springhouse.

She had left the milk until the last minute because the day was hot and she didn't want it to spoil. Besides, there was nothing better than ice-cold milk after a day's work, especially with hot, buttered biscuits.

Slipping into her bedroom, she took a moment to check on Robbie. The boy had passed a restless afternoon, but an hour ago he'd taken some warm broth and fallen into exhausted slumber. Now he lay curled on his side, his splinted arm resting on a pillow. Aching with love, Laura leaned over the bed and brushed a kiss where one damp golden curl fell across his forehead. He was her boy, her perfect, precious son.

What if she'd lost him today in that terrible fall from the tree? For the space of a heartbeat she'd feared... But no, Laura forced the thought from her mind. Robbie was safe now. His arm would heal, and soon he'd be good as new.

The springhouse, a sturdy log building the size of a very small room, stood just a few steps from the back door. Laura's husband had built it over the creek, which he'd diverted from its true channel by means of a timber dam, covered with earth and sod. Inside the springhouse there was a perforated tin cool box set into the water, as well as shelves and hooks for hanging meat. It was a clever piece of engineering. Mark had been proud of his work; but after his death, Laura had come desperately close to dousing the structure with kerosene and burning it to the ground. Only practical need, coupled with the danger of setting the house on fire, had stayed her hand.

Even after five years, she could not step into that clammy darkness without feeling sick. Her hand shook as she turned the key in the steel padlock. The door creaked softly as it swung inward.

Her skin began to crawl as she forced herself across the threshold. There was no sound except the gurgling of water, but the buried echo of a gunshot lingered in the wooden heart of each log that formed the walls. The mossy earth was rank with remembered odors—gunpowder, blood, and the awful aftermath of death. Steeling herself against a rush of nausea, Laura bent and lifted the milk from the tin box. The jug was cold and dripping wet between her hands. She hurried outside with it, gulping fresh air into her lungs. For a moment she stood still, letting the twilight settle around her. The fading sun was warm on her face. A rock wren piped from the foothills beyond the tool shed.

Balancing the jug on her hip, she used her free hand to hook the padlock through the hasp and squeeze it firmly closed. Only then did her pulse slow to its natural rhythm. She would be all right now. The horror was locked away…until next time.

A furtive glance told her that Caleb McCurdy was no longer at the pump. An instant later she spotted him at the corral fence, filling the water trough. His arms lifted the big bucket as if it had no weight, pouring the water carefully so that none would spill and be wasted. In the fading light, his wet hair gleamed like polished jet.

Turning, he gave her a nod. "Anything you need?" he asked, raising his voice to be heard across the distance.

"Supper's on." She forced the words, her throat so tight that it felt as if she hadn't spoken in months.

"I'll be in as soon as I finish here." He sounded as uneasy as she did. Laura imagined their mealtime conversation as a series of stilted comments on the weather, interspersed with long, awkward pauses. She'd forgotten how to make small talk, especially with a man.

But what did that matter? The only man in her future would be her son. As for Caleb McCurdy, he was nothing but a saddle tramp. As soon as the work ran out—sooner if he grew weary of it—he'd be over the hill and gone like a tumbleweed in the wind. By then, she'd probably be grateful to see the last of him.

In the kitchen, she set the milk on the counter while she checked on Robbie. He was still sleeping, his breathing light and even, his lashes wet against his rosy cheeks. With a grateful sigh, Laura hurried back to the kitchen, poured the foamy milk into earthenware mugs and took the tin of biscuits out of the warmer above the stove. She was arranging the biscuits on a plate when she heard the light rap at the door.

Her heart lurched. Her hands flew upward to smooth back the wind-tousled tendrils of her hair, only to pause in midair like hesitant butterflies.

What in heaven's name am I doing? Laura forced her hands down to her sides. Arranging her features into a prim expression, she strode across the parlor, turned the latch and slowly opened the door.

The aromas wafting from the kitchen beckoned Caleb to enter. But the sight of Laura, flushed and trembling, stopped him like a bayonet to the heart. He hesitated at the threshold. Her eyes were large and bright, her face glowing in the amber light that slanted through the window. Her mouth, however, was pressed into a grim line, as if her lips had been sealed to keep any emotion from spilling out. Was she frightened, angry, or simply unsure of herself, as he was? For the life of him, Caleb could not read her.

Lord, what was he doing here? What had made him think he could help this woman, when he was part of the nightmare that had scarred her face and driven her wild with terror? If he had any sense, he would turn around, ride away and never look back.

But her lips were moving now, opening like soft pink petals. "Come in," she said in a taut little whisper. "Your supper's on the table."

"It smells mighty fine." He took a tentative step inside, letting the aromas of meat, onions, and fresh biscuits shimmer through his senses. He was tired and hungry. The food smelled damned good, and he'd earned every bite.

"How's your boy?" Remembering his manners, Caleb pulled out her chair and waited until she'd seated herself before taking his own place—Mark Shafton's place—at the head of the table.

"Better. He ate an hour ago and went to sleep." She ladled the stew into big bowls with her small, chapped hands. It would have been easier with the boy here, Caleb thought. Alone with Laura, he would have to make conversation for the length of the meal. He'd never been good at talking to women, and five years in prison hadn't helped that any.

"I…hope you like rabbit stew," she said, passing him a plate of flaky, golden biscuits.

"I was raised on it back in Texas. But my ma's rabbit stew never smelled this good." He dipped a bit of biscuit in the broth, wondering if it was the proper thing to do. "Or tasted this good," he added after savoring the morsel on his tongue. "Did you shoot the rabbit yourself?"

As soon as it was out of his mouth, the question struck him as inane. And Texas. Noah had mentioned Texas on that day, five years ago. Even the word could spark Laura's memory. Why couldn't he just keep his mouth shut?

"I didn't exactly shoot it." She buttered a chunk of her own biscuit. "Bullets are expensive. Snares are cheap. When I first came west, I couldn't imagine harming helpless little wild animals. But when you're raising a child, and you have to put meat on the table every day..." She shrugged. "It's amazing what necessity can make you do. I did shoot the grouse you had for lunch. Early this spring, I even brought down a deer that wandered into the yard. Butchered it myself. We ate like royalty until the weather warmed up and the meat went bad."

Caleb studied her over his mug, trying to imagine how she'd managed to survive the past five years, out here alone with a small child. In the fading light she looked as delicate as a rose and just as beautiful. Her eyes were the color of clouds before a storm, and her tawny hair clung in tendrils to her blooming cheeks. The neck of her gown was open to the heat, revealing the creamy skin of her throat and the slight swelling at the top of one breast.

He drank her in, filling his senses with the sight of her.

She shifted in her chair, turning the scarred side of her face away from him. He burned to tell her that the damned scar didn't matter—that it wouldn't matter to any man in his right mind. But that, he sensed, would only make her more self-conscious.

"Don't you have anyone who looks in on you, Laura?" he asked. "Neighbors? Friends?"

Caleb saw her eyes widen and he realized that once more he'd put his foot in it. A strange man, asking if she was alone. No wonder she looked as if she were about to bolt for the shotgun. Swiftly he changed the subject.

"My mother used to make jerked venison—salted and dried. I could show you how. That way, if you get another deer, the meat won't go to waste."

"I'd like that." She paused to swallow a bit of stew. "Is that how they preserve meat in Texas?"

Texas again. Caleb's throat tightened. "My mother was Comanche. Her people always made jerky. When I was a boy, I used to eat it like candy. Robbie will, too. It's good, and you can take it in your pocket."

She studied him with doe-like eyes. Caleb wondered how she felt about half-breeds. "Is your mother still alive?" she asked.

Caleb shook his head. "She died when I was twelve. My father's gone, too."

"Any other family? Brothers or sisters?"

"None that I've seen in a long time—or want to see." Caleb's mouth had gone dry. Her curiosity was cutting dangerously close to the truth. But he could not lie to those eyes—eyes like silvery crystal that seemed able to look right through him.

"I just got out of prison," he blurted, seizing on a different truth. "I did five years in Yuma for my part in a bank robbery."

Laura's spoon clattered to the table. She was staring at him in horror, her eyes huge in her pale face. Maybe she'd throw him out now. That would make everything easier.

"Just so you'll know, I didn't hurt anybody," he said. "And I didn't take any money—never even laid eyes on it. I was just in the wrong place at the wrong time, with the wrong people. I've paid my debt, and now I'm going straight." He pushed himself away from the table and rose to his feet. "I'd never hurt you or your boy, Laura. But if you don't feel safe with me around, just say the word and I'll leave now. It's up to you."

Caleb waited, forcing himself to meet those fathomless gray eyes. His innards crawled with self-loathing. What he'd told her was bad enough. But what he hadn't told her was a hundred times worse. Using one truth to cover another was more heinous than a lie. It was a crime against innocence and trust.

Her silence lay heavy and cold in the room. Caleb could hear the slow ticking of the pendulum clock in the parlor, counting the empty seconds, and still she did not move or speak.

At last, when he could stand it no longer, he cleared his throat. "Well, I guess that says it," he muttered. "I'll be going now, as soon as I can saddle up. Much obliged for your hospitality and the good food."

Tearing his eyes away from her he strode out of the kitchen and across the parlor. It was for the best, Caleb told himself. The longer he stayed, the deeper the lie and the greater the risk that Laura would discover the truth. He had the answer to the question that had brought him here. Wasn't that enough?

He had reached the front door when he heard her voice.

"Come back here, Caleb McCurdy. You haven't finished your supper."

He froze with his hand on the doorknob. Open the door and walk out of her life, that would be the smart thing to do. But Caleb knew that wasn't going to happen. With a sigh, he turned around and ambled back into the kitchen.

Laura was sitting where he'd left her, one hand resting lightly on the edge of the table. The fading light caught windblown tendrils of hair, framing her face in a soft, golden halo.

"Please sit down," she said. "There's something you need to understand."

Caleb lowered himself onto his chair, waiting in silence. Even before she spoke, he knew what he was about to hear.

"Five years ago I thought my life was perfect. I had everything I wanted—a home, a loving husband and a baby on the way. Then one afternoon three rough-looking men rode in through the gate. Just the sight of them made my flesh crawl. I begged Mark to send them on their way, but he was a man who lived by the Golden Rule. We welcomed them, even gave them a meal. Then, just as they were getting ready to leave, things got ugly." She stared down at the table for a long moment. "One of them caught me alone in the springhouse. He gave me this when I fought him." Her fingers brushed the scar as she flashed Caleb a view of her left profile, then turned full face once more. "When my husband came rushing in and tried to save me, they shot him and rode off. He died in my arms."

She made an odd little strangled sound, closing her eyes and clasping her hands until the knuckles went white. Then the breath went out of her in a long exhalation. She opened her eyes, composed once more. "I'm telling you this so you'll understand how I feel about strangers. It hasn't been easy for me, having you around the place today. But you've been honest about your past, Caleb. You're a hard worker and you were here when I needed help with Robbie. You're welcome to stay—until the work is done and you're ready to move on, of course."

Caleb gazed at her numbly, feeling as if he'd been kicked in the face. Lord, why hadn't he walked away while he had the chance? If she'd run him off the ranch with the shotgun, he'd have been fine with it. But her declaration of trust, however reluctant, had undone him. Guilt knotted his innards with a pain so physical that he wanted to double over and groan.

Part of him wanted to know more. Had Laura been able to get help? Had she gone to the law with descriptions of the three men? Were he and his brothers wanted for the crime? But this was no time to ask. He'd pushed her far enough.

"I'm right sorry for what happened," he muttered, taking a bite of food that had lost its taste. "I'll be glad to stay, and grateful for the work. But if I do anything to make you nervous, just say so. I'll be gone in the time it takes to saddle my horse. Understood?"

"Yes, and thank you." She nibbled at a biscuit, then set it back on her plate. Both of them, it seemed, had lost their appetites.

The silence in the darkening room grew long and heavy. Caleb was relieved when Robbie woke up in the bedroom and began to whimper. Laura flitted away from the table. Moments later he could hear her through the open doorway, crooning a velvety lullaby to her son. Caleb forced himself to finish the stew and biscuits on his plate. He had a hard day's work ahead tomorrow, he reminded himself. And he certainly didn't want Laura to think there was anything wrong with her cooking.

He was sopping up the last of the gravy when she came back into the kitchen. By now it was almost dark. She paused to light the lamp on the counter. The match flickered in the gloom; then the golden light flooded her face, making her look as softly beautiful as the Madonna Caleb had once seen in an old Spanish church.

"Just a bad dream," she murmured. "I got him into his nightshirt, and he went back to sleep. There's pie if you're still hungry." When Caleb shook his head, she added, "You must be tired. Will you need a lantern to lay out your bedroll?"

It was a clear dismissal. Caleb slid back his chair and rose to his feet. "I cleared away a spot in the toolshed before I came in," he said. "I'll be fine. But let me put the milk and butter back in the springhouse for you. It's getting dark out there. Might not be safe for a woman alone."

The words were out of his mouth before he remembered. He'd made the same offer on that long-ago day when Zeke had cornered her in the springhouse. If she'd accepted his help then, the tragedy might never have happened.

This time she nodded and fumbled in her apron pocket. "Thanks. I'll give you the key to the padlock. You can leave it on the nail by the back door when you're finished."

Again those firm words of dismissal, making sure he knew that she didn't want him coming back inside. Caleb understood her reasons all too well. Still, it pained him that she felt the need to speak.

The miniature brass key glimmered as she drew it out of her pocket. Caleb reached out to take it from her. For the barest instant, his fingers touched hers.

Her fingertips were as callused and rough as his own. But the warmth of her flesh went through Caleb like a flash flood of raw need. He had touched her before—surely he had—when they were tending to Robbie's arm. But this time the awareness of her, of every sweet, womanly part of her, left him dry-mouthed and dizzy.

For that instant, the only thing on his mind was wanting more.

The clatter of the key, dropping to the tiles, brought him back to his senses. With a muttered curse, Caleb dropped to his knees and fumbled in the darkness under the table. Laura bent close with the lantern. He could hear the silky rasp of her breathing behind him. Lord help him if he didn't find that key—

"Got it!" His hand touched metal. He clambered to his feet, his fingers gripping the key, pressing its small, cold shape into his palm. Laura's eyes were smoky in the lamplight. She took a step backward, widening the distance between them.

"Sorry," he muttered, jamming the key into his own pocket. "Are you sure you want to trust these hands with your precious milk and butter?"

She forced a weary smile as she thrust the milk jug and the covered butter jar into his hands. He'd be all right now, Caleb told himself. He wouldn't be tempted to brush his knuckle along her cheek as he left, or to lay a too-casual hand across her shoulder. He couldn't allow himself to touch her again; that much he knew.

"Have a good night's rest," she said, opening the kitchen door for him. "When I see you up in the morning, I'll call you in to breakfast."

"That's right kind of you. I'm looking forward to more of your good food." Caleb moved out into the twilight. The door closed behind him, then jerked open again, flooding the stoop with light.

"Close the door of the shed before you go to sleep," she said. "We get skunks in the yard, looking for eggs and food scraps. One morning I even found a rattler in the corral. I killed it with the shotgun. They like warm places where they can crawl in and hide. Believe me, you don't want one of those for a bed partner."

Caleb gave her a nod. "Thanks for the warning. We had skunks and rattlers back in Texas, too. Some of them were the two-legged kind. Don't worry, I'll be fine. And you'll be safe with me here."

This time, when she closed the door behind him he heard the sharp, metallic click of the bolt.

Enough light remained for Caleb to see his way to the springhouse, but night was falling fast. He balanced his burden against the wall while he fumbled with the lock, turned the key and released the hasp. The door creaked inward and he stepped into the shadows.

The hair rose on the back of his neck as the nightmare memories crept around him. Laura's anguished screams echoed off the walls, ripping through his senses. He felt the awful snap of bone and his own sick helplessness as Zeke's blade opened her beautiful face. His eyes recoiled from the glint of light on Mark Shafton's rifle and from Noah's dark bulk in the glare of the sunlit doorway. The air was thick and smothering like a foul hand clamped over his face, shutting off his breath. It was as if the fear and evil born in that dank place had taken on a life of its own. All Caleb wanted was to get out of there.

His hands shook as he replaced the milk and butter in the cool box and stumbled out into the night. His mother had warned him about the spirits that lingered in places where some awful event had occurred. As a man, Caleb had chalked her stories up to Comanche superstition—until now.

Laura went in and out of the springhouse every day, he reminded himself. Did the horror of the place haunt her as it had haunted him? Or had she managed to wall it off into some forbidden corner of her mind? Caleb's jaw clenched at the thought of what she must have suffered and the courage it must have taken for her to stay here alone.

Filling his lungs with the cool evening air, he closed the padlock and hung the key on the nail beside the back door. Lamplight flickered through the window as Laura went about her work in the kitchen. Caleb pictured her small, quick hands, washing, wiping, putting everything in order for tomorrow. What would it feel like, he wondered, to stand behind her, wrap his arms around her shoulders and cradle her gently against him? He wouldn't ask heaven for more—just holding her would be enough, feeling her warmth and smelling the sweet, clean aroma of her hair. That was what he'd missed most in the past five years. In most any town there were whores who could be had for a few dollars, but simple tenderness was beyond any price he could pay.

Frustrated, he turned away from the house and

walked toward the shed where he'd laid out his bedroll. In the east a waning teardrop of a moon hung above the horizon. Clouds floated across its pitted face. The moon was scarred, and yet it was the most beautiful object in the sky. What would Laura say if he told her that?

But what was he thinking? He was a half-breed and an ex-convict. Even if his family's crime could be rubbed out and forgotten, a woman like Laura wouldn't be caught walking down the street with him.

He crossed the yard, keeping an eye out for skunks and rattlesnakes. His horse stood dozing in the corral. Its ears twitched as Caleb passed the fence. He could saddle up and go tonight, he thought. Maybe he'd ride south, skirting the foothills, all the way to Mexico. He could build a new life there, with his own little ranch and a fiery-eyed *señorita* who didn't give a damn about his past as long as he bought her pretty things to wear.

But no, he had fences to mend, firewood to chop and ditches to clear. He had an injured boy who could still take a turn for the worse, and a brave, beautiful woman who could only do so much without his help.

With every day he stayed here, the risks would mount. But Laura needed him. And while she needed him, he wouldn't leave her. Not tonight. Not tomorrow. Not until he could leave her safer, happier and better off than he'd found her.

Wispy clouds were streaming over the mountains.

Dark against the indigo sky, they floated like tattered silk on the evening breeze. Caleb's eyes traced the path of a falling star. He was bone tired, but something told him he wouldn't get much sleep tonight.

In Laura's window, the light had gone out.

Chapter Four

Laura lay with her eyes open, staring up into the darkness. Beside her Robbie curled in slumber, his splinted arm still resting on the pillow. Usually he slept in his own room, like the little man he was so determined to be. But tonight she wanted him near in case he woke up frightened or in pain. Tonight he was still her baby.

From outside in the yard, she could hear the light creak of the windmill in the nighttime breeze. She recalled how Caleb McCurdy had climbed up to replace the broken vanes with pine slabs he'd cut and shaped from logs in the woodpile. She remembered the sureness of his long, brown hands and the easy power of his body, a savage's body, beautiful in its lithe, catlike way.

Watching him was like watching a dangerous animal. He had a brawler's face, but the broken nose and the puckered scar across his eyebrow lent him a cynical, off-kilter expression that drew her eye and piqued her fascination. Laura had found herself wishing she could draw him out, learn more about who and what he was. But the secrets that blazed in those dark, intelligent eyes had warned her to keep her distance.

His whole way of moving and speaking was a study in tightly reined ferocity. Yet she'd never known anything from him except gentleness.

The man had been in prison, she reminded herself. And his self-confessed part in the robbery that landed him there had likely been played down for her benefit. He didn't act like a criminal. But then, how was a criminal supposed to act? How would she know?

Restless, Laura turned onto her side and bunched her pillow under her head. She would be wise to watch his every move, she cautioned herself. Not only was Caleb McCurdy an ex-convict, he was also half Comanche. She didn't know much about Indians, but Mark had warned her about half-breeds. They had the worst traits of the white race and the worst of the red, he'd told her. That was why decent folks didn't like having them around.

Blurred by darkness now, Mark's silver-framed photograph gazed at her from its place on the nightstand. What a handsome man he'd been—so bright and anxious to do well for himself. As a young bride, Laura had hung on his every word. Only in later years had she come to realize that, in many ways, Mark had been no wiser than she was. They'd been two innocents, little more than children, at the mercy of an untamed land and its people.

Laura twisted the thin gold band on her finger. Mark had been wrong about so many things. Had he been wrong about half-breeds, too?

With a sigh, she eased onto her back once more. Her arm slipped around the shoulders of her sleeping son. Robbie was her one sure, solid truth. His life gave meaning to every breath she took, every beat of her heart. All the rest was so much dust in the wind…even the tall, dark stranger who'd appeared like a phantom out of nowhere.

One day soon he would move on, and Laura sensed that she wouldn't see him again. Caleb McCurdy didn't strike her as a man who formed ties to any place—or to any person. He would simply ride away and never look back.

"What're you doing now, mister?"

Caleb fitted a board into the empty slot and used his free hand to pick up a nail and press the tip into the soft pine. He didn't mind the question at all. After the lonely years in prison, it was pure pleasure being tagged around the yard by a curious little boy.

"I'm putting new wood on your chicken coop so the skunks won't get in and eat the eggs at night. Do you think that's a good idea?" He picked up the hammer and sunk the nail with a few sharp blows.

Robbie watched him, wide-eyed. "Won't the skunks get hungry?"

"They'll find other things to eat." Caleb glanced

down at the nails scattered on the ground. "You can help me if you want. Pick up a few of those nails. When I need one, you can hand it to me."

"You bet!" Robbie scrambled for the nails, eager in spite of his splinted arm, which Laura had cradled in a sling made from a faded bandanna. The boy had bounced back from yesterday's fall. Except for some soreness in the arm and some awkwardness with the splint, he seemed to be doing fine.

Caleb accepted a second nail from Robbie and hammered it into place. Out of the corner of his eye, he could see Laura hanging a muslin sheet on the clothesline. She'd had wash hanging out the day before, he recalled. Today she didn't seem to have more than a small batch, just some bedding and a few dishcloths. Caleb suspected that the long process of boiling, scrubbing, rinsing, wringing and hanging was little more than an excuse to be outside where she could keep an eye on Robbie, and maybe on him as well.

He remembered the very first time he'd set eyes on her, standing in that very same spot, with yellow ribbons fluttering in her hair, so sweet and perfect that she'd reminded him of a brand-new store-bought doll just lifted from its tissue-paper wrappings.

Today she was dressed in threadbare calico, faded to a washed-out blue-gray that was worn almost colorless where the fabric strained against her breasts. Her sun-streaked hair hung down her back in a single braid, with loose tendrils blowing around her face. Her deep gray eyes were as luminous as ever, but they were framed by shadows of grief and worry. Laura Shafton was no longer a doll. She was a strong, capable woman who had stared death in the face and survived. A woman who could shoot a snake, skin a deer, chop her own firewood and raise a son with loving firmness.

In Caleb's eyes, she was more beautiful than ever.

"Can you shoot a gun?" Robbie asked, handing him another nail.

"If I have to."

"Will you teach me how?"

Caleb shook his head. "A gun isn't a toy. You can learn when you're older."

"How old?"

Caleb drove the nail in with a half-dozen ringing blows. "Maybe thirteen or fourteen, if you've got somebody to teach you. You need to be strong enough to hold the gun steady. And you need to be smart enough to know when and what to shoot."

"I'm strong and smart. My mama says so."

"Maybe so. But you're not old enough to shoot a gun."

The boy's lower lip thrust outward. "But what if bad men come around, like the ones that killed my papa? What if I have to shoot them?"

Caleb felt his stomach clench with a pain so physical that it stopped his breath. He knew the boy's question needed an answer, but words had deserted him. A bead of sweat trickled down his temple. The sun had suddenly become too warm, its light so bright that it made his eyes water.

"Ka-pow!" Robbie aimed his imaginary pistol toward the corral and pulled the trigger. "*Ka-pow! Ka-pow!* Take that, you dad-blamed varmints!" Laura glanced around, an expression of concern on her face. The boy turned back to Caleb. "That's what I'd do if bad men came!" he announced. "I'd shoot them all!"

Caleb found his voice. "I'll tell you what, Robbie. Let's finish nailing on these boards. Then maybe your mother will let me take you fishing this afternoon."

"Fishing?" The round blue eyes brightened. "Can I catch a fish?"

"Maybe. I'll show you what to do. The rest is up to the fish."

"I'll ask her now!" The boy spun away, then swung back toward Caleb, looking crestfallen. "But how can we go fishing? We don't have a fishing pole."

Caleb's face relaxed into a grin. "Leave that to me," he said.

Laura had agreed to let her son go fishing, but only on condition that she come along. Caleb seemed to get on well with the boy, but water could be dangerous. It would be all too easy for a man to become distracted and turn his back at the wrong moment. That aside, fishing would also be a useful skill for her to learn, one more way to put food on the table in times of need.

The problem of finding a pole and tackle had

been solved when Caleb delved into one of his saddlebags and came up with a small canvas pouch. Inside was a coil of fishing line and an assortment of hooks and sinkers. All that remained was to find a long, stout willow with the right amount of flex and to dig a few worms from the garden. By then Robbie was dancing with excitement.

Willow, cottonwood and box elder cast dappled shade as they followed an old game trail uphill along the path of the creek. Caleb, with the fishing pole, led most of the way except when Robbie bounded ahead of him. Laura, ever watchful, brought up the rear.

Laura had never seen her son so happy. What a tragedy Mark hadn't lived to raise his boy. Robbie was only a few years beyond babyhood, but she could already see how much he'd missed having a man around. She would be wise to make sure the boy didn't get too attached to Caleb. Otherwise he could end up with a broken heart.

Robbie scampered ahead, waving his worm can toward a spot where white water cascaded over steep rocks. "Let's fish here!" he shouted.

"Hold your horses, boy," Caleb chuckled. "Fish like to hang around where the water's slow and deep, in places we call holes. When we find a good hole, that's where we'll find our fish." He paused long enough for Laura to catch up. The trail had widened here. There was no longer any need to walk single file.

"So you've never fished before?" he asked, making polite conversation.

"Mark—my husband—didn't care for fishing. And, believe it or not, I grew up in a household where young ladies didn't get their hands smelly. So, no, I've never tried fishing."

"Then maybe it's time you did."

She glanced up to find his fierce dark eyes studying her. Up close they were brownish-black with flecks of coppery green, set deep into shadowed sockets. They were striking eyes—unusual eyes, really. Why did she have this strange feeling she'd seen them somewhere before?

But she was imagining things, Laura told herself. Surely if she had met a man like Caleb McCurdy, she would remember him.

"It's Robbie's turn to fish today," she said. "I'll watch and learn."

"Fine. If you change your mind, just say so." He glanced at Robbie, who'd darted up the trail to snatch a handful of ripening blackberries and stuff them in his mouth. "I know it's none of my business, but your boy seems pretty lonely. Doesn't he have any friends near his own age?"

"Not now. There used to be a family of homesteaders out on the flat. Sometimes they'd stop by on their way into town and Robbie would play with their boys. Last month they pulled up stakes and moved on." She sighed. "Not everything Robbie learned from those boys was good, but I know he misses them."

Caleb's left eyebrow quirked upward. "That makes sense. I figured he didn't get 'take that, you dad-blamed varmints' from you."

"Wait till you hear some of the other things he didn't get from me." Laura shook her head in mock despair, then decided to broach an idea that had been simmering all morning. "I was wondering if you'd mind driving us to town in the buckboard tomorrow. It's a long day's trip there and back, but I'm low on baking supplies and grain for the chickens, and Robbie really should be checked by the doctor..."

She trailed off, struck by Caleb's expression. For a flicker of time, it was as if a cold wind had passed across his face, chilling his features. Then the strangeness passed. He shrugged, cleared his throat and spoke.

"Can't argue with that. I know you won't rest easy till you know the boy's all right."

"I drive the road myself every couple of months," she said. "But it can be dangerous, and I always worry about something going wrong. With a man along, it'll be safer, and we'll be able to load more..." She paused, suddenly aware that she'd been babbling. "I'm sorry," she murmured. "I didn't mean to beat you down with words. If you don't want to come—"

"No, it's fine. Just let me know how early you want to leave, and I'll have the team hitched." His eyes had narrowed to unreadable slits. "And now I'd better see what your son is up to. Maybe he's found that fishing hole we're looking for."

He strode up the trail and around the bend, where Robbie had vanished a moment before. Laura could hear them talking, Robbie's voice high-pitched with excitement, Caleb's a low rumble. Laura quickened her own steps, battling the vague uneasiness that had settled over her spirit. It was a beautiful day. The air was sweet with the scent of wild roses. Meadowlarks were trilling on the grassy hillside, and her son was as happy as she'd ever seen him. Wasn't that enough for now?

Wasn't it?

They'd found their fishing hole at the foot of a low waterfall where the stream widened into a pool. Here the water had undercut the bank, carving out deep, dark lurking places for the cutthroat trout that lived in these mountain streams. They were small fish but full of fight, and the taste of them, grilled fresh over an open fire, was pure heaven.

Robbie's splinted left hand was too clumsy to bait the hook, so Caleb did it for him. Laura sat on a flat rock, watching them with her quiet gray eyes. The sunlight filtered down through the aspens, warming her hair to the spun-gold hue of wild honey. Her cheeks were rosy from the climb up the slope, her full lips flushed and parted.

Caleb stole a glance at her as he seated Robbie on the bank and showed him how to let the baited hook drift under the lip of the pool. Right now Laura looked as sweet and innocent as an angel. But what could be going on in that beautiful head of hers?

Her suggestion that he drive her into town had come out of nowhere, throwing him off balance. He'd had little choice except to agree. But he was still wondering what to make of her request. Did she simply need his help? Or was Laura guiding him into a devilishly laid trap?

He studied her furtively as he helped Robbie balance the pole. Laura Shafton was not a stupid woman. If she'd recognized him, she wouldn't let on. A confrontation of any kind would be too risky, especially with Robbie around.

It made more sense that she'd play the fool, pretending to trust him. Then, when the time was right, she'd make an excuse to get him into town where she could point him out to the sheriff.

A drop of sweat trickled between Caleb's shoulder blades. He had no proof either way. But the more he weighed what she'd said and done, the deeper his suspicions grew. To carry out a scheme like that, Laura would have to have ice in her veins. But then, the woman's husband had been gunned down before her eyes. He'd died a bloody death in her arms. After living through such an ordeal, she might be capable of anything.

Caleb glanced back toward her. The brief smile she returned tore at his heart. Maybe he was wrong. Maybe she was every bit as innocent and trusting as she appeared. But even if she had no secret plan, going into town would be risky. There was no telling who might be there—some lawman passing through, or someone who knew his brothers and might remember him from those wild days before his arrest.

Caleb's nerves began to tingle, then to crawl. No,

he couldn't take the chance. There was too much danger of something going wrong—something that could land him back in prison or even at the end of a rope. But he'd already agreed to go with Laura. How could he break his word now without rousing her suspicions?

"A fish!" Robbie squealed. "I've got one!"

Caleb caught the jerking pole just in time to save it from the creek. "Hold on tight, Robbie!" He braced the pole while the child's hands got a better grip. "That's it! What a fighter! Now ease back... Bring him in slow and steady..."

Robbie whooped as the fish broke water and burst into the sunlight. Moments later it lay quivering in the grass, a small treasure of living silver. Laura clapped her hands. Robbie touched the fish with a cautious finger, his expression blending wonder, elation and sadness. For a moment Caleb was afraid he might burst into tears. Then the boy grinned. "I want to catch another one!" he said.

"You're on your own this time, so keep a cool head, hear?" Caleb re-baited the hook and handed him the pole. Robbie settled happily onto the bank and dropped the line in the water. Laura's face wore a tender little smile.

He would leave tonight, Caleb resolved. While Laura and her son were asleep, he would saddle up and ride off into the darkness. There was no other way to avoid what might happen if he drove the buckboard into town tomorrow.

Caleb hated the idea of sneaking off at night, especially if Laura truly needed him. But every day he stayed raised the odds of betrayal and tragedy. To leave now, before any more harm could be done, would be the smartest thing he could do.

Robbie sat happily on the bank, dangling his line in the water. Caleb's gaze wandered from the boy to his mother. Laura's braid had come undone. She sat with her hands clasping her knees, her head flung back to let her hair fall down her back in thick, silky waves. Caleb imagined tangling his fingers in that honey-gold mass, lifting it to his face and inhaling its womanly scent—*her* scent—clean and honest and so sensual that just being near her made his throat ache with need.

But touching her hair wouldn't be enough, he knew. Once he began, one thing would lead to another. He would stroke her skin, running a fingertip down her arm to caress the contours of her tough little hand, shaping each finger with his own. He would kiss a tender path along the white scar, from her temple to the corner of her rosebud mouth, then nibble his way down the curve of her throat to where her bodice closed and her satiny skin turned from gold to ivory. He would play with each button, testing, teasing, brushing a knuckle along the curve of one breast as if by accident…

Damn! Caleb cursed silently as he forced the forbidden images from his mind. Yes, it was time to leave. Now, tonight, before he drove himself crazy thinking about her. There were other women in other towns, women whose troubles had nothing to do with him. Maybe there were even one or two out there who could make him forget a heart-stopping pair of dove-gray eyes.

She shifted her position, and suddenly those eyes were fixed on him. Caleb resisted the urge to look away. He'd been caught devouring her with his gaze. There was nothing to do but make the best of it.

"You should wear your hair down more often," he said. "It seems such a waste to braid it up the way you do."

Self-conscious, she raised her hand and brushed a straying lock back from her face. "You mean I should wear my hair down to milk the cow and hoe the garden and do the wash? Why? It would just be in the way." Her tone was neutral, as if she couldn't decide whether to be flattered or offended. "I haven't worn my hair loose since..." Her voice caught slightly. "Since my husband died. Not much reason to, is there?"

Her hands fluttered up to her hair, reached back and finger-combed it into three sections. With hurried, jerky motions she began to braid.

"You don't need to do that," Caleb said.

She paused in mid-motion, her lips parted, her eyes moist and glimmering. "Yes, I do," she said softly, and continued the braiding.

"Hey, it's stuck!" Robbie's shout was a welcome distraction. Caleb hurried to help him free the hook, which had snagged on a mossy log.

"Here you go," he said, dropping the hook back into deep water. "Let's give this hole a few more tries. If nothing bites, we'll hike upstream and find another spot. That's what fishing's all about."

"I like fishing!" Robbie waggled the hook and was instantly rewarded by another strike. This fish was larger and put up a spirited tussle. Laura's son was ecstatic as he dragged it onto the bank. "Can we eat my fish for supper tonight?"

"You catch 'em and I'll cook 'em!" Caleb flashed the boy a grin. Tomorrow he'd be gone. There wasn't much he could do to make things right with Laura, but he could give her lonely little boy a few good memories before he rode out of their lives. It was the least he could do.

The evening meal was a grand occasion. Robbie had caught seven fish that afternoon. Caleb had cleaned them and grilled them outdoors, on a rack of green willows over a bed of glowing red coals. Their smoky aroma was mouthwatering, their skins crisp, their flesh pink and succulent.

Laura had done her share by frying up a mess of potatoes and onions, served with a salad of fresh lettuce, baby carrots and parsley from her garden. She'd added hot biscuits, butter and wild strawberry jam, with fresh-baked oatmeal cookies for dessert.

On impulse, she'd set the table with the good china from her wedding and picked a bouquet of dark blue gentians for the centerpiece. She wanted Robbie to know that this was a special meal and to give Caleb her wordless thanks for making it possible.

All three of them were ravenous, so there was more eating than talking. But Laura couldn't help pausing to study the contrast of Caleb's dark head bent next to Robbie's thatch of golden curls. Both of them were absorbed in the fine points of lifting the tiny fish skeleton clear of the delicate pink meat. "If you're careful," Caleb was saying, "you can get the backbone and ribs out all in one piece, so you won't be spitting out all those little bones. Here, try it. Careful, now…"

He was so gentle, she mused. There had to be more to Caleb McCurdy than a battered face and a prison record. He was well mannered, well spoken and, from what she'd observed, the very soul of kindness. Who was the man behind that bruised and taciturn mask? Wasn't she entitled to know? She'd taken him under her roof, trusted him with her precious son. Surely she had the right to question him.

And question him she would, Laura resolved. She would demand his story tonight—and she wouldn't be satisfied with anything less than the truth.

Chapter Five

By the end of the meal, Robbie was so tired that he nodded off over his half-eaten oatmeal cookie. Laura eased him into her arms, wiped the crumbs off his face and carried him into his room.

Caleb stood and began to clear away the dishes, scraping the fish bones into the rubbish pail. The afternoon and evening had been a bittersweet interlude in his life, almost—but not quite—like being part of a family. Now it was time to end it. He would stay long enough to thank Laura for the fine supper. Then he'd bid her good-night for the last time. By sunrise he'd be miles away, never to see her beautiful, scarred face again.

Finding the key next to the door, he carried the milk and butter out to the springhouse and put them in the cool box. Only the gurgling stream broke the quiet within the thick log walls. Still, the evil lingered, lurking in the dark silence. By the time he locked the door behind him, Caleb's skin was beaded with cold sweat. He stood at the corner of the house for a moment, watching the last threads of crimson fade into the indigo sky. Only when the warmth had crept back into his bones did he turn and go back inside the house.

He found Laura in the kitchen wiping down the tabletop with a damp cloth. He held out the key. She took it, her fingers skimming his. Even after their contact ended, the warmth of her skin flowed through him.

Caleb cleared the tightness from his throat. "I would've left the key outside and gone, but I wanted to thank you. For a man who's spent the past five years where I have, a day like this one, a supper like this one..." His voice trailed off into a breath. He'd said enough, maybe too much. It was time to leave before he made a fool of himself.

He turned away, but her hand caught his sleeve. "It's early yet. Come out onto the porch and sit with me awhile." The nervous little sound she made might have been a laugh. "Robbie's a bright boy and good company, but sometimes I miss talking with another grown-up."

Caleb followed her through the parlor and opened the front door. Outside the twilight had deepened to purple dusk. Crickets sang in the willows along the creek. The faint aroma of wood smoke floated on the night breeze.

Laura settled herself on the edge of the porch, her feet resting on the bottom step. Caleb hesitated, then sat beside Laura, keeping a proper distance between them.

"You don't have to be so alone, Laura. You could go into town more often, go to church, go to parties and dances. You could make new friends, maybe even find yourself a good man—"

"No." Her voice was flat, adamant.

"Why not? You're a beautiful woman. Any man would be happy to—"

"Balderdash!" She spat out the word. "Spare me your pretty lies, Caleb. Back in St. Louis, before I was married, I had more friends and beaux than I could count. Now, when I walk down the street, the people I pass turn and look the other way, and I don't blame them. Who wants to look at *this?*" She turned sideways and yanked her hair back to give him a full view of her scarred profile.

Zeke's blade had done its ugly work. Twilight gleamed on the jagged white line, bordered by puckered flesh where the edges of Laura's healing skin had pulled together. The scar stopped just short of her mouth, tugging the corner into a slight upward slant. Caleb checked the impulse to seize her face between his hands and tell her how beautiful she was. That, he sensed, would only frighten her.

"We all have our scars, Laura," he said softly. "Some of them are on the outside. Some are on the inside. But we can't change them. All we can do is accept them as part of who we are and go on living."

Laura let her hair fall back to shadow her cheek. Her fingers toyed with her thin gold wedding band, turning it restlessly. A nighthawk flashed across the rising moon, a swift, dark shadow.

"And what about *your* scars?" she asked. "I can't see them, but I know they're there. Have you learned to live with them? Or are you just better at lying to yourself than I am?"

Caleb let the silence fall around them while he digested her question. "My mother died in childbirth when I was twelve. My father spent the next five years drinking himself to death. Our home and the land with it went to pay off what he owed. But I've known others who fared worse. At least I had my mother in my growing-up years. She was a fine woman."

"Any brothers or sisters?"

At the mention of brothers, he felt the familiar sinking in the pit of his stomach. Was she trying to back him into a corner, or was it just an innocent question? Caleb decided to err on the side of truth.

"Two half brothers. Gone their own way—to the devil for all I care." He stirred, shifting his bones on the hard wooden edge of the porch. "My life story hasn't been a pretty one. I've made mistakes and I've paid. Take it for whatever it's worth to you."

She released her breath in a raspy little sigh. "I don't mean to pry. But I need to know what sort of man's been sitting at my table and spending time with my son. So far, you've been the very soul of decency. But you've been arrested. You've spent time in prison, and who knows what other things you haven't told me..." Her voice trailed off. Her deep gray eyes seemed to plead for understanding.

"You're saying you need to know that you and Robbie will be safe with me."

"Yes."

Caleb swallowed hard. What could he tell her? That he'd rather cut off his arm than hurt one hair on her or her son's head? That he'd gladly die fighting to protect them from harm?

Would she think he was spouting empty words? Or worse, would she remember how he'd failed to protect her before? Only one thing was certain—Laura had no reason to believe anything he told her.

"What you see is who I am," he said. "You can trust me or send me away. That's your decision. Nothing I tell you is going to make a bean's worth of difference."

"Maybe not." She gazed into the deepening twilight, her hands clasped on her knees. Her silence hung between them, demanding to be filled. Caleb sighed and stretched his legs, bracing his dusty boots against the bottom step. He'd never told anyone about the gift he'd received in prison. Maybe now was the time.

"Let me tell you a true story," he said. "Again, it's not pretty. But it might help you understand a few things."

Laura turned toward him, still silent and waiting. Moonlight silvered the sun streaks in her loose-braided hair.

"Being in prison's about as bad as anything you can imagine," he began. "Yuma was purgatory on earth—hot, miserable, and filled with the sorriest excuses for human beings you ever saw. I know. I was one of them."

Laura's lips parted. For a moment Caleb thought she might speak, but she simply nodded, her gaze holding his.

"When they first threw me in that place, I was young and stupid and mad at the whole world. I handed my soul over to the devil and vowed that when I got out of that place I was going to raise bloody hell. I'd help myself to whatever I wanted, and heaven save any do-gooders, psalm-singers and law-keepers who got in my way."

"What happened?" Laura's question was a breath on the wind.

"Nothing for the first couple of years. I was known as a hard case, a bad-mouther and a brawler who'd take on any man who looked at me sideways, even if it meant getting beaten to a bloody pulp. As the months went by, I put on muscle and learned to hold my own in a fight. But inside, I was the same scared young fool I'd always been."

Caleb sucked in his breath. He'd never shared the things he was telling Laura. With her pure eyes burning through the darkness, burning through *him,* it was like ripping out a piece of his soul.

"I was too far gone to pray for a miracle," he said. "But fate or destiny or whatever you want to call it was waiting to smack me in the head. Toward the start of my third year, I was put in with a new cell mate. His name was Ebenezer Stokes. He was doing time for attempted murder."

Laura's eyes widened. She had drawn her feet up under her skirt and was sitting with her hands clasped around her knees. "Go on," she said in a taut whisper.

"Ebenezer's wife had been running around with a gambler. Ebenezer found out and went after the man with a pistol. Lucky for them both, Ebenezer couldn't shoot for sour apples. The judge gave him five years, but any fool could see that he'd never live to finish his sentence. He was sick—his kidneys, he said, although he swore he'd never been a drinking man. By the time I met him, he was too weak to go out on the work gangs. He helped in the kitchen for a while, but finally even that got to be too much."

"And he was your miracle? An attempted murderer with kidney disease?"

Caleb rose to his feet, too agitated to sit. "I'd never been to school. I was raised by a Comanche mother who couldn't read or write a word, and a father who couldn't do much better. I could print my name and do a few sums. That was about it." For a moment he stared up at the half-veiled face of the moon. Then he turned back to face her. "Ebenezer Stokes was a schoolmaster."

Her mouth formed a pretty little *O* of astonishment. At that moment, to Caleb, the light in her eyes was worth more than gold. Warmed by her response, he chuckled wryly and shook his head.

"Lord help me, the man was a tyrant! Our first night together, he told me he reckoned he'd be going to hell soon, but he wanted to leave one good thing behind. That one good thing was going to be me!

"We started right then, first with reading, then with writing, then with arithmetic. Somehow he'd gotten his hands on a big paper notebook and some pencils that I had to sharpen by chewing away the wood. I filled every inch of that paper on both sides and wore the pencils down to nubs. Still he wouldn't let up. We went on to history, geography, science, literature. Because we didn't have books, he'd pour out what was in his head, and I'd have to recite it back to him, sometimes word for word.

"The worse his health got, the harder he pushed me. He must've known time was running out. I'd come in from pounding rock on the work gang, dead dog tired and just wanting to sleep, and he'd be waiting for me. 'Who was Socrates?' 'Where's the Danube?' 'Name the planets in the solar system.' Sometimes we'd be up all night."

"Didn't that make you angry?"

"Madder than spit, especially at first. But I couldn't hit a dying man. And I couldn't refuse to learn. Even at the worst times I knew what he was giving me, and what it was costing him.

"Sometimes I thought he must be crazy. Sometimes I wondered if I might be crazy, too. I'd catch myself recollecting things he'd taught me and trying to fit them together like the pieces of a puzzle. After he'd gone, there were nights when I'd lie awake just thinking…

"We shared a cell for about ten months. Then he took a turn for the worse. They took him to the infirmary while I was out on the work gang, and I never saw him again. I didn't even get a chance to thank him."

Laura sat in silence, her knees drawn up against her chest. Did she believe him? He wanted her to, Caleb realized. He wanted it with a desperation that made him ache. It didn't matter that he'd be gone in a few hours, never to see her again. Right now, all he wanted was to see a flicker of trust in those silvery eyes.

"I know this sounds like a cock-and-bull story. You're probably thinking I made it up." The words stumbled out of him. "But if you want proof, ask me anything—anything you might've learned in school."

She stirred, releasing her knees. "No, I believe you. Mark Twain himself couldn't have invented a story like that."

"Then believe this, Laura. I'm not the person I used to be. To hurt you or Robbie or anybody else would betray a good man's gift. I owe it to Ebenezer to make something of myself. Someday I will, but it's going to take time. Right now I'm just a grubby saddle bum trying to find his way in the world."

She stood, pressing her hands to the small of her back, stretching out the soreness. The arch of her body, head thrown back, breasts thrusting upward, was so innocently sensual that Caleb had to turn away. It was impossible not to imagine clasping her in his arms and molding her body to his, feeling the sweet pressure of her nipples against his chest, the tapered curve of her waist, the solid little mound where her thighs came together, hard against his own hard heat. He swore under his breath.

"So where do you go from here?" she asked. "Back to Texas?"

Texas again. And her tone had been almost too casual, too conversational. Caleb had hoped the story of his redemption would win her trust, but maybe that was too much to ask.

"Can't say," he answered truthfully. "Right now I'd settle for any place where I can make good honest money. Someday, when I'm ready to put down roots, I'd like to buy a spread of my own. But that's still a dream. It'll take a lot of blisters to make it come true."

She seemed to hesitate, then took a step toward him. "Show me your hands," she said. "My grandmother always said she could read a man's future in his palms. Maybe I can do it, too."

Caleb held his hands toward her, palms up. She cupped them from below, her fingers cool against his skin. Moonlight shone on the horny calluses, the half-healed cuts and blisters, the smashed thumb that had come between a rock and a hammer. They were rough, ugly hands, convict's hands. Half-ashamed, he fought the urge to tug them away from her.

Her fingertip traced the lines and contours of his palm. He felt the contact as a tingle that shimmered up his arms. Caleb bit back a groan. Even in this simple, strangely intimate way, he couldn't get enough of her touching him.

"I see ambition." Her voice was a throaty whisper. "I see stubbornness and stoicism—the willingness to endure pain, suffering, humiliation… I think you'll get your dream, Caleb McCurdy. With hands like these, you'll get whatever you go after."

Even a woman like you? The words sprang into Caleb's mind, but he knew better than to speak them. No matter how much he might want her, Laura could never be his.

"What about you?" he asked, capturing her hand in a deft move. "If I could read your palm, what would it tell me about your future?"

She gazed down at their joined hands, her face masked by the shadow of her hair. "My future is what you see—this place and my boy. If I can raise him to be a good man, that's enough for me."

"Is it, Laura?" He held her fingers imprisoned in his fist. "What about something for yourself? What about finding some good man to care for you and build a life with you, maybe give you more children?"

Laura shook her head and pulled her hand away. "Robbie's enough. He loves me the way I am because he doesn't know any better. As for finding a man—why should any man choose me when he could have a pretty woman, a *perfect* woman?" She made a little choking sound. "That's what Mark—my husband—used to say. He told me I was perfect, and that was why he loved me."

"Then your husband was a damned fool, and so are you!" The words exploded out of Caleb before he could stop them. His hands cupped her face, gripping hard, forcing her to look up at him. "No man in his right mind could help loving you the way you are, Laura! No man..."

Driven by an urge too deep to resist, he lowered his mouth to hers. The first kiss was little more than a nibble, a tentative, tasting brush of lips. She stiffened at his touch. He felt the leap of her pulse beneath his thumbs and he half expected her to pull away, but she stood as if rooted to the ground, trembling like an aspen in the wind.

He kissed her again, letting his hands slide down her shoulders to her back. Her lips were like the petals of a storm-blown rose, cool and soft and yielding. Her heart thundered against his chest as he pulled her close. Hunger flashed through his body, igniting a current of liquid heat that pooled in his swollen, aching loins.

Caleb could feel the exquisite tension in her body, the heart-pounding fear that could send her bolting into the house at any moment. Holding her was like stroking a wild fawn. He struggled to keep his hands gentle, his kisses tender, but it wasn't easy. He wanted her so damnably much. It was all he could do to keep from crushing her in his arms, yanking open the neck of her threadbare gown and burying his face in the heavenly hollow between her breasts.

Her hands crept up to his shoulders. Little by little her body began to relax, her womanly curves melting against him, her warmth going through him like a fever.

"You're so beautiful, Laura..." he whispered, letting his lips caress her cheeks, her eyes, her throat. "Don't you know that? Don't you know what I see when I look at you?" His mouth skimmed the faint puckered ridge of the scar. Suddenly she went rigid in his arms.

"All women are beautiful in the *dark!*" Tearing loose from him on the last word, she spun away and stood quivering in the moonlight. "The fact that I'm disfigured, and that I've been out here alone for five years, doesn't make me an easy mark for any man who wanders by! I'll thank you to remember that, Caleb McCurdy! Take your pretty lies someplace else!"

She wheeled, raced up the front steps, crossed the porch and vanished into the house. Caleb heard the unmistakable click of the bolt. Hellfire, did the woman think he'd be coming after her?

Cursing out loud he turned away from the house and ambled toward the shed. His blood was still on fire, he was hurting like blazes and he knew exactly how the evening was going to end. He should've had the sense to keep his hands off Laura. Whatever he'd done tonight, it wasn't good.

But at least he'd created a reason to leave. When Laura came outside in the morning to find him gone, she wouldn't have to wonder why.

The wail of a coyote drifted down from the foothills, a plaintive, lonesome song. Caleb stood by the corral fence, his shadow long and solitary in the moonlight as he listened for an answering call. When no answer came he strode into the shed to pack his saddlebags and wait until the house went dark.

Laura could not sleep. The air inside the house was warm and sticky. She twisted in the clammy sheets, electric sparks still racing through her veins. Why had she let Caleb touch her? Why had she let him kiss her? And why, against all reason, had she kissed him back?

Until tonight she'd managed to forget how it felt, the leap of flame from skin to skin, the surging pulse, the warm liquid weight that shimmered and tightened in the secret depths of her body…

She must have experienced those sensations as a young bride with Mark—surely she had. She'd enjoyed their loving once the soreness healed. But nothing had ever shaken her like the heat that had rocketed through her body when Caleb McCurdy took her in his arms. Sweet heaven, it had terrified her. She'd frozen against him, fearful that if she let herself respond she might spiral completely out of control. Only when he'd kissed the scar on her face had she come to her senses and broken away.

How could such a thing have happened? Because she'd *let* it happen, that was how. She was the one who'd led him on. Moved by the story of his prison education, she'd taken his hand and pretended to read his future. It had been a game, a silly excuse to touch him, that was all. But Caleb had clearly taken it as an invitation. She should have known where it would lead. Oh, why couldn't she have left well enough alone?

Laura had no illusions about why he'd kissed her. It wasn't because he was in love with her or because he thought she was pretty. A man fresh out of prison would take any female he could get his hands on, even a woman with an ugly, scarred face. He'd seen her as an easy mark, a woman who'd be hungry and grateful for a man's attention. Well, Caleb McCurdy had a few lessons to learn about women—especially about *this* woman!

Tomorrow he'd be driving her and Robbie into town. They'd be spending hours together in the buckboard. She would make it clear at the outset that Caleb was to keep his hands—and his sweet talk—to himself. She had too much at stake to humiliate herself with a rootless drifter—even a drifter whose kisses lit bonfires in her veins.

Bunching her pillow beneath her head, she turned onto her side. From where she lay, she could see Mark's photograph on the nightstand. It was too dark to see his face but that made no difference. The handsome image, with its wavy blond hair, earnest eyes and classically chiseled jaw had long since been burned into her memory. But she could no longer remember his voice or how it felt to be touched by him. Now when she closed her eyes, it was Caleb's lean, dark face she saw, Caleb's raw-pitched voice she heard, Caleb's hungry kisses she felt on her mouth.

From the parlor, the pendulum clock chimed the hour. It was one o'clock, the very dead of night. Even with the window open, the room was so stuffy she could barely breathe. What was wrong with her? How could she face the difficult day ahead without a decent night's sleep?

Swinging her legs over the edge of the bed, she stood, padded over to the window and leaned her elbows on the sill. The night breeze was pure bliss on her damp face. She unbuttoned the neck of her nightgown, letting it cool the sweaty furrow between her breasts. The air still smelled faintly of wood smoke from Caleb's fire. She filled her lungs in long, gulping breaths.

A movement near the corral caught her eye—a dark figure near the horses. Her heart dropped as she realized it was Caleb. He was fully dressed, carrying a saddle in his arms.

Laura's mouth went dry as she realized he was leaving.

She drew back from the window, not wanting to be seen. Fine, let him leave, she told herself. Let him leave now, before things got any more complicated than they already were. She'd be better off without him! As for tomorrow, she could hitch up the buckboard and drive the twenty miles to town by herself. She'd been doing it for five years, so why should she depend on some man to help her?

Weak-kneed, she sagged against the edge of the window frame. It was her doing, of course. She'd driven him off, sure as the sun rises. And why not? Why stay around if he knew he wouldn't be getting anything for his trouble?

All women were beautiful in the dark—that's

what she'd told him and that's what she believed. But no man could look at her in the daylight and want her as a woman—not even a man as woman-hungry as Caleb McCurdy.

Peering around the window frame, she risked another glance outside. At first she couldn't see him. Then she realized he was crouching low to fasten the cinch under the horse's belly. A minute more and he'd be gone.

Well, good riddance! She would check on Robbie and go back to bed. When she woke up at dawn, things would be just as they'd been before Caleb came into her life....

Except that the corral gate wouldn't sag anymore, the windmill would work as it should and the skunks wouldn't be able to get at the chickens.

Robbie would know how to fish for the rest of his life.

And her own memory would be seared by the burn of a stranger's kiss.

The door of Robbie's room stood ajar. As Laura tiptoed inside, she could hear him whimpering beneath the covers. She flew to his bedside and helped him sit up.

"What is it, Robbie? Your arm?"

He shook his head. "Tummy hurts," he muttered. "Gonna be sick—"

Laura barely had time to grab the empty chamber pot before he became violently ill.

Chapter Six

Caleb had finished loading the horse and was mounting up when he heard Laura shout his name. She'd burst out of the back door and was flying toward him across the moonlit yard, her feet bare, her white nightgown fluttering against her body. For a moment he entertained fantasies of her running to his arms and begging him to stay. But then, as she came closer, he saw the look of anguish on her face.

He plunged toward her, catching her by the shoulders. Her eyes were pits of fear in the darkness. The neck of her nightgown had fallen open but she seemed unaware of it.

"What is it?" he demanded.

"Robbie!" she gasped. "He's sick, throwing up everything! Get the buckboard ready, we need to get him to town—to the doctor—"

"Any blood?"

"I can't tell. But he's in a lot of pain."

"Let me have a look at him." Caleb released her and she spun away. He followed her as she sprinted back toward the house. The timing of this drama was a little too neat, he mused. If this was some kind of trick to get him into town, then Laura was a damned good actress. But he would reserve judgment until he saw the boy. Robbie had taken a nasty fall. A serious internal injury like a ruptured liver or spleen could take time to manifest itself.

The door to Robbie's bedroom was standing open. As soon as Caleb stepped inside he knew that Laura had told him the truth. Even with the window open, the room smelled of vomit. Robbie lay in a patch of moonlight, his face white, his eyelids drooping. Caleb's heart dropped at the sight of him. With the doctor hours away, the boy could be in real danger.

"How are you doing, pal?" he asked, smoothing back the matted blond curls.

"My tummy hurts," Robbie whimpered. "It hurts bad."

Laura had flung herself down beside the bed and was sponging her son's face with a damp cloth. "Please, Caleb," she whispered. "The buckboard—hurry!"

Caleb took a step toward the door, then paused as he remembered something. "My mother used to boil pine pitch into a tea for stomach problems. There's a clump of piñon trees up the hill. Get some water boiling while I gather some pitch. We can take the tea with us."

He'd half expected her to argue, but she simply nodded and flashed into the kitchen. Caleb raced uphill to where stubby piñon pines grew among the sage and junipers. With his knife he scraped off beads of pitch from their trunks. He came back into the house to find Laura at the stove, shoving kindling into the smoldering firebox. Her eyes were huge in the flickering light.

An open kettle sat on the front burner. Caleb dropped the pitch into the water, which was just starting to simmer.

"How long will it take?" Laura's white nightgown was smudged with soot. The buttons at the neck had been hastily done up, leaving the collar askew.

"Keep it covered and boiling while we get ready to go. We can let it steep longer on the way. By the time it cools, it should be strong enough."

"Will it really help?"

"It might make him feel better. For now, it's the best medicine we've got. Bring a basin and some towels." Caleb lit a lantern and strode outside to put his own horse away and hitch Laura's team to the buckboard. He didn't have a good feeling about being in town, but there wasn't much he could do about it. He could hardly ride away and leave Laura with a sick child. And he couldn't turn his back on a little boy who needed him.

For better or for worse, he was trapped.

A wan half-moon floated overhead as the buckboard rumbled across the sagebrush flat. Laura cradled her blanket-wrapped son in her arms to cushion him against the bumpy ride. She'd managed to get a few spoonfuls of the pine pitch tea down his throat but Robbie had battled every swallow. It was too soon to know whether the bitter liquid was doing any good. But at least he'd stopped whimpering and fallen into a fitful sleep.

Caleb sat beside her on the bench seat, driving the team as fast as he dared over the rutted lines of earth that barely qualified as a road. His dark hands plied the reins with patient skill—the same skill that could mend a gate, thread a fishing line or caress a woman—as Laura had learned all too well.

Except for a few terse sentences, the two of them had scarcely spoken in the past hour. The memory of their stolen kisses lay like a ravine between them, a lapse in judgment that Laura had no wish to discuss. Nor did she want to bring up the fact that she'd caught him leaving. It seemed unimportant now. Nothing mattered except her fear for Robbie's life.

"How's the boy?" Caleb's voice was soft, his glance no more than a flicker.

"Asleep for now." Laura shifted wearily on the bench seat. "I don't have much experience with sick children. What do you think is wrong with him? Perhaps the fall—"

"It could be anything, or nothing. The doctor will know." Caleb spoke with a studied calm that didn't fool her for a minute. He was worried, too.

She shuddered, holding her son close. "When I was eight, my little sister died from a fall. She was just…Robbie's age." Laura's voice broke. She swallowed a sob.

"Don't dwell on it," Caleb said. "You'll only wear yourself out worrying. Youngsters get sick. Most of the time they come through it fine. Otherwise there wouldn't be so many adults walking around."

"Oh…I know you think you're making sense, Caleb." Laura laid her cheek against Robbie's curls, feeling the feverish heat of his scalp. "But you've never been a parent. You can't imagine what it's like. If anything happened to Robbie…" She drew in a shattered breath. "My life would be over. Loving somebody this much…it's heaven and hell rolled into one."

"Was that how much you loved your husband, Laura?"

His question startled her. Likely as not, he was just trying to distract her from Robbie, but for a moment Laura felt as if she'd been punched. Her mind scrambled for some clever evasion, but she could find none.

"I loved him as much as a seventeen-year-old girl is capable of loving. But that love never had the chance to grow. It had barely begun when it ended. All I had left of Mark was his memory—and Robbie."

"And you're willing to settle for that?" Caleb shot her a look that reminded Laura of a disapproving father. "One day that boy's going to grow up and get a family of his own. And you'll be left wondering what you might've had if you'd been brave enough to reach for it."

Laura stared at the bobbing rumps of the horses. Caleb's words had rankled her. She'd barely known the man two days, and here he was telling her how to live her life, unlocking doors she never wanted to open again. Why couldn't he just drive the team and leave her alone?

Setting her jaw, she resolved to change the subject. "I have a question for you," she said. "Why are you pretending to care what becomes of me? As I recall, when I came outside tonight you were about to mount up and ride away! Explain that if you can, Caleb McCurdy."

Caleb groaned inwardly feeling like a rabbit caught in one of her snares. He'd realized that Laura would question him, but what could he say to her? What explanation could he offer that wouldn't get him in deeper trouble? Hellfire, he couldn't even explain things to himself!

Had he made the decision to leave because he didn't trust her, or because he didn't trust his own feelings? Either way, there were no easy answers. He only knew that underneath the whole muddled mess lay one gleam of truth—he felt responsible for Laura and her son.

Five years ago he'd been part of the tragedy that had stolen their chance for a happy, prosperous life. Now all he wanted was to see that chance given back—a crazy, impossible dream. He had no money to help them. And as for loving Laura, or being a father to Robbie, that betrayal could destroy them all over again.

"I'm waiting." Her voice was taut and edgy.

Caleb exhaled. "I do care what becomes of you, Laura. That's why I was leaving."

She made a derisive little sound. "That's a pat answer if I ever heard one! What were you really thinking? That I was planning to meet you in the morning with a preacher and a shotgun? That because of one reckless kiss you might end up having to look at me for the rest of your life?"

"Don't be silly," he growled. "You're a beautiful woman with a lot of love to give. You need a man who'll return that love, somebody who can take care of you and Robbie and give you all the things you deserve."

"And that man isn't you, right? For heaven's sake, Caleb, I know that! What kind of fool do you take me for? You kissed me, and I let you. That didn't mean you had to take the coward's way out and sneak off in the night. I'd have let you go with my blessing!"

She spoke in a whisper, but she was madder than a hornet. Caleb couldn't blame her. As she saw it, he'd insulted her intelligence and behaved like an abject coward. Worse—far worse—he had very nearly not been there when she needed his help. What if he'd left her alone and the worst had happened to Robbie because of it? A cold shudder passed through Caleb's body. That would have been unforgivable.

"So you've pinned me to the wall," he muttered. "Fine. The truth is, I'm not very good at saying goodbye."

"Try a handshake, or a tip of the hat. You can leave anytime you've a mind to, Caleb. I'll never try to stop you. But for the sake of common courtesy—"

She broke off as Robbie began to stir in her arms. The boy's eyelids fluttered. He mewled softly.

Laura gathered him closer. Her eyes flashed an alarm to Caleb. Clearly he was still in distress. "It's all right," she crooned. "Here, sit up. Let's see if you can drink more tea."

"My tummy hurts," Robbie whined. "And I hate that old tea. It's nasty!"

Caleb halted the team. Moon-paled clouds of road dust settled around them. "Why not let me take him while you drive for a while? I might have better luck getting that tea down him."

Laura sighed. "For a little while, maybe. Here, be careful—" She eased her son into Caleb's arms, took the reins and brought them down with a slap on the backs of the horses. The buckboard shot forward, lurching over the bumps in the road. Caleb bit back a word of caution as he caught Robbie close. Laura knew the road better than he did, and she was in no mood to take his advice.

Robbie curled in his arms, so small and so sick that his vulnerability tore at Caleb's heart. Laura was right. He had no idea what it meant to love a child. Heaven and hell, she'd called it. He was beginning to understand.

The tea in the kettle had long since cooled, but Robbie wanted no part of it. He choked and spat and struggled in Caleb's arms, wasting his meager strength. Caleb knew the old Indian remedy was the best thing for stomach problems, but trying to get it down the boy was doing more harm than good.

Sick with frustration, Caleb rocked the exhausted child in his arms. "All right, we'll have some water," he murmured, reaching for the canteen. "Drink all you can, then we'll try the tea again."

Robbie nodded and took a few feeble sips, but he'd thrown up everything in his stomach and he was getting weak. While Laura drove like a demon, Caleb pondered what to do next. Dehydration could take a child's life in a matter of hours. Somehow he had to get more fluids down the boy.

"Let me tell you a story, Robbie," he said. "When I stop talking, you'll have to take a swallow of tea before I go on. Understand?"

The child managed a faint nod, and Caleb began. "Once upon a time an Indian boy named Red Arrow was hiking up a mountain trail. As he walked he sang 'hi-yah, hi-yah, hi-yah.' The song made him feel very brave. All at once, he came around a bend in the trail, and there, right in front of him, was a great big…" Pausing he tipped the spout of the tea kettle to Robbie's feverish mouth.

The boy glanced up. Caleb pressed his lips together, a sign that he was waiting. Robbie grimaced, then took a sip of the tea and swallowed it. Caleb continued, "…a great big mother bear with a little cub. Now, the song had made Red Arrow very brave, but he knew better than to mess with a mother bear, so he turned around and started back down the trail, still singing, 'hi-yah, hi-yah, hi-yah.' For a while he thought everything was fine. Then he looked back over his shoulder. There, trailing along right behind him was…"

He paused. Robbie took a hasty swallow of the tea.

"Right behind him was the baby bear cub. It was acting like it wanted to play with him. All at once…"

Caleb stole a glance at Laura. Her grateful smile glowed like a candle in a darkened church.

The town of Benbow emerged from the flat with the paling dawn. Laura's spirits rose as the buckboard rounded the last bend and she sighted the distant clump of low-slung wood and adobe buildings, surrounded by a clutter of outlying homesteads. The long, fearful ride was almost over.

Her son slumbered peacefully in Caleb's arms. Thanks to the cleverly told story, Robbie had swallowed most of the tea before he drifted off. It seemed to have eased his discomfort. But Laura knew she wouldn't rest until she knew the boy was out of danger.

Stretching a little, she shifted her tormented buttocks on the seat. She'd driven through the night while Caleb tended to Robbie. Neither of them had planned it that way, but once the boy was asleep it didn't make sense to move around and disturb him.

Glancing to the side, she caressed her son with her eyes. Robbie was still in his nightshirt. His bare legs, startlingly long and pale, dangled off Caleb's lap. His rumpled head lolled in the hollow of Caleb's shoulder. Caleb sat slumped against the back of the seat. He looked as if he might be dozing but Laura knew better. He would be alert to every sound and sensitive to Robbie's every move.

The man would make a wonderful father, she mused. Somewhere there had to be a girl just waiting to give him love and a home and children of his own. Laura could only hope he'd meet her someday soon and find the happiness he deserved.

As if he'd sensed her thinking about him, Caleb raised his head and looked at her. His eyes were bloodshot and lined with shadows. His hair and clothes were coated with dust. She probably looked even worse than he did, Laura reminded herself. But what did appearances matter?

They'd arrived safely and, with luck, the doctor would be minutes away.

"We're almost there," she said softly, not wanting to wake the boy.

"I know." He cleared his throat. His whisper was a dusty rasp. "It might be a good idea if you dropped me off on the edge of town and let me walk in on my own," he said. "Driving in with a strange man who's been living at your ranch might cause some talk."

"I can handle talk. You're my new hired man and there's nothing more to it. I'll make that perfectly clear."

"You're sure that's what you want?"

"I'm sure. While Robbie and I are at the doctor's,

you can take the horses to the livery stable for some feed and water. After that, I'll need your help loading some supplies in the buckboard. Oh, and while we're in town you'll need to leave that pistol at the marshal's office. Unless you're a lawman, packing a weapon in the city limits is illegal."

Caleb glanced down at his holstered pistol as if he'd forgotten it was there. He hadn't worn the gun belt while he was working at the ranch, but he'd evidently put it on to leave and never taken it off. Now, suddenly, his face wore a slightly startled look, as if he'd just come fully awake.

"Is that a problem, leaving your gun?" she asked.

"Of course not." He shifted on the seat, causing Robbie to stir. Laura could have sworn the move was deliberate.

With a little groan, the boy opened his eyes. "Hullo," he muttered. "Where are we?"

"Getting close to town." Caleb gave him an easy smile. "Your mother's a right fine driver. How are you feeling?"

"My tummy's better, but my head hurts a little. Will you tell me another Red Arrow story?"

"Maybe on the way home. We'll see. For now let's get some water down you." Caleb reached for the canteen, and tipped to Robbie's dry little mouth. Would he be around long enough to tell the boy another Red Arrow story? Or would he be behind bars before nightfall, jailed for his part in the murder of Mark Shafton?

He found himself wishing he'd brought along his

own horse. Last night he'd almost suggested it. But he'd known that wouldn't set well with Laura. Besides, he'd begun to trust her—trust her *almost* completely. Who wouldn't trust those sweet gray eyes and that tender mouth, especially a man who wanted to believe every word she said?

Last night he'd put his fate in her hands and felt fine about it. Now she was saying that he needed to report to the marshal's office. Caleb swore silently. Even if the marshal didn't figure out who he was, he'd be stuck in town without a horse or a gun. He was completely at Laura's mercy. All he could do was cross his fingers and be on his best behavior.

The doctor's office was built on to his home, a fine-looking structure of brick and wood with a shaded front porch that swept the full width of the house. A carefully tended climbing rose, just bursting into pink bloom, wound its way up a trellis to meander along the edge of the roof. As the buckboard pulled up to the gate, a dark-haired young woman who looked to be about nineteen, opened the front door and came out onto the porch. Caleb, who'd taken over the driving, figured she must know Laura because she gave her a friendly wave. Then, when she noticed that Robbie was still in his nightclothes, she came rushing down the path. She reached the gate just as Caleb was helping Laura and her son to the ground.

"Oh, my stars, what's wrong?" She had dancing brown eyes and a perky, slightly pug-nosed face.

Her daffodil-yellow gown was cinched to an impossibly tiny waist.

"He took a bad fall, and last night he started throwing up." Laura glanced at Caleb. "Clarice, this is Caleb McCurdy, my new hired man. Caleb, this is Miss Clarice Trimble. Her father's our doctor."

"Pleased to meet you, Miss Trimble." Caleb gave her a polite nod. The girl was pretty and well aware of her charms, but this morning he couldn't have cared less.

"Likewise." Clarice turned her attention back to Laura. "Papa's at breakfast. Come on in, and he'll see you as soon as he's finished. You look like you could use a bite yourself."

She ushered Laura and Robbie up the path toward the house. Grateful to have been ignored, Caleb climbed back into the buckboard and headed for the main part of town. Laura had given him both directions and instructions. First he was to go by the marshal's office to leave his pistol in compliance with local law. Then he was to drive around the corner to the livery stable and see that the horses were fed, watered and left to rest for the trip back to the ranch. That done, he could take his time walking back to the doctor's place. The rest of the day would depend on how Robbie was doing.

The businesses along Main Street were just opening as Caleb pulled up to the marshal's office. He sensed people's eyes watching him as he climbed down from the seat and looped the reins over the hitching rail. Evidently, strangers weren't a common sight in these parts. Or maybe the townsfolk recognized Laura's team and buckboard and wondered if he'd stolen them.

Pausing by the rail, he unbuckled his gun belt and wrapped it around the holster. Then, fighting panic, he strode toward the marshal's door. It would be all right, he told himself. He and his brothers had never been to this town. In fact, they'd given the whole area a wide berth after Mark Shafton's death. And even if Laura had described the three of them, he bore little resemblance to the skinny youth he'd been five years ago. Hellfire, his own mother wouldn't recognize him now. So why was he so edgy?

What if Laura and the marshal had some sort of prearranged signal, say, the lawman was to hold anyone who came to turn in his gun—but no, that idea was far-fetched beyond belief. Everything would be fine. All he needed to do was keep a cool head.

Heart pounding, Caleb opened the door.

The marshal, a lean man in his fifties with a drooping mustache, sat at his desk drinking his morning coffee. He glanced up, taking Caleb's measure with sharp blue eyes. "That's Laura Shafton's rig out there. I hope you can explain why you're drivin' it."

"I've been doing some work at her place. Her boy got sick in the night so we brought him in. She's got him at the doctor's now. McCurdy's the name, and I'm here because she told me to leave this with you." Caleb slid the gun belt across the desk.

"Thank you kindly. Benbow is a quiet, law-abiding town. We want to keep it that way." The marshal opened the bottom drawer of his desk, put the gun belt inside and locked the drawer with a small brass key. His movements were slow and deliberate. A careful man, Caleb surmised.

"Coffee?" Without waiting for a reply, the marshal rose, took a chipped white china mug from a shelf and filled it from the blue enameled pot on his desk. "It's fresh," he said, thrusting the mug toward Caleb. "The lady who runs the boarding house brings it by every morning. It'll just go to waste if you don't drink it."

"Thank you." Caleb wanted nothing more than to be on his way, but the coffee did smell good. He took a sip. The mellow heat curled down his throat to ease his crawling nerves, if only for the moment.

"Have a seat." The marshal indicated a straight-backed wooden chair next to the desk. "When I see a stranger in town, I like to know what he's about. Makes my job easier in the long run." He took another sip of his coffee. "Go on—sit down, Mr. McCurdy. Tell me what it is you're doing out at Laura's."

Caleb lowered himself onto the chair, which was just as uncomfortable as it looked. "Just some odd jobs," he said. "I was passing by, knocked on her door and offered to fix her gate for a meal. She's a fine cook and she needed a lot of things done. But I never meant to stay long. I'll be moving on in a few days."

The marshal scowled thoughtfully. "I'd best warn you that Laura's well thought of in these parts. She keeps to herself, but folks understand her reasons. They wouldn't take kindly to any man that caused her harm." He leaned forward, his eyes like steel. "Did she tell you what happened to her husband?"

The coffee turned to acid in Caleb's mouth. "In a few words. I didn't push for more."

"Lord's mercy, what that woman must've gone through. Locked in that springhouse for two days, watching her husband die, then being in there with his body, in the dark. By the time she clawed her way out, her hands were nothing but bloody shreds. And her face—it was too late for the doctor to do anything about the scars. It's a miracle she didn't lose her sanity. I think she might have, if it hadn't been for the baby." The marshal's fist tightened around his cup. "By heaven, if I ever catch up with those three unholy bastards..." The words trailed off. His shoulders sagged as he exhaled.

Caleb stared down at his coffee, feeling as if he'd been stabbed in the gut and was slowly bleeding to death, spilling his life onto the tobacco-spattered floor. He forced himself to speak. "So they were never caught?"

The marshal shook his head. "By the time Laura got free, hauled herself onto a horse and rode into town to get help, they were long gone. She gave me a description, but it wasn't much to go on. They were just drifters. Probably didn't even give their real names."

Caleb sipped his coffee, struggling to look as if none of what he'd heard had affected him. Inside, the invisible knife probed and twisted.

"Laura was in shock when I spoke with her," the marshal continued. "She never did remember much, even after she recovered. All she could tell me was that two of the men cornered her in the springhouse and tried to rape her. When her husband ran in to stop them, the third man shot him. The next thing she remembered was the click of the lock, the sound of horses riding away and her husband dying in her arms. The doctor confirmed she hadn't been raped. Bastards probably got scared after they shot the husband and figured they'd better light out. At least she didn't have to endure that."

The marshal slid back his chair and rose to his feet. "You probably think I'm nothing but an old gossip, Mr. McCurdy. But I'm telling you all this for a reason. I won't pry into your past, but you have the look of a man who's lived rough and maybe done a few things he shouldn't. Laura Shafton is one damned fine woman. She's worked hard to hold on to her land and raise her boy. But she's been through the kind of hell most of us can't even imagine. Emotionally she's as fragile as a snowflake." The blue eyes pierced Caleb like shards of ice. "If you do anything to hurt her, this whole town will be riding after you with a rope. I'll be in the lead, and when we catch you we won't bother with a trial. Understand?"

Chapter Seven

Caleb worked the pump handle until he heard the gush of water. Then he bent his body over the horse trough and let the cold stream splash onto his head. He shivered as it trickled through his hair and down his face, washing away layers of gritty dust. Too bad it couldn't wash away his sins as well, he thought. Right now there was nothing he wouldn't do to erase the past, not only for his own sake, but for Laura's.

The marshal's story would haunt him to the end of his days—Laura locked in the darkness with her husband's dead body, and all the horrors that implied. Laura clawing her way through wood and rocks and earth, her hands torn, her face bleeding…

It was a mercy, Caleb supposed, that she didn't recall everything that had happened. But the devil of it was that Laura seemed to have no memory of his trying to help her. Two men had trapped her in the springhouse and tried to rape her—that was what she'd told the marshal. The fact that one of those men had fought to rescue her, then talked her husband's killer into leaving her alive, was lost in the shadows of her memory.

"Haw!" A raucous voice broke into Caleb's thoughts. Two of the livery stable hands loitered by the fence, grinning as they watched him. "Look at that feller, Lem! I reckon if I'd spent the night in a buckboard with that Shafton woman, I'd need a cold splash myself!"

Caleb glowered at them through the water that drizzled off his hair. The pair appeared to be brothers, big-bellied, unkempt and none too bright. Having recognized Laura's rig when he'd brought it in, they'd been goading him about her, probably looking for an excuse to gang up on him and stomp him into the manure.

"What's it like, livin' out there with nobody but her and that young 'un? You get a look at her yet—I mean anythin' most folks don't get to see?" The bigger of the two men spat a stream of tobacco. "Her face don't look too good with that scar and all, but by God, that body would drive a man crazy! Them perky little titties—"

"Watch your mouth!" Caleb snapped. "Mrs. Shafton's a lady, and you're way out of line!" Damn it, he needed to get away from this place. The last thing he needed was to call attention to himself by getting into a fight. But he could feel his temper seething, on the verge of explosion. If those sons of bitches said one more thing about Laura—

"Oh, so she's a lady, now!" the smaller man hooted. "Crap, man, her bein' a widow, and out there alone all this time, I lay good money you've had yourself a poke or two already. I sure would if I had the chance. It ain't like she's a virg—"

Caleb's fist exploded into the man's chin. The man staggered backward, clutching his broken jaw as his brother attacked from behind, wrapping his arms around Caleb's throat.

The larger bully outweighed Caleb by a good forty pounds, but Caleb had learned to fight in the hell pits of Yuma against the murdering scum of the earth. There was no trick, dirty or otherwise, he hadn't mastered. A backward jab of his elbow crunched into the big man's solar plexus triggering a burst of pain that left him gasping. A catlike twist and a solid blow to the gut finished the job. Both men cowered against the manure pile, gasping and moaning. They were jackasses and they'd gotten off far too easy. But at least they might think twice before mentioning Laura again.

Reining in the urge to do more damage, Caleb raked his dripping hair back from his face. "Have Mrs. Shafton's horses ready when I come back to pick them up," he said icily. Then he turned and walked out of the stable yard.

He cut through the block to a back street, avoiding the main part of town. The doctor's house was only a few blocks away, and Laura had told him to take his time getting back. All the same, Caleb found himself striding hard. His long legs ate up the road as his heart pumped nervous energy through his body.

He was no good for Laura—if he hadn't known it before he knew it now. To build a future in this community she needed friendship and support. His presence at the ranch, and here in town, had already tarnished her reputation. To stay would be to make her an outcast and a target.

He would get her safely back to the ranch. Then, as soon as Robbie was out of danger, he would bid her goodbye and ride out of her life.

Dr. Horace Trimble frowned as he fingered Robbie's bare belly. His eyes, overhung by shaggy gray eyebrows, met Laura's. "You say he fell out of a tree?"

"Yes. It was two—no, three—days ago. Yesterday he seemed fine. Then late last night he started vomiting."

The doctor's scowl deepened. "I don't feel any swelling. There's no tenderness, no bruising, and his color looks all right. What was the boy doing yesterday?"

"Caleb took me fishing!" Robbie interjected. "I caught seven fish! And we had a picnic! It was the best day ever!"

"So you had a picnic, did you, lad? What did you eat?"

Robbie frowned. "Sandwiches, I think. I can't remember what else. And I ate some red berries off a bush. They were sour." He made a puckery face.

"Oh, dear!" Laura shook her head in dismay. "I remember those berries now. I think they were blackberries, but they weren't ripe. Could they have made Robbie sick?"

"Maybe. They're not poisonous, but they could have caused a bad reaction. You say your hired man dosed him with pine pitch tea?"

Laura nodded. "He said it was an Indian remedy. It did seem to help."

"Indians had some good ideas about medicine," the doctor muttered, buttoning up Robbie's nightshirt. "And somebody did a nice job of splinting that arm, as well. All the same, I'd like to keep this boy overnight and see how he's doing tomorrow." He glanced at Laura. "The two of you can stay here. It'll be a pleasure to have you. And your hired man can bunk out back if he wants. There's a cot in the tack room."

"Oh, but I wouldn't want to put you out," Laura protested, although she knew she could barely afford a room at the boarding house. "We can manage—"

"Nonsense! We'd love to have you!" Clarice waltzed into the room. "And say—there's a dance in the town square tonight. Why don't you come with me, Laura? It would do you a world of good to have some fun!" Her sarsaparilla eyes took Laura's measure. "You and I are close to the same size. I have a blue gown that would look stunning on you, and I'd love to fix your beautiful hair."

Laura felt the blood drain from her face. Her pulse drummed an aching tattoo in her head. "Oh, no, I really couldn't—how could I leave Robbie?"

"Robbie will be fine. Rosa, our housekeeper, can watch him for a couple of hours. She adores children, doesn't she, Papa?" Without waiting for her father's reply, Clarice seized Laura's shoulders. "You absolutely must go! I won't take no for an answer!"

"She means it." The doctor gave Laura a weary smile. "I've long since learned not to argue with my daughter. I always lose."

Robbie, who was sitting on the table between them, tugged at her sleeve. "You go to the dance, Mama," he said. "I'm a big boy. I can stay here just fine."

Laura felt panic's clammy fingers tighten around her throat, shutting off her breath. To walk into the dance, to feel those pitying eyes on her—no, she couldn't do it! The very idea was unthinkable!

She was scrambling for another excuse, any that might save her, when the knocker on the outside office door rapped sharply. Clarice flew to answer it.

"Why, Mr. Caleb McCurdy, come right in!" she sang out. "I was just persuading Laura to go to the dance tonight. Why don't you come, too?"

Laura glanced around to see that Caleb had washed the trail dust from his face and hair. His color was high and he had a dangerous look about him, like a sleek, black panther. Clarice had ignored him earlier. She was not ignoring him now.

"I mean it," she said. "I was on the planning committee, so I know you'll have a dandy time. There'll be a fiddle and a guitar, punch and cookies, and lots of pretty girls. A handsome man like you, why you'll be showered with attention!"

"Sorry, but I'm not much for dancing," Caleb murmured, catching Laura's eye. "How's Robbie?"

"He's doing better. The doctor can't find anything wrong, but wants to check him again in the morning. I'm afraid we'll have to be here overnight."

"But don't you worry, it's all arranged," Clarice broke in. "Laura and Robbie are staying here with us, and there'll be a place for you to sleep out back—*after* the dance, of course." She flashed him an impish grin.

Laura felt something sink in her heart. Had she ever been that pretty, that sure of herself? The time when she could smile at a man and invite him to a dance seemed like a hundred years ago, in a different world.

The doctor made some notes in an open book on his desk. "What this boy needs now is a sponge bath, plenty of fluids and a day of bed rest. Clarice, would you show Laura to the guest room and see that she has everything she needs?"

"Certainly, Papa." Clarice flashed Caleb another enticing glance. "And I'll have Rosa cook up more bacon and eggs. You're invited for breakfast, of course, Mr. McCurdy. And then I'll show you to your bunk in case you want to stretch out for a few hours. After driving most of the night, you must be ready to drop!"

Caleb took a step toward the door. "Thank you kindly, but Mrs. Shafton did most of the driving. You tend to her and Robbie—no need to bother with me. I'll see myself out and be back here first thing tomorrow."

Clarice looked adorably crushed. "But you

won't forget the dance tonight, will you? It starts at seven-thirty!"

Caleb's eyes flashed toward Laura. "I'll be here in the morning," he said, stepping out the door and closing it behind him.

"What an arrogant man!" Clarice huffed. "I hope he does show up at the dance just so I can ignore him!"

"Well, if he does, he's yours to ignore. I have absolutely no claim on him." Laura gathered Robbie into her arms, wondering why Caleb had left so abruptly. He could have stayed for breakfast, at least. He'd certainly been invited. But Caleb was a proud man. It wouldn't set well with him to accept a meal or a bed he'd done nothing to earn. He would see it as charity. Then again, maybe pride wasn't the issue at all. Perhaps he just didn't want to be questioned about his past, especially by a pretty girl like Clarice.

So where was he going to spend the night? On the street? Or maybe in one of those scandalous rooms above the saloon? The idea of Caleb in bed with a whore, doing what men do, triggered a sickly, fluttering sensation in the pit of her stomach. The man had just gotten out of prison and would have his needs, of course. Still... Laura forced the thought from her mind. What Caleb did on his own time was his own business. Right now she had a sick boy to look after.

"Close your eyes, Laura!" Clarice tucked one last stray curl into place and added a dab of rouge to Laura's cheeks. "I'm going to turn you around now, toward the mirror. When I count to three, you can open your eyes and look. Ready?"

Laura closed her eyes tightly. She must have been crazy to let Clarice talk her into dressing up, she thought. But Robbie had slept peacefully all afternoon. Clarice's suggestion that she borrow the tub to bathe and wash her hair had been too much to resist. One thing had led to another—the loan of clean underthings and a dress while her own dirty clothes went into the day's laundry. Then the hair, then a touch of jewelry. It had become a game, with Clarice pushing every step of the way. Now Laura was about to see herself in a mirror for the first time in five years.

Her heart was pounding and her palms were clammy with sweat. She was sick with the dread of it, but she was trapped. Without hurting Clarice's feelings, there was no way she could refuse to look.

"One, two, three! Open your eyes, Cinderella!" Clarice let go of her shoulders and stepped away. Trembling, Laura willed her eyes to open.

Standing before her, framed by the gilt-edged mirror, was a stranger. Slender, almost elegant in a modest frock of sky-blue batiste with a silvery sash, she stood quivering with one hand at her throat. Her upswept hair framed her face in soft waves, accented by simple pearl earrings. The reflection staring back at Laura with haunted eyes was nothing like she remembered or had expected. The young bride who'd taken such pleasure in her own beauty was gone. But so was the slashed, twisted creature she'd imagined herself to be for so long. She was simply a woman with a scar—a white, puckered line that pulled a bit at her mouth, giving her face a slightly off-kilter look. She would never be pretty again. But she was no monster. That in itself was a comfort.

But if Clarice thought she was going within a country mile of that dance tonight…

"Laura, you're shaking. Are you all right?" Clarice laid a steadying hand on her arm.

"It's just that I've kept away from mirrors for so long. It's a bit…overwhelming."

"But look at you! You're lovely! Your eyes, your hair, your figure—why, you'll be the belle of the ball tonight!"

"No—" Panic welled like nausea in Laura's throat.

"Oh, Laura—"

"I'm sorry, Clarice. You've been so kind to me, but it's…it's just out of the question."

"Why, for heaven's sake? You'll be fine! You'll have plenty of partners, I promise."

"You mean, men will ask me to dance because you talked them into it, or maybe because they feel sorry for me?" Laura shook her head. "I know you mean well, but I don't want pity. I'm staying here with my son, where I belong."

She raised a fumbling hand to remove one of the pearl earrings. Clarice caught her wrist. "Don't be silly, Laura. I saw the way Caleb McCurdy looked at you. Believe me, there was no pity in those fascinating dark eyes of his. If you can charm him, there's no reason you can't charm others."

The unexpected rush of heat and color left Laura's knees limp. "Be sensible, Clarice, you saw no such thing," she sputtered. "Mr. McCurdy's fond of Robbie, and he was concerned about him, that's all. Girls your age see everything in terms of romance!"

"Girls my age, indeed!" snorted Clarice. "You're no dowager yourself—certainly too young to lock yourself away like a hermit. Your husband's been gone five years, Laura. You have a boy who needs a normal family with brothers and sisters and a good man to help you raise him. You know I'm right!"

Laura stared down at the floor. Yes, Clarice was right. And Caleb had been right last night. Robbie deserved better than to grow up on a lonely, rundown ranch with a recluse for a mother. She owed it to her son to move ahead with her life.

But why did it have to be tonight, with the whole town looking on? Why couldn't she wait a few weeks, or even a few months, while she built up her courage? Maybe next year, when Robbie was older, she'd be ready. But tonight, at a dance—no, she couldn't face so many people. Not yet.

"*Señora?*" The doctor's grandmotherly Mexican housekeeper had appeared in the doorway. Her face broadened into a grin as Laura turned around. "*Que bonita!*" She clapped her hands, then added, "*El niño*—the boy, he's awake."

"Oh—thank you, Rosa. *Gracias.*" Laura darted past her, out the door and down the hall to the guest room. Robbie, looking damp and rumpled was sitting up in bed. His eyes brightened as he caught sight of her.

"Mama! You look so pretty!" He held out his arms. Laura lifted him for a hug. His cheek was soft and cool against hers.

"How are you feeling?" she asked him.

"Better. But no more berries."

Laura gathered him close again, but he squirmed free to gaze at her.

"You look like a princess," he said. "Are you going to the dance tonight?"

Laura shook her head. "I thought I'd just stay here and keep you company. Would you like that?"

"No!" His vehemence was startling. "I want you to go to the dance, Mama! I want people to see how pretty you are!"

Clarice chuckled from the doorway. "You can't say no to that kind of logic, Laura. Papa and I will be leaving after supper, around seven. It'll be fine, you'll see."

"Go to the dance, *señora!*" Rosa peered around her employer. "I will watch your boy. He and I are friends already. *Amigos, sí?*"

"Sí, amigos!" Robbie grinned, delighted with the new Spanish words he'd learned. "You can dance till midnight, Mama, just like Cinderella. Promise me you'll go."

Laura blinked back a rush of tears, overcome by feelings of love, gratitude and gut-clenching fear. Walking into that dance would be like walking up the steps of a gallows. But she was outnumbered. Even Robbie was pushing her.

"Mama, do you promise?"

Laura swallowed a rush of nauseating panic. "All right," she murmured, "I promise."

The Town Square, as it was grandly called, was little more than a vacant patch of ground behind the school where the children played tag and mumblety-peg at recess. But the dance committee had taken pains to make it look nice for the evening. The weedy ground had been mowed and leveled. Wires strung between poles held dangling lanterns with colored shades. In one corner a platform with two stools had been set up for the musicians. Music as light and earthy as ale foam drifted on the twilight air. Dancing couples crowded the floor. Skirts swung, petticoats flashing in polkas, waltzes and old-fashioned reels.

Along one side of the dance floor a refreshment table, festooned with bunting, held an immense cut-glass punch bowl and trays heaped with homemade delights—cookies, candies, sweet rolls and little squares of cake. The sight of so much bounty made Caleb's mouth water. He was sorely tempted to meander past the back side of the table and help himself to a treat or two. But no, he reminded himself, he wasn't really attending the dance. And the last thing he wanted was to be noticed. He would stay where he belonged, in the darkness beyond the ring of light, watching for Laura.

At first he hadn't expected her to come. But then, with the evening still young, she'd arrived by buggy accompanied by the doctor and his lively daughter.

The sight of her—the simple blue frock that set off her eyes, the glorious mane of hair twisted and pinned to fall from the crown in a cascade of curls—had stopped his heart for an instant. But then he'd always known Laura was beautiful. What mattered was that *she* know it.

So what was he doing here tonight? He certainly hadn't come here to dance—in fact he scarcely knew how. And the last thing he wanted was for Laura to be seen with him. His only intent, Caleb told himself, was to make sure she was all right and to be here in case she needed him.

Now he watched from the shadows as a lanky young cowhand whirled her around the floor in a rollicking polka. She danced well enough, but even from a distance Caleb could sense the resistance in her body. Her face, which she kept slightly averted from her partner, was fixed in a rigid little half smile. Her eyes were like a cornered calf's at branding time. She was enduring—barely. It had taken all Laura's courage to come here tonight. Now her courage seemed to be failing.

Caleb ached to stride to her rescue and sweep her away. But that, he knew, would only cause talk and make matters worse.

"So you're Laura Shafton's new hired man."

Caleb whipped around, his hand jerking reflexively for the gun that wasn't there. Standing a few steps away was a prosperous-looking stranger in a brown suit and tie. He was, perhaps, an inch short of Caleb's own height and looked to be in his early forties. Gray-streaked hair framed a square face that was pleasant if not quite handsome.

"Tom Haskins," he said, extending his hand. "You don't know me but I heard about you in town today. I'm Laura's neighbor. Her land borders mine."

"Then you must be the man who bought her cattle." Caleb introduced himself and accepted the proffered handshake. The stranger's grip was firm—firm enough to put Caleb on alert. This was no accidental encounter. Clearly, Tom Haskins had sought him out and had something to say.

"So she mentioned the cattle. Did she tell you anything else about me?"

"Not that I recall. We haven't spent that much time talking. All I've done is fix a few things around the place in exchange for meals. When night comes I lay out my blankets in the toolshed." Caleb's eyes narrowed. "Laura Shafton is a lady in every sense of the word. There's nothing going on between us, and I'll fight any man who says there is."

"From what I heard, you already have."

"Word gets around fast."

"Don't worry about it. From what I know of those two galoots, they had it coming." Haskins stood watching the dance floor, where Laura had changed partners for a reel. "How long do you plan to stick around?" he asked.

"Not long. Providing the boy's all right, I'll be moving on in the next few days. Maybe head for Texas, or even Mexico." Caleb thrust his hands in his pockets, remembering a concern he'd had. Tom

Haskins seemed a decent sort. Maybe he could be of help.

"I know Laura's short on money," he said. "She needs a way to make a living off that ranch of hers. I've been thinking, since you bought her cattle, maybe you could loan her back a few calves to raise and sell. She could pay you out of the profits, maybe buy more, get a start on a herd. What do you think?"

Tom Haskins glanced toward the dance floor, a tentative smile twitching at the corner of his mouth. "It's not a bad idea, McCurdy. But something tells me Laura's money problems will soon be a thing of the past."

"What?" Caught off guard, Caleb stared at him.

Haskins glanced down at his well-polished boots. "I've been thinking about Laura for the past six months, since my wife passed away. Now that the proper time's gone by, I'll be calling on her at the ranch."

"Calling on her?" Caleb felt his pulse skip.

"You heard me right. I'll be courting her. If she'll have me, I plan to make Laura my wife."

Chapter Eight

The punch was lukewarm and sickly sweet. Laura tried to smile as she forced it down her throat. She knew she was supposed to be having a good time—she owed that much to Clarice and to Robbie. And she'd certainly had no lack of partners. But every single dance had been an ordeal. She didn't belong here. She belonged back on the ranch with her son, far from the torment of prying eyes, groping hands and gossiping tongues.

"Can I get you something else—say, a slice of that prune and walnut torte?" The pimpled young clerk from the government land office hovered at Laura's elbow. He had asked her to dance three times, and she'd been kind to him because his face was nearly as flawed as her own. Now she was beginning to wonder if she'd been too kind—and whether people showed kindness to her for the same reason.

"Thank you, no," she said, eyeing the sticky torte. "I'm not hungry just now. What would really taste good to me is a drink of cold water."

"Your wish is my command!" The young man practically clicked his heels as he seized an empty glass from the table and made for the pump that stood outside the schoolhouse, beyond the mass of waiting buggies. Laura sighed, wishing she could just melt into the ground and disappear. In the months ahead, she would seek out new friends for Robbie's sake. But she was never going to another dance as long as she lived.

"Hello, Laura. I was hoping I'd catch you between partners."

Laura's eyes traveled up the brown suit and neat white shirt to a face that was at least familiar—her nearest neighbor, Tom Haskins.

She found her voice. "I—didn't expect to see you here, Tom. What a nice surprise. Is your wife here, too?"

"You must not have heard." He shifted his feet a bit awkwardly. "Grace passed away six months ago."

Laura stared at him in dismay. "Oh, Tom, I'm so sorry. I can't believe nobody told me. I never even heard about the funeral—"

"And I'm sorry no one let you know. You and Grace didn't see much of each other, but she considered you a friend. We both did."

The musicians had struck up a lively polka. Without asking permission he took her hand, caught her waist and swung her out into the stream of dancers.

She gazed up at him, forgetting her own shyness for the moment.

"I don't know what to say. If I'd known about Grace, I'd have come to the service or at least sent some food—"

"No, it's all right. Grace was doing poorly, so I sent her to her sister's in Ohio, where she could get better medical treatment. It..." He paused, sucking in his breath. "It didn't make any difference in the end. She was buried there with her family. Not many folks around here knew when it happened."

"So how have you been?"

"Lonesome." His hand tightened against the small of her back. "With my daughter married now and the boys away at school, it's just me and the hired help—along with a pack of hounds and a few thousand head of livestock!" He chuckled, a bit uneasily. "I was wondering if you'd mind a visit now and again."

"A visit?" She glanced up, startled by his question.

He gazed down at her expectantly, then shook his head. "Blast it, girl, I was never any good with words. I'm asking your permission to come calling."

Laura went numb in his arms. She could hear the music but she could no longer feel its pounding rhythm. She was dimly aware of Clarice, winking over her partner's shoulder as they whirled past on the dance floor, and the young clerk, standing at the refreshment table with a glass of water in his hand and a doleful expression on his face. But her brain refused to form coherent thoughts, let alone put them into words.

"Is that so surprising?" Tom Haskins asked. "You're a lovely woman, Laura, and we're both alone. You can have all the time you want. I won't press you. But I may as well make my intentions clear from the start."

Laura struggled in silence as the dancers blurred around her. She knew he was waiting for an answer, some word of encouragement, at least. And she'd be a fool not to give it. Tom Haskins was a decent man. He had the means to give her a comfortable life and ensure a promising future for Robbie. As for looks, he was attractive enough, despite the fact that he was old enough to be her father. So what was holding her back?

He wanted her land, of course. No man would want her for herself alone. But the land was Robbie's legacy from his father. At some point she would have to make that clear. Once he understood that the ranch wasn't part of her dowry Tom Haskins would surely lose interest. But she could hardly bring that up now.

"Laura?" His light brown eyes sought hers.

"I'm sorry, Tom, but this is so…so sudden," she heard herself saying. "Until a few minutes ago, I thought of you as a married man. I'm afraid I'll need some time—a few weeks at least—to get used to the change. If you'd allow me that, maybe we can begin again where we started tonight. Of course, if you find someone else in the meantime—" She managed a feeble smile. "We can always be friends, can't we?"

A bead of sweat trickled down Laura's temple. Heavens, what was wrong with her? First she'd been speechless; now she was babbling like a fool. She didn't want this man, or any other man here. Why couldn't she just say so and leave with her dignity intact?

"Take all the time you need, Laura. I'll understand. But you're looking distressed. Are you all right?" He bent close, his forehead creased with concern. Above the line where his hat usually fit, his skin was as pale as the underbelly of a fish. For an instant she feared he was going to kiss her. Then she realized that the music had stopped. Couples were separating to find new partners.

"I'm getting a bit of a headache," she murmured, which was true. "Don't worry, I'll be fine. I just need a few minutes of peace and quiet."

"How about a walk? Wait—I'll go with you." He reached for her hand, but Laura, pretending not to see the gesture, slipped away and zigzagged through the crowd to the edge of the dance floor. A few more steps carried her beyond the edge of the light. As she passed into the darkness she broke into a run.

Where was she going? Heaven help her, it didn't matter. She only knew that she couldn't face being at the dance a minute longer—the talk, the prying eyes, the abrupt transformation of her married neighbor into a widowed and eager suitor—her fragile nerves were threatening to snap. She should never have let Clarice talk her into coming here tonight.

She had passed through the maze of buggies and

reached the corner of the schoolhouse before she noticed that the echo of her footfalls had taken on its own rhythm. A hand seized her shoulder from behind and whipped her around. Caleb loomed over her, his eyes blazing into hers. "What happened?" he demanded. "If anybody's hurt you, so help me—"

"No!" Laura reached up and pressed a finger to his lips, signaling quiet. Strange, how safe she suddenly felt with him here. Her panic was receding like the water of a flash flood after a storm.

But she'd be a fool to feel secure with Caleb. He was as restless and unpredictable as the wind. Just last night, right when she needed him, she'd caught him preparing to sneak out the gate. She'd be better off with a man like Tom Haskins than with a volatile, footloose wanderer who'd only ride off and leave her with a broken heart.

But what was she thinking? When had her heart become part of the stakes here?

"Are you sure you're all right?" His clasp, warm and hard through the sleeve of her gown, sent ripples of awareness through her body.

"I'm perfectly fine. Everyone's been very nice. I'm just tired of pretending to have a good time, that's all." She twisted loose and stood glaring up at him. "And what about you, Caleb McCurdy? What are you doing out here in the dark? Spying on me, for heaven's sake?"

He stood his ground, denying nothing. "I just wanted to make sure nobody gave you any trouble."

"I don't need a babysitter, Caleb. I can take care

of myself. It's just that—" She released her breath in a ragged sigh. "I should have stayed at the house with Robbie. I don't belong here, with all these people."

He made a reflexive move, as if to take her in his arms, then checked himself. "I met your friend Haskins. Not a bad sort, but he pretty much told me he'd staked his claim on you."

"Tom Haskins told *you* that?"

"He was just being cautious, I suppose, wanting to make sure there was nothing going on between us. I set him straight, told him I was just hired help and I'd be leaving in a few days."

Laura sucked in her breath, feeling stung. Somewhere, on the fringe of her awareness, the musicians were playing a waltz. Its melody was so sweet and wistful that she wanted to weep. "So you're really leaving."

"People are starting to talk, Laura. You can't afford to let that happen."

"I see." She forced back a rush of emotion. Why should she care if he left? After all, who was Caleb McCurdy to her? Just a handsome saddle tramp who'd stopped by the ranch to help out. If his presence was causing gossip, wouldn't she be better off without him?

"So, is that why you're slinking around out here in the dark?" she demanded. "Why not go to the dance and give the girls a thrill? Pay them some attention. That might stop the talk about you and me!"

He hesitated in uneasy silence.

"Why not?" she pressed him. "I'm sure Clarice would be happy to dance with you! And there are others, so many pretty girls—"

"Stop it, Laura, it's not that simple."

"Why not, for goodness sake?"

"Well, for one thing, I'm not cleaned up. For another, some people don't take kindly to socializing with half-breeds."

"Clarice invited you. She said you'd be welcome. And not everyone is dressed up. You'll have to do better than that."

"All right, if you want to know the truth, I don't know how to dance."

"What?" She blinked up at him, then laughed. "Oh, don't joke with me, Caleb. Everybody knows how to dance!"

"Not me. I was raised by a Comanche mother, I didn't go to school, and I've told you where I spent most of the past five years. Where was I supposed to learn?"

He stood facing her in the moonlight, long-limbed, graceful and alert, as Laura imagined his mother's people must have been. She pictured him growing up in an illiterate family, grubbing an existence off the land with none of the things she'd taken for granted in her youth—no school, no books or music, no nice clothes, parties or dances. Who had Caleb been before a dying convict gave him the gift of an education? If she'd known him then, would she recognize him now?

"You know," she ventured, "dancing isn't all that hard. I could teach you the basics in a few minutes."

"You mean here? Now?"

"Why not? Who knows when you'll have another chance, especially with music?" She moved to his side. "The first thing you need is to recognize the rhythm. Listen—" She paused to let him hear the lyrical strains that drifted through the darkness. "The tune they're playing now is a waltz. You can hear the beats on the guitar—ONE, two three, ONE, two three, and so you step like this…" Laura lifted her skirt to show her borrowed dancing slippers. "One big step, then two small, almost like walking. Try it, ONE, two three, ONE, two three…"

He complied, stumbling over his boots as he tried to match her steps. The expression on his face told her he felt utterly foolish but he kept at it for a moment without complaining. Then, abruptly, he halted.

"This doesn't feel much like dancing," he muttered, and swept her into his arms.

The hand that caught the small of her back was firm and strong. The rest took a bit of fumbling, but in very little time they were moving together through the silken darkness. He held her close, following the subtle cues of her legs and body until he felt sure enough to take the lead. Then there was nothing more for her to teach him about waltzing.

Neither of them spoke. The throb of the music crept around and through them, its melody as poignant as a tear. Laura could feel the light brush of his arousal through her skirt and the sweet, wet burning of her own response, but the ache was nothing more than a part of the dance—a fleeting sensation of something that could never be.

His jaw rested lightly against her temple. She closed her eyes as his lips brushed her hairline and nuzzled her forehead. Laura was dimly aware that the music had ended, but that didn't matter because they were no longer dancing. They stood holding each other, both of them trembling in the darkness.

His mouth skimmed hers. She responded hungrily, her lips opening for more, her body arching upward to press against his. Her senses swam with the clean, salty taste of his skin and the texture of his lips, like firm, wet velvet. Her hands clasped the back of his head, fingers working into the damp tangle of his hair. Had she felt this way with Mark—the hot hungers racing through her body like the licking flames of a prairie fire? Heaven save her, she had no memory of it. Here, in Caleb's arms, might well have been the first time—except that now there was no strangeness, no fear, only need.

His hands molded her body against his, pressing his hardness into her belly. She rose on tiptoe to heighten the sensation. He lifted her off her feet and she hung suspended against him, the contact triggering exquisite spasms between her thighs. Holding her there, he kissed her mouth, her face, her throat…

Abruptly he groaned, raised his head and lowered her to the ground.

"Laura." His voice was thick and hoarse. "Laura, you need to go back to the dance now."

She stiffened in his arms, still quivering. "Why?"

"Because otherwise there'll be hell to pay. If you stay out here one more minute, I won't be held responsible for what I do to you. And that's not the half of it. Don't think you haven't been missed back there. Plenty of folks will be wondering where you've run off to."

"Let them wonder."

He released her and stepped back, dropping his arms to his side. "Don't be a child. You've got a reputation to guard—for your boy's sake, if nothing else. If anybody sees you out here in the dark with your half-breed hired man…" He shook his head. "Go back, dance out the evening and pretend the past few minutes never happened. Don't take any chances."

His argument made sense. Laura realized that, even as her simmering blood began to cool. But so many things had happened tonight. The thought of going back to face all those curious eyes sent waves of panic crashing through her body.

She shook her head. "I'm in no condition to stay. I'll have someone tell Clarice and the doctor that I went back to the house. They'll understand that I want to be with Robbie."

She turned to go but he blocked her way, his face a mask of cold disapproval. "I've never known you to be a coward, Laura Shafton. If you want to go, I won't stop you. But you'll be taking the easy way out. And you'll be teaching your son that if he doesn't like what he's facing, he can just run away. Is that what you want him to learn?"

"Who gave you the right to lecture me?" She flung the words at him.

"Somebody's got to do it. Until you stop being a damned fool, I guess it'll have to be me!"

"Oh, you—" Her hand went up as if to strike him. Then she checked the motion, spun away from him and flounced back toward the dance floor. Caleb was right, of course. But why did he have to be so high-handed about it? Oh, she'd show him, all right. She'd dance with every man who asked her! And she wouldn't stop until the lanterns went out and the musicians stumbled home to bed.

And that, she realized, was exactly what Caleb wanted her to do. He'd played her like a blasted hurdy-gurdy!

I've never known you to be a coward, Laura Shafton.

Only now, as she reached the edge of the light, did the oddness of that phrase strike her.

Caleb had only known her a few days. But he'd spoken as if he'd known her for years.

Caleb had borrowed a spare blanket from the buckboard and hiked into the foothills above town. There, on a patch of sandy ground he scooped out a comfortable hollow and eased himself down to spend the night.

For Caleb, sleeping in the open was anything but a hardship. At Yuma, his only view of the night sky had been through the holes in the strap iron door of his cell. On his first night as a free man he'd been thunderstruck by the glittering expanse above him. He would never again look up at the stars without feeling a sense of awe.

For a time he lay on his back, picking out the constellations and trying to recall each of their names—first the Comanche names his mother had taught him, then the Greek names he'd learned from Ebenezer Stokes. But it was a useless diversion. Thoughts of Laura seeped through his resistance like water through a failing dam until, at last, there was no point in looking at the stars. She was all around him, her passionate mouth, her sensuously curved little body, her searing need to love and be loved—a need that burned as deep as his own.

He had kept an eye on Laura long enough to determine that she was really staying at the dance. Then he'd forced himself to leave. His wanderings had taken him to the town's only saloon where he'd nursed a single whiskey. A blond wisp of a whore who couldn't have been more than sixteen had tried to catch his eye. But Caleb had finished his drink and left.

Now he swore as his body responded to the memory of holding Laura in his arms. Hellfire, he'd been so out of control that he could have taken her right there with her body arched over the back of some buggy. He should never have let himself get close to her, never let her set him on fire with her touch.

He needed to be gone from here. And Laura needed a good, stable man in her life, somebody like Tom Haskins, who could offer her everything that a penniless drifter couldn't. He could only hope Laura would have the good sense to see that.

If he had any sense of his own, he'd head for new territory tonight. Unfortunately he'd left his horse and saddle back at Laura's ranch, and his gun belt was locked up in the marshal's office. He'd never get far unarmed and on foot. Nor did he want to leave Laura the way he'd nearly left her before, without even saying goodbye. He owed her that much.

But what could he say to her in the morning? How the devil was he supposed to behave after what had happened between them?

He was hired help, Caleb reminded himself. He would do his job, keep his words to a minimum and his hands to himself. That would be the only way to get through the remaining days.

Stretching, he turned onto his side and closed his eyes. He was weary beyond belief but sleep was a long time coming. When dreams drifted in they were like black fog, darkly sensual, filled with murky images and a torment of desires that left him drained and frustrated.

At dawn he awoke to a sky that matched the color of Laura's eyes.

After breakfast the doctor examined Robbie and pronounced him well enough to travel back to the ranch, as long as he continued to rest. The stomach cramps and nausea were gone. Laura's son was his curious, lively self again.

Caleb brought the buckboard around to the doctor's house, loaded with the supplies Laura had requested from the general store—sacks of grain and oats for the animals, flour, salt, baking powder, beans and a big slab of bacon.

There was also a small bag of horehound and peppermint sticks for Robbie. Glancing at the receipt, Laura realized he'd bought the candy himself instead of putting it on her account. "Thank you, that was very kind," she said, giving him a strained smile.

Caleb's only response was a curt nod as he turned away to adjust the harness. Beneath the brim of his dusty Stetson, his bloodshot eyes were framed in shadowed creases. Laura didn't want to think about how he must have spent the night.

Not that she was any spring blossom herself this morning. Last night's dance had lasted till nearly eleven. She'd returned to the house exhausted and slept fitfully at best. Now, dressed in her own plain frock, her hair braided beneath a dowdy sunbonnet, she looked like a pioneer woman on the last leg of crossing the plains. Caleb was probably wondering what madness had possessed him when he'd taken her in his arms and kissed her. Well, the ball was done and Cinderella had turned back into a scullery maid. The whole ridiculous fairy tale was over.

Only Robbie was animated. Dressed in his nightshirt and a straw hat, he perched on the seat of the buckboard, sucking a peppermint stick and firing questions at Caleb. "Will you take me fishing when I'm all better?... What's the biggest fish you ever caught?... Can I shoot your gun just once?"

Caleb grunted his answers. He'd reclaimed his gun belt and was wearing it this morning, slung low around his lean-muscled hips. He looked as surly and dangerous as the ex-convict he was, but Robbie didn't appear to notice.

Clarice, fresh and pretty in mint-green calico, came out of the house with a basket of sandwiches and a Mason jar filled with cold lemonade. Laura put the treats in the bed of the buckboard, then hugged her warmly. "Thank you for everything," she murmured. "I can't recall when anyone's been so nice to me."

"It was my pleasure," Clarice responded, then leaned closer to Laura's ear. "Tom Haskins is such an attractive man, and with money to boot. I can't tell you how many women have set their caps for him. Nobody missed the fact that he danced with you four times last night. I think you've made a conquest!"

Laura flashed a glance at Caleb, who was studiously pretending not to hear. "Oh, honestly, Clarice, he was only being kind. With so many women after him, I'm sure he can find someone more desirable."

"Well, whatever you think, the man seems to have set his sights on you. I'll bet you haven't seen the last of him. What will you say if he proposes?"

Caleb was adjusting the harness once more. His back was as rigid as a poker. Was Clarice playing a game, making herself heard just to pique him?

"I can't imagine Tom Haskins would be fool enough to do such a thing," Laura said. "Now we really must be going. The sun's already getting warm. Thank you again, Clarice, and please thank Rosa for all her help."

"There'll be another dance next month. You're welcome to join us again—unless Tom wants to escort you, of course." Clarice grinned, enjoying the drama as Caleb helped Laura into the buckboard, balancing her as if she were a porcelain doll. Laura settled her skirts and gathered Robbie close to her side.

Caleb swung into the driver's seat, tipped his hat to Clarice and flicked the reins over the sleek brown backs of the horses. Was he playing the hired man for the sake of appearances, or were there deeper emotions flickering behind those stony eyes—emotions he was determined to keep hidden?

Oh, how could she have made such a mess of things? Why couldn't she have stayed with Robbie last night instead of letting that minx Clarice talk her into dressing up and going to the dance? What she wouldn't give to have her drab, simple life back again!

The buckboard rolled through town, past the general store and the saloon, past the post office and the jail, where the marshal gave them a friendly wave, and past the livery stable where the surly brothers who tended the place were shoveling manure into a wheelbarrow. Shielded by her sunbonnet, Laura gazed straight ahead. Caleb drove in pensive silence. The memory of last night lay between them like a keg of gunpowder, threatening to explode at the first touch of heat.

Robbie chattered happily, waving to occasional passersby and sucking on his peppermint stick. Laura could only hope that her son's presence would act as a buffer on the ride home. Otherwise she and Caleb would be in for a long, wearying day.

Chapter Nine

The sun hung like a ball of dripping butter against a torrid griddle of a sky. The sultry air lay like a thick blanket over the sage flats, forcing everything that flew or crawled to seek out the meager shade. Only one stubborn vulture defied the heat, soaring against the sky with its huge black wings outstretched to catch the rising currents of air.

To the west, thunderheads boiled above the Sangre de Cristo Mountains. But there was no welcome scent of rain. Any moisture that fell from the sky would vaporize before it reached the ground.

Caleb drove the team at a plodding pace. Between the heat and the loaded buckboard, a faster speed would overtax the horses. Two nights ago they'd made the trip to town in less than five hours. The return trip would take nearly seven.

Two hours short of the ranch, Robbie fell asleep.

Laura lowered him tenderly onto the grain sacks behind the seat and used the quilt to improvise a canopy, protecting his delicate skin from the sun.

The boy had been cheerful all morning, drinking lemonade and shooting questions at Caleb, whose answers had been brief but patient. As the day crawled on, however, his small head had begun to nod. Finally he'd dozed off in Laura's arms.

Laura had said little, preferring to let her son chat with Caleb. But now that Robbie was fast asleep, there could be no more evasion. She could hardly expect to sit in silence for six tedious miles.

She eased him onto a blanket in the wagon bed, taking an extra minute to cushion his splinted arm. Then she settled herself back onto the seat of the buckboard. "He's fast asleep," she said, stating the obvious. "I hope you didn't get too tired of his questions."

"How can a boy learn if he doesn't ask questions? The lad's bright and wants to know things. Count it as a blessing that he asks." Caleb squinted into the light. His hands fidgeted with the reins, twisting the leather in restless fingers.

Laura stared down at her own work-worn hands. Such pathetic hands, she thought, the palms chapped, the nails cracked and broken. But there was no use wishing them soft and dainty like Clarice's. Her life, like her hands, was what it was. Crying about it would only be a waste of tears.

"So, is it true, what Clarice said? Are you going to marry Tom Haskins?"

Caleb's question, coming out of nowhere, hit her like a slap.

She stared at him for an instant before recovering her voice. "Clarice doesn't know what she's talking about. I shared a few dances with Tom. That doesn't mean the man's going to propose."

"That's not what Haskins told me." He studied her, his eyes narrowed against the sun. "He made it clear that he'd marked you as his territory and I was to stay away."

"And so you took that as a challenge? Was that what last night was about?" Her voice shook with wounded defiance.

He glanced away. "Last night never happened, Laura. If you're smart you'll marry Tom Haskins, or someone like him who can give you and Robbie a decent future. The sooner you do it and forget about me the better."

"You haven't told me anything I didn't already know." She spoke out of wounded pride. "But it isn't me Tom wants. It's the ranch. He'd propose to a cow if he thought it would get him more land!"

"You can't know that for sure. He didn't seem like a bad sort, maybe a little too pushy for my taste, but then I'm not the one he wants to marry."

"Oh, stop it!" Laura shoved her sunbonnet back onto her shoulders, letting a stray breeze cool her sweaty hair. "Don't you see? The ranch is for Robbie, to be held in trust until he's of age. I paid a lawyer in town to draw up the papers after he was born. Once Tom understands that, he'll be showing me his heels in no time. And so will any other man who thinks he has something to gain by courting me. In the end they'll all walk away."

"If they do, they're fools," Caleb growled. "Any man worth his salt would know that the real treasure isn't the land, it's you."

"Don't, Caleb—" Laura averted her face to hide the hot rush of color. "You can make free with words because you know you're leaving. After you're gone, you won't be held accountable for anything you've said to me."

"I don't find that very flattering."

"But it's true. My grandmother used to tell me that the things a man says to a woman are only on loan. He can take them back anytime he wants to. So you can stop wasting your breath. I don't need your pretty lies. I know what reality is—I feel it with my fingers every time I wash my face."

With a mutter of frustration, Caleb hunched over the reins and sank into silence. Laura pulled her sunbonnet over her hair once more, screening her profile from his view. She was too contrary for her own good, she knew. But why did her happiness seem to matter so much to Caleb? Why was he so determined to change her life when he didn't plan to be part of it?

Laura was about to ask him when she heard the sound of stirring behind her. Robbie was awake, she realized. She and Caleb had kept their voices low, but some of their conversation may have reached his ears.

Yawning, the boy sat up and dragged himself back onto the seat between his mother and Caleb.

Laura cushioned him against her side, hoping he'd go back to sleep, but he seemed determined to talk.

"Why do you have to go away, Mr. Caleb?" he asked plaintively. "I don't want you to go. Mama needs you to fix things, and I need you to teach me shooting and fishing and stuff like that."

"Somebody else can teach you those things, partner," Caleb said. "It's time for me to be moving on."

"But why?" Robbie persisted. "Mama likes you. I can tell."

"And I like her," Caleb said, causing Laura to flush beneath her sunbonnet. "We're good friends, your mother and I. But I need to find a place of my own somewhere. And the two of you need to get on with your lives. I know that doesn't mean much now, but you'll understand when you're older."

Robbie fell silent, fiddling with a button on his nightshirt as he pondered what he'd just been told. He was too young to understand the things that happened between men and women, Laura knew. But he was not too young to feel loss.

"When will you go?" he asked.

"In a day or two, when I finish mending the sheds and fences."

"Will you take me fishing again before you go?"

Laura heard the slight catch of Caleb's breath before he answered. "You can't go fishing until you're feeling strong enough."

"Then you'll have to stay till I'm all better." He fixed Caleb with eyes that would melt basalt. "You can do that, can't you, Mr. Caleb?"

Caleb hesitated, then shrugged. "I'll think about it, but only if you'll behave yourself and rest when your mother tells you to. Do that and I'll take you fishing when you're well enough to go. All right?"

"Yahoo!" Robbie whooped and clapped his hands.

Laura murmured a quiet thank-you. When it came to Caleb's leaving, her emotions were hopelessly jumbled. This fiercely gentle stranger had turned her world upside down, awakening hungers she'd never known she possessed.

Maybe if she had a few more days to straighten things out between them, she'd be better prepared to see him ride out of her life. But no, her sensible side shrilled. Caleb McCurdy was like a bad tooth. The only way to get beyond the pain was to yank it out. And the only way to get over Caleb was to have him gone for good.

The road had begun its upward climb from the burning sage flats to the long sweep of brushy foothills. In the heat-blurred distance a faint ribbon of green meandered down from the mountains, marking the path of the stream that ran through her ranch—her piece of the earth, her home.

The ranch was where she belonged, Laura thought, not in town and not planted in some man's house, however fine. Her future was here, on the land she and Mark had purchased with her inheritance, the land where they'd built their dreams.

When she buried Mark she'd buried most of those dreams with him. For the past five years she'd lived in poverty, hoarding the cash from the sale of her cattle, pinching every cent to make the money last. Alone, with a baby to raise, she'd let the place fall into disrepair.

It had taken Caleb to show her the possibilities that were right under her nose. Now that Robbie was growing up, it was time to start rebuilding the value of the ranch.

Caleb had given her a good start on the repair of the outbuildings and fences. But now, before the season passed, she needed to get some calves and start a new herd. Raising cattle wasn't an easy proposition, but maybe she could lease some of her fine pastureland to neighboring ranchers. As part payment, they could lend her a man or two to help with such chores as branding and castrating. Of course she'd have to do much of the work herself. But Robbie was already big enough to ride with her, and before long he'd be old enough to help.

Tonight, or maybe tomorrow, she'd get Caleb's advice. If he could stay long enough to help her get started… But no, Laura resolved. She couldn't ask Caleb to stay. Not when every day they spent together heightened the tension between them. For both their sakes, she had to let him go.

Tom Haskins, then… But no. Laura sighed. That would only give him an excuse to spend more time with her. And it wouldn't be in Tom's best interest to see her succeed at running her own ranch. Not when he wanted the ranch for himself.

But there were other neighbors she could turn to.

Some of them had growing families. What if she were to open a little school for their younger children? The ranchers could repay her by making sure she had the help she needed. It was such an exciting idea, Laura wondered why she hadn't thought of it before. Not only would she be doing a service, but also Robbie would have the chance to make new friends.

Laura was still spinning plans when Caleb drove through the ranch gate. As the buckboard pulled up to the house, however, her daydreams scattered in the flurry of things to be done. The cow was bawling to be milked and the hens had pecked the ground clean of grain. The supplies had to be unloaded and put away, the horses unhitched and fed. But first Robbie would need to be sponged down, given water and tucked into bed. And even before that could be done, the windows and doors would have to be opened to air out the stifling house.

When Laura came outside after settling her son, Caleb was unhitching the horses. She hurried past him to the granary where she scooped up a bucket of feed and scattered it for the chickens. Then she raced for the cowshed and herded the cow into the milking stall.

When Caleb found her a few minutes later she was crouched on the three-legged milking stool with her hands pulling expertly at the cow's long pink teats. Milk flowed in foamy streams that spattered rhythmically into the bucket below.

"If you don't mind putting things away, the feed

sacks go in the granary," she said. "The bacon goes on one of the hooks in the springhouse and you can leave the other things on the kitchen table. If you're hungry, help yourself to some oatmeal cookies. There are plenty left over. When I'm done here, I'll be in to start supper and—"

"Laura." He laid his right hand on her shoulder. She fought back a surprising surge of tears as his fingers began to knead her taut shoulder muscles. "You're worn out," he said. "Everything's put away except for your cooking supplies. I can do that and finish the milking. Go inside and rest."

"I'll be fine," she muttered, her forehead brushing the cow's satiny side. She willed herself to focus on her task, ignoring the delicious pressure of his massaging hand. But she hadn't realized how tense she was, or how easily she could be undone by a simple touch. If he continued, she would melt. If he didn't, she would shatter.

"Thank you for staying around," she said, struggling to sound calm and civil. "I know you're anxious to go, but it means a lot to Robbie."

"He's a fine boy. There's not much I wouldn't do for him." Caleb's left hand had joined his right, thumbs working the sore muscles on either side of her spine. Laura bit back a moan of pleasure.

"You'd make a good father, Caleb. Maybe someday you'll have a boy of your own."

"I'll have to find a mother for him first." Caleb chuckled wryly, his fingers moving outward along Laura's shoulder blades. "But being around Robbie's started me thinking about how it would be to have a family. Can't say the one I grew up in was any great shakes, with my brothers out raising hell and my father coming home drunk to beat up my mother. But maybe I can give the next generation a better chance."

"You will, I know." She closed her eyes. The cadence of squirting milk slowed as her hands began to relax. "What ever happened to your brothers?" she asked, making conversation. "How long's it been since you last saw them?"

She heard the sudden catch of his breath, as if a noose had jerked around his throat. "Not long enough," he muttered, lifting his hands from her shoulders. "I'd better get the rest of your things inside. Where's the key to the springhouse? I'll hang that bacon for you."

"Don't worry about the bacon. I'll take care of it when I put the milk out. I'm nearly finished with old Bessie here."

In truth, Bessie's swollen udder had a good deal more to give, but Laura sensed that her exchange with Caleb had taken a turn in the wrong direction. He seemed to have a sore spot where his brothers were concerned. Instead of prying into his past, she should have brought up her plans for the ranch and asked him for ideas. But the timing wouldn't have been right, she realized. They were both too tired, too raw.

Let him go, she told herself. His private demons were none of her concern. Heaven knows she had enough demons of her own.

Laying her cheek against the cow's smooth tan side, she reached for the teats and willed her flagging strength to flow into her hands. Milk spurted into the pail, warm and rich and creamy. Life should be more like milk, filled with simple goodness, Laura thought. But then, even milk could sour and go bad. Nothing was ever quite what it seemed.

Pausing to rest, she glanced back over her shoulder. Caleb was gone, as she'd known he would be. From the direction of the corral came the ring of hammer blows. From the mountains beyond, faint but ominous, dry thunder rolled across the sky.

By the third day home, Robbie's nonstop energy had returned. He could no longer be kept in bed. Laura didn't want to overtax the boy, but it was all she could do to confine him to the house and the shaded front steps.

An hour after breakfast, Laura carried her rocking chair out onto the porch and sat down with a basket of mending to keep an eye on him. Robbie was playing on the top step, building a miniature fort for his toy soldiers with empty wooden spools. But he'd soon be getting restless, wanting to swing or tag after Caleb. Keeping the boy quietly entertained was an ongoing challenge.

The day promised to be hot again, but the morning air was pleasantly fresh. Redwing blackbirds called from the overgrown pastureland. Bees hummed in the yellow clumps of blooming chamisa that grew around the house. From the granary, where he was boarding up the log foundation to keep out rodents, came the familiar sound of Caleb's hammering.

Laura had darned one stocking and was starting on a second when Robbie jumped to his feet, pointing toward the wagon road. "Look, Mama! Somebody's coming!"

Laura shot out of her chair on full alert. She was always uneasy when someone approached the house, and her first impulse was to snatch Robbie inside, bolt the door and race for the shotgun. But as the distant speck materialized into a single rider on a big black-and-white pinto, she gave a sigh of recognition. Her visitor was Tom Haskins.

Minutes later he rode in through the gate. He was dressed in clean work clothes—a plaid shirt with a denim vest, twill trousers and recently shined boots. He grinned as he doffed his Stetson and dropped it over the saddle horn. From the granary, Caleb's hammering paused momentarily, then started up again, a trifle louder than before.

As Tom dismounted Laura saw that he was holding something in a cotton flour sack. He kept it under his arm as he approached the porch.

"Now, Laura," he began before she could speak, "I know what you told me at the dance, and I plan to respect your wishes. This is just a neighborly visit. I wanted to see how your boy was doing and to bring him a little present."

"A present? For me?" Robbie's eyes lit up. He

squirmed with anticipation. Tom's eyes flickered toward Laura, who was looking hesitant.

"I'm sorry, I know I should have asked you first," he said. "But it just seemed right, and I didn't think you'd mind."

As he neared the porch, Laura could see that something in the bag was moving, wriggling in an effort to escape. Smiling, Tom lowered the sack into Robbie's lap.

The top of the sack fell open and a fuzzy, golden-brown head emerged. Robbie gave a squeal of delight as the puppy's wet pink tongue assailed his face. Grappling and giggling, the two of them tumbled together onto the porch.

Laura sighed and shook her head. Tom had been way out of line, bringing the puppy over without consulting her. But she'd never seen her son so happy. A dog was exactly what Robbie had needed. And the pup was a little charmer with deep chocolate eyes and huge paws. She could feel herself beginning to melt.

Tom grinned knowingly. "One of the bitches in my pack had pups a couple of months ago. This one's the biggest and smartest of the litter. When he's older I can help your boy train him. He'll make a right fine hunting dog."

Laura's heart sank as she realized how she'd been outmaneuvered. Tom had agreed not to come courting until she gave the word. But he was already courting her son.

"What do you say to Mr. Haskins, Robbie?"

"Thanks!" Robbie beamed as the pup licked his chin. "What's his name?"

"I thought I'd let you name him." Tom stepped to Laura's side and rested a casual hand against the small of her back. "You can call him anything you like."

"Can I call him Caleb?" Robbie's eyes shone with innocence. Laura bit back a groan.

"Oh, Robbie, why, for heaven's sake?" she asked, sensing Tom's displeasure.

"I want to remember Mr. Caleb when he goes away. If I name my dog Caleb I won't ever forget him."

And neither would she, Laura thought. But she didn't want to remember Caleb every time she stood at the back door and called the dog. "A puppy should have his very own name, not somebody else's," she argued.

Robbie looked crestfallen, then brightened. "Can he have Caleb for his *middle* name?"

Laura sighed, surrendering to her son's logic. "All right, I don't see why not. Just give him a good first name—like Buster or something."

"Dogs don't have middle names," Tom said.

"This one does," Robbie said, grinning. "His name is Buster Caleb Shafton. Do you like that, Mama?"

"I like it fine." Laura rumpled his curls.

"Dogs don't have last names either," Tom groused.

Laura chose to ignore the remark. "Goodness,

it's already getting warm," she said, fanning her face with her hand. "What do you say we invite Mr. Haskins to sit down in the rocker and have some cold cider, Robbie? You and Buster can visit with him while I fetch the jug from the springhouse."

She turned to go, but Tom caught the bow on her apron, pulling her back. "Hold off on the cider," he said. "First I'd like to see the repairs that hired hand of yours is doing on the property. I can hear him hammering, but somebody needs to make sure you're not getting shoddy work for your money."

"My money!" Laura twisted out of his clasp, loosening her apron ties. "That's a joke, Tom. Caleb's been working for three meals a day and a place to sleep. He's making do with whatever tools he can find, and the lumber he's using is mostly split from the woodpile. For all that, he's been doing a good job."

"Probably using up all your firewood," Tom muttered. "I'll have to chop some more while I'm here so you won't run out."

"Caleb showed me how to fish," Robbie piped. "I caught a lot of fish and we cooked them for supper! It was the best day ever in my whole life!"

"Was it, now?" Tom's eyes narrowed. He scowled as he turned in the direction of the hammering. "Don't bother coming with me, Laura. I'll only be a few minutes. Then I'll take that cider."

Weak-kneed with premonition, Laura watched him stalk around the corner of the house. The only thing worse than a confrontation between Caleb and

Tom would be her getting into the middle of it, she told herself. With luck it wouldn't amount to much and would soon be over. But riled-up men had no more sense than donkeys. That's what her grandmother had always said, and Laura believed it.

Retying her apron strings, she cautioned Robbie to stay on the porch with the puppy. Then she bustled off to the springhouse to get the cider jug out of the cool box.

Caleb had paused to wipe the sweat from his forehead when Tom Haskins came striding around the house. His expression was as dark as yesterday's thunderclouds. If the man had been an Indian, he'd have been wearing war paint, Caleb observed wryly. Maybe he'd just found out the hired man had been kissing his woman.

Caleb had heard him ride up and hoped that he'd simply come to see Laura. Alas, that was not to be. An otherwise fine day was about to be blown to hell.

"Hello, Haskins," he said in an even tone. "I'd offer to shake hands, but—" He shrugged, showing a dirt-stained palm.

"Never mind," Haskins growled. "I just came back to make sure Laura wasn't being cheated. She's such a trusting soul, and so's that boy of hers. He seems to think you hung the moon. Even wanted to name his damned dog after you!"

"Robbie's a good lad," Caleb said. "But you don't need to worry about him getting attached to me. In a couple more days I'll be saddled up and on the trail.

"That's what you told me in town," Haskins fumed. "I came out here this morning expecting to find you gone, and here you are, still hammering away. I'll bet good money you're scheming to settle in here—get yourself a ranch and a pretty woman in the bargain."

Caleb picked up his hammer again and positioned a nail in place. "Make that bet and you'd lose your money. Laura deserves better than the likes of me. I've got sense enough to know that much, at least."

"Then you'd better have the sense to clear out of here before you tarnish her reputation and break her boy's heart."

"That's just what I plan to do." Caleb raised his hammer for the blow.

"Then do it today," Haskins said. "I'll send one of my men over to finish this work, or even do it myself, but I want you gone."

Caleb lowered the hammer slowly, reining in his annoyance. The last thing he needed was another fight. But he'd be damned if he'd let this big bag of wind order him around.

"I promised Robbie I'd take him fishing when he was better," he said, meeting Tom Haskins's bland, brown eyes. "I mean to keep that promise. Then I'll be moving on. But not before."

Haskins's neck reddened, the color creeping upward into his face. "You listen up, McCurdy," he hissed. "Coyotes like you leave dirty tracks everywhere they go. I've got friends who can find out all there is to know about a man's past. If you're not gone the next time I come here, so help me, I'll see that Laura and that boy know every rotten thing you ever did—even if it's enough to get you hanged. Do I make myself clear?"

Caleb studied the man in silence. Haskins was likely bluffing, he knew. But could he afford to count on that? His relationship to Zeke and Noah was public record in Arizona, where he'd been arrested and tried. If Haskins and the marshal knew that much, it wouldn't be that hard to tie the three of them to Mark Shafton's murder.

Laura had failed to remember him. But Zeke and Noah would be far easier for her to recognize. If any law office could supply wanted posters of his brothers with their pictures and their real names—Lord, it would all be over for him.

"So there you two are!" Laura's voice, artificially cheerful, broke into his black musings. She was coming around the corner of the house balancing two mugs on a tray. "I thought maybe you could both use some cooling off."

Tom Haskins had been waiting for an answer, but he was all smiles as he turned his attention to Laura and accepted one of the mugs.

Caleb blessed her interference as he gulped the cold cider. But he knew his rescue was no more than a reprieve. Haskins's threat was all too real, and he wouldn't feel safe until he was beyond the reach of the law.

Tomorrow he would keep his promise to Robbie. Then, before the day was over, he would bid goodbye to Laura, mount up and ride for the Mexican border.

Chapter Ten

Tom Haskins left after the midday meal, surveying the ranch from his big spotted horse as if he were already the owner. Caleb, who'd declined Laura's invitation to eat at the table in favor of a sandwich in the yard, was relieved to see him go. The visit had cast a shadow over an otherwise pleasant day. Caleb detested being controlled by the man's threats. But he knew he'd be a fool to ignore them.

By now it was late afternoon. Caleb had finished work on the granary and was shoring up the corral fence, replacing the weaker posts and hammering the rails securely between them. Sweat drizzled down his face and soaked through his chambray shirt. He kept the canteen close by, gulping water whenever he paused to rest. The heat was draining. But this job was a picnic compared to breaking roadbed in Yuma. And it was sweetened by the promise that Laura would have more cold cider waiting at the end of the day.

"*Kapow!* Take that, you no-good varmints!" Robbie was playing lawman in the shade of the big cottonwood tree, ducking around the trunk to shoot at imaginary outlaws. His new sidekick Buster had trailed him for much of the afternoon, then curled up in the hollow of a tree root and drifted into puppy dreams.

Even Caleb had to admit the dog had been a great idea. Tom Haskins might be a tad too possessive, but his heart seemed in the right place. All in all, Laura could do worse. But would she be happy? Would the security Haskins could offer be enough to give her real joy?

It was joy he wanted for her, Caleb thought. He yearned to give back the happiness his family had stolen from her on that awful day. He ached to see the sparkle of sunlight in her somber gray eyes, hear the laughter in her voice and know that it came from a deep, true center of love and peace.

But that gift was beyond his power to give. The best he could hope for was to improve her lot in a few small ways and ride out of her life before he caused her any more grief.

"Have you seen any low-down sneakin' varmints, Mr. Caleb?" Robbie's question startled him out of his reverie. "I'm on the trail of some real bad 'uns."

Well, you just found one right here, Caleb thought, looking down into the small, earnest face. "Tell me something, Robbie. What'll you do when you catch those bad men? You can't just shoot them, especially if they throw down their guns and give themselves up."

Robbie's brow creased as he pondered the question. Then he brightened. "I'll just lock them in my jail—right over there!" He pointed to the springhouse. "They'll have to stay for a long, long time, all the way till Christmas!"

"Sounds good to me." Caleb chuckled as the boy darted off. With an imagination like that, Robbie might grow up to be a writer as well as a rancher.

Hearing a muted ripple of thunder, he glanced up at the sky. Afternoon clouds were milling in a restless herd above the peaks of the Sangre de Cristo Mountains. Maybe this time they'd bring a little rain to the sun-parched foothills. Lord knows they needed it. Last time he'd checked, the creek was down to a trickle. But at least Robbie should have good fishing tomorrow. With the water as low as it was, the trout would be crowded into the deeper holes. They'd be hungry and fighting over the bait. It wouldn't take the boy an hour to catch a nice mess of fish for supper.

Caleb planned to stay and eat one last meal with them. Then it would be time to say goodbye.

His throat tightened at the thought of leaving. Laura and Robbie had become the only people in the world he truly cared about. But in the long view of their lives, leaving was the best thing he could do for them.

He would remember that, and all the rest, as he rode away.

Laura glimpsed her son through the kitchen window as she scooped the freshly churned butter into an earthenware crock. He was racing around the yard as usual, shooting his make-believe pistol at imaginary bandits. She should probably have kept him inside for the rest of the day, but he'd seemed so well, and he'd been so eager to romp with his new puppy. By the end of the day, boy and dog would both be worn out. At least they ought to sleep well tonight.

The four loaves of bread she'd mixed that morning had risen to plumpness in the warm kitchen. She would take the butter out to the springhouse and fetch the rabbit she'd skinned to fry for supper. Then she'd put the bread in the oven. It would still be warm when Caleb and Robbie came inside to eat.

Glancing out the window, she saw Robbie talking with Caleb by the corral. They exchanged a few words. Robbie pointed to the springhouse, then darted away. She shook her head, recalling the name her son had given his pup. It touched her that Robbie had accepted Caleb's leaving and wanted to remember him. But poor Tom had looked to be on the verge of apoplexy.

Sooner or later she'd have to decide what to do about Tom Haskins. He was a decent man and he'd been a good friend to her. But the thought of being in his arms, letting him kiss her and take her to his bed… No, she couldn't even imagine such a thing.

It would be a kindness to let him know how she felt and to explain the ownership of the ranch. The sooner she did it the sooner Tom would feel free to look elsewhere.

As for Caleb's leaving, she wouldn't let herself dwell on that now. She had one more day to fill her eyes with the sight of him, one more day to hear his voice before he rode away, leaving her world drab and colorless once more.

It would tear at her heart, seeing him go. But she couldn't depend on a man to give her the life she wanted. That power was inside her, and she would learn to use it. She was through wallowing in self-pity, through hiding her face from the world. God had given her a good mind and a pair of strong hands. She would put them to work, by heaven, and she wouldn't rest until her ranch was a showplace of prosperity.

As for love…that part of her life was behind her. Love had gotten her Robbie. Wasn't that enough? Wouldn't a second time be asking too much?

Still musing, Laura scraped the dasher clean and put the lid on the butter crock. The key to the springhouse was in her apron pocket. She fumbled for it with one hand, holding the crock against her chest with the other as she stepped outside and walked around to the door of the springhouse.

Hot and sultry as the weather was, the air felt cool after the heat of the kitchen. Laura glanced around for Robbie, but he was nowhere in sight. He was probably pestering Caleb again. Not many men would be so patient with a busy little boy.

Working the key into its tiny slot, she turned it until the padlock snapped open. As was her habit, she returned the key to her apron pocket and hung the open lock on the hasp. Only then did she nudge the door inward and step into the springhouse.

The clammy darkness surrounded her as she closed the door behind her, leaving an inch-wide crack that would admit a finger of light without letting the cool air escape. Goose bumps rose on her skin as she crouched to place the crock inside the cool box. Would she ever get over her fear of this place? Would she ever be able to step inside these thick log walls without hearing the echo of her own screams?

Closing the box, Laura rose to her feet and made her way to the hook where she'd hung the skinned rabbit carcass. She could hear her heart pounding in the gloom and feel the familiar rise of panic. She willed it away. A few more seconds and she'd be out in the sunlight again—safe from the nightmare.

A bit of the rabbit's flesh had dried around the hook. Laura was working it loose when suddenly the light vanished. Plunged into darkness, she heard the most blood-chilling sound of all—the metallic click of a closing padlock.

Too startled to scream, she sucked in her breath. That was when she heard the childish voice, faint through the heavy planks. "Ha, you low-down varmints! You'll never escape now! Nobody gets out of my jail!"

Laura's heart dropped. She flew to the door, attacking it with her fists. "Robbie!" she shouted. "Let me out!"

"Mama..." Her son's voice quavered, as if he'd

just realized what he'd done and expected to be punished.

"Open the door, Robbie," she coaxed, pressing desperately against the planks. "It's all right. I know you didn't mean to shut me in here."

"I can't open the door," he wailed. "It's locked, and I haven't got the key."

Laura groaned aloud as she remembered. The key was in her own pocket and there was no spare. She was truly locked in.

Cold waves of nausea swept over her, churning the bile in her stomach. She struggled against them, resisting with all her strength. "Listen to me, Robbie," she gasped. "Go get Mr. Caleb! Run!"

There was no answer.

"Robbie?" A sickening fear began to seep through her body. Had her son gone for help or was something else happening beyond the locked door—something awful beyond imagining?

"Robbie!" She began to pound on the door again, smashing her knuckles against the splintery wood. *"Robbie!"*

She held her breath, listening. Only the gurgling stream broke the silence.

Exhausted she sagged against the door. She could feel the old ghosts creeping out of the darkness. There was the big man, the monster, with the knife in his hand and the look of madness in his odd, yellowish eyes. There was the older one, nerveless and cold, gunning Mark down without a flicker of remorse. And the young one, the boy, who was no more than a shadow in her mind—he'd been here, too. But what had he said? What had he done? The memory was a blur. But surely he'd been as evil as his brothers. Why else would he have come into this place except to get his turn at her?

They were all around her now, circling like a pack of hungry beasts. Mark's body lay at her feet, his awful wound soaking the earth. She could smell the blood in the darkness. She could smell the sweat, smell the lust as the hellish trio surrounded her, closing in…

She began to scream.

"Laura!" Caleb's voice shocked her back to reality. He was pounding on the door, shouting her name. "Laura, can you hear me?"

"Yes." Her voice emerged as a whimper.

"We've got to get you out of there. Have you got the key?"

"Yes."

"Try to slide it under the door." His deep voice was calm and soothing. Laura clung to the sound of it as she fumbled in her pocket. It would be all right, she told herself. Caleb would never let anything happen to her.

Her fingers found the key. It felt cold and slippery in her shaking hand. Despite its tiny size, Laura had her doubts that the key would fit under the door. Mark had built the springhouse to keep out heat and vermin. The door fit so tightly that when it was closed not so much as a sliver of light could get through. In the pitch-like blackness Laura couldn't even see her own hands.

She crouched low, feeling for the base of the door. From outside, she could hear Caleb talking with Robbie. The stream whispered in the darkness. Her beating heart seemed to echo against the walls.

"Laura?" Caleb's voice washed through her senses. "Laura, are you all right?"

"Yes...but it's so dark. I can't—" She gave a little cry as the key slipped through her fingers. Bouncing off a stone, it dropped into the water with a splash.

"Oh, no—please, *no*—" Falling to her knees she plunged her hands into the water. Summer heat had shrunk the stream to a depth of just three or four inches. But the streambed was loose and gravelly, the current swift enough to carry a small object away. Although Laura groped frantically in the darkness, the key was nowhere to be found.

She sank back onto her heels. The murky air pressed in around her, brushing her skin. She could feel the lurking horror, feel the sick panic rising in her chest once more.

"Laura, what's wrong?" Caleb's worried voice filtered through the heavy planks.

"The key—it's lost," she gasped. "You'll have to break in somehow...hurry, please."

There was a tick of silence. "Robbie, run and get the hammer," Caleb barked.

Silence again, a small eternity of it. Laura huddled in the darkness, her heart exploding in her chest. Even greater than her fear of that awful darkness was the fear that she might be losing her sanity. *Hurry...oh, please hurry...*

She heard a scraping, bumping sound, followed by the splintering of wood as the hasp was pried loose from the frame. The door swung inward. Dazzling sunlight flooded the springhouse as Caleb plunged inside.

Half blinded, Laura was jolted by an inexplicable flash of memory—the door crashing open, the lanky figure flying through, only to crash against the far wall and crumple to the earth. Her heart seemed to stop. She gasped for breath. Then, in the next instant, the image was gone. Caleb had gathered her into his arms and was holding her close, murmuring little sounds of comfort.

She shrank into him like a wild creature seeking safety. His arms were so strong, his chest so solid and warm. He smelled of wood shavings and clean, honest sweat. Laura buried her face against his shirt. Little by little, the tears began to flow. Convulsive sobs racked her body.

"It's all right," he murmured, clasping her fiercely. "Go ahead and cry, Laura. You're safe now. Those men will never hurt you again."

Laura felt a tug at her skirt. Robbie was looking up at her, teary-eyed. "I'm sorry, Mama," he said. "I was just locking the bad men in jail. I didn't mean to shut you in, honest."

Caleb released her. She knelt on the ground and wrapped her arms around her son, being careful not to hurt his splinted arm. "It's all right, Robbie," she whispered. "I know you didn't mean any harm. And just think of it, you found Caleb and you brought his hammer so he could open the door. You helped save me! I think that makes you a hero!"

"It does?" His eyes widened.

"You bet it does!" Laura kissed the little swirl of hair at the crown of his head. "Now what do you say I take this rabbit into the kitchen and cook it so we can celebrate at supper?"

Caleb rumpled the boy's hair as Laura let him go. "We can celebrate tomorrow, too, by catching some fish," he said. "How does that sound?"

"Yahoo!" Robbie whooped, waking the puppy. The two of them raced wildly around the tree.

Laura forced herself to chuckle as she lifted the skinned rabbit off the hook. "Well, it looks like things are settling down again. Supper will be ready in about an hour."

"I'll find the key and fix the lock," Caleb said. "If you want, I'll nail the hasp higher up so your boy can't reach it."

"Please do. If he'd played this game when we were alone—" Laura's knees weakened as she thought of what could have happened. She turned away to hide the welling of unexpected tears. After tomorrow, Caleb's calm, quiet presence would be nothing but a memory. There were no words for how much she would miss him.

Caleb watched her walk away, filling his eyes with the brave tilt of her head and the long stride that failed to disguise the feminine sway of her hips. His shirtfront was soaked with her tears. He could feel their salty wetness drying in the afternoon heat. The sensation of holding her lingered as a subtle burn along his arms.

His eyes followed her until she disappeared into the kitchen. Leaving her and the boy would be the hardest thing he'd ever done. But he couldn't risk any more delay. The look that had flashed across Laura's face when he charged into the springhouse had jolted him. It was as if, for a split second, her memory had awakened and she'd remembered who he was. Caleb had braced himself for an onslaught of hysterical rage, but it hadn't come. Instead she'd crumpled in his arms, and he'd realized the danger was over—for now, at least. But what had happened once could—and likely would—happen again. It was only a matter of time.

For supper that evening they feasted on fried rabbit with fresh bread, potatoes, and greens from Laura's withering garden. Robbie, half-asleep on his feet by now, fed the scraps to Buster. Then, with the pup hanging under his good arm, he staggered off to get ready for bed.

Caleb was clearing the table when Laura returned from tucking him in. Shadows framed her eyes, but her face wore a tired smile. "I never thought I'd let my son sleep with a dog, but I didn't have the heart to separate them. I only hope Buster doesn't have fleas." She shrugged and sighed. "If he does, I suppose I'll find out, won't I?"

She moved toward the stacked dishes on the counter, but Caleb stopped her with a hand on her wrist. "You've had a rough day. Sit down and relax. I can finish cleaning up."

"I have a better idea," she said. "Leave the cleanup and come outside with me. It's cooler on the porch, and I want to ask you about my plans for the ranch. This might be my last chance to get your advice."

"I'm flattered that you'd ask a poor Texas farm boy anything." Torn by mixed emotions, Caleb followed her out into the dusk. He desperately wanted to spend time with Laura. But the episode in the springhouse had roused all his danger instincts. Caution whispered that from here on out, the less she saw of him, the better.

She sat down on the edge of the porch with her feet on the third step. Caleb settled himself beside her, his body not quite touching hers. He could feel the brush of her skirt against his leg and smell the clean aroma of the homemade soap she used. Drawing her close and cradling her head in the hollow of his shoulder would have been the most natural thing in the world. It was all Caleb could do to keep from reaching out to her.

Twilight lay around them like thick blue velvet, cool and sweet after the long, hot day. The rising moon cast liquid shadows across the yard and painted the blossoming clumps of chamisa with silver. A nighthawk darted low, flashing its white-barred wings in the darkness.

Sitting beside Laura, Caleb couldn't help wondering how it would feel to belong in a place like this—to have his own land solid beneath his feet, his own children slumbering in the house and his own woman beside him, her body warm with the promise of the night to come. But he knew better than to wish it could be this land, or this woman.

Caleb's lips moved in a silent curse. It would have been better for him if he'd never come back to this place. But it was too late to change things now.

He cleared his throat. "So tell me about your plans for the ranch," he said.

"I will." She gave a nervous little laugh. "But first I want to apologize for the way I behaved this afternoon. The fact that Robbie locked me in the springhouse was no excuse for hysterics."

A prickle of unease crawled like a centipede up Caleb's spine. "The last thing you owe me is an apology, Laura. The marshal told me what happened to you in the springhouse. Nobody could blame you for getting upset when you were locked in there again."

She shook her head. "Upset isn't the word for what I was feeling. It was closer to sheer terror. There's an evil presence in that springhouse, Caleb. I feel it every time I go in there. If I could spare the money, I'd have that cursed pile of logs torn down and rebuilt in a different spot, with everything new. Maybe someday I will." She glanced at him as if for reassurance. "You probably think I'm crazy, don't you?"

"No, I've sensed something in there, too," he said. "My mother's people believe that spirits will haunt a place where evil's been done. I've never had any reason to doubt the truth of it."

"Until five years ago I would've called that belief superstitious nonsense. But not anymore. That's why I keep the door locked. I don't want Robbie going in there, not ever." She leaned forward, wrapping herself in her arms. Caleb gazed into the twilight, his mind groping for an easy way to change the subject. He didn't like the way their conversation was going. The last thing he wanted was to relive that awful day in the springhouse. But that was what Laura seemed to have in mind.

"They were monsters, those three men," she said, staring into the gloom. "I wanted Mark to send them away, but he insisted on feeding them. Afterward, I was in the springhouse, and the crazy-looking one came in and swung the door shut. He had a knife, and he held it at my throat while he put his hand up my skirt—" She shuddered at the memory. "I begged him not to hurt my baby, but he only laughed. Then the younger one came in and they started fighting over me. I tried to get away. That was when *this* happened."

Her fingers brushed the left side of her face. Caleb stared down at his hands, afraid to meet her eyes. Lord, was that the way she remembered it—that he and Zeke had fought over her? Hadn't she known that in his bumbling way, he'd been trying to rescue her?

"You don't need to tell me the rest," he said, wanting to end the painful tale. "The marshal told me how your husband came in with his rifle and how he was killed."

She went on as if she hadn't heard him. "The man who shot my husband in the back had the coldest eyes I've ever seen," she said. "They were like a snake's—he didn't even blink when Mark went down. I thought he was going to shoot me, too. If it hadn't been for the baby, I wouldn't have cared."

Laura's hands clenched in her lap, fingers bunching a fold of her skirt. Caleb studied her rigid profile, almost afraid to breathe. Surely she'd remember how he'd stepped into the line of fire when Noah was about to shoot her, and how he'd talked his brother into letting her live.

"I went down on my knees next to Mark and tried to stanch the blood," she whispered. "So much blood—it was like trying to dam a river with a handkerchief. The next thing I knew, it was dark. I heard the sound of the lock closing..."

She'd begun to tremble. Sick with dismay, Caleb stared into the shadows. "It's all right, Laura. It's over. You don't have to talk about it."

But she plunged ahead, the words spilling out of her. Caleb sensed that she'd never told anyone some of the things he was hearing now.

"Mark took a long time to die. The bullet missed his heart and lungs but it tore up the lower organs. I kept thinking that if I could just get to the house I might be able to save him. I ripped off my petticoat and held it against the wound, but it didn't help. I don't think anything would have helped, except maybe some laudanum to ease the pain. So much pain..."

The tears had begun to trickle down her face.

"Toward the end, it was so bad that he begged me to find his rifle and put him out of his misery. But the rifle was gone. The murderers had taken it. And even if I'd had the gun, I don't know if I could have used it. All I could do was hold him."

Her shoulders shook with quiet sobs. Caleb ached to cradle her in his arms, but the horror of her story had paralyzed him. How could he reach out to her, knowing the hell that his family had put this woman through?

"The marshal told me you dug yourself out with your bare hands," he said gently. "I can't even imagine the courage that took."

She sucked in her breath. "I could just as easily have given up and died in there with my husband. But I knew I had to survive for my baby. Robbie was the only thing that kept me going."

Laura gazed down at her clasped hands for a long, silent moment. Caleb watched in wonder as she pulled herself erect, shoulders squaring, head lifting. It was as if she were gathering the shards of her broken spirit and forging them into steel.

When she turned toward Caleb her tear-mottled face wore a determined smile. "Robbie's still the only thing that keeps me going," she said. "So tell me, how can I make this ranch pay enough to raise him right?"

Chapter Eleven

Caleb lay on his bedroll, staring up into the dark rafters and wondering how he could have gotten himself into such an infernal mess. Laura owed him her life. She owed him the life of her son. But her memory had painted him as evil as his brothers. Now, things being what they were, there was no way he could tell her the truth.

Not that he blamed her for the mistake. When he'd burst into the springhouse and broken his shoulder, Zeke's blade had been cold against her throat. How was she to know that he'd arrived to save her and not to join in the deviltry? By the time he'd talked Noah out of shooting her, she'd been in shock. Her world had shrunk to the sight of her husband and his hellish wound. She wouldn't have remembered much of anything else.

Cursing, Caleb yanked on his boots and went outside. He hadn't bothered to undress. He'd had a premonition that this would be a sleepless night, and he'd been right.

Restless, he ambled over to the corral. Leaning his elbows on the fence he watched the horses drowsing in the moonlight. Bats flitted through the darkness, swooping and diving after night-flying insects. The drawn-out wail of a coyote echoed across the foot-hills.

He and Laura had spent nearly an hour discussing her plans for the ranch. Caleb had done his best to listen and to contribute his own suggestions, but he'd lost his enthusiasm for talking. The story of her ordeal had left him drained, with little to offer in the way of ideas. But what did it matter? Laura would get along fine without his help. She was a smart woman with ambition to match her intelligence. What she didn't know about ranching she could learn. And if she had questions, there was always Tom Haskins.

A midnight breeze fluttered the aspens and shimmered through the moon-silvered willows along the creek. Clouds billowed across the sky, veiling the stars as they passed.

The house was dark and silent, with lace curtains fluttering at Laura's open window. Caleb imagined her asleep in her bed, her glorious hair spilling over the pillow, her bravely beautiful face at rest. How would it feel to stretch out alongside her and pull her close, cradling her body spoon-fashion against his? Caleb was no virgin, but he'd never spent the night with a woman in his arms. Right now, he couldn't imagine anything sweeter than the satin heat of her buttocks tucked against his thighs, the intimate aromas of her skin and the innocence of her quiet breathing. He wouldn't even have to make love to her. Just holding her until they awoke, warm and sleepy in the dawn, would be enough.

He cursed the swelling erection that strained the crotch of his trousers, making lies of his tender thoughts. He wanted her, damn it. He wanted her so badly that every minute he spent with her was torture. And there was nothing he could do about it except leave.

If he had any sense he'd mount up and ride out now. Laura would be madder than spit, but she'd get over it and be fine. However, it wasn't just Laura he was concerned about.

"...That boy of hers, he seems to think you hung the moon. Even wanted to name his damned dog after you!"

Tom Haskins's words came back to taunt Caleb as he gazed toward the house. Laura might understand his reasons for running out. She might even forgive him in time. But Robbie was young and impressionable. The lessons he learned about promises and betrayals would stay with him, shaping his character for the rest of his life.

Caleb sighed and thrust his hands into his pockets. He would stay and take Robbie fishing tomorrow afternoon, as he'd promised. Then he'd saddle up and ride for the border with a clear conscience. Maybe in some sleepy Mexican town that fiery little señorita would be waiting for him. Maybe he'd even settle down and learn to be content with her. But whatever the future held, one thing was certain—Laura's lovely, tragic eyes would haunt him until the end of his days.

The wind had freshened, heralding a spill of angry clouds that poured over the mountains like an invading army. Lightning danced above the peaks. Caleb counted twelve seconds before the distant cannonade of thunder boomed across the horizon. The flash had been more than two miles off. But maybe the clouds would come this way. Maybe this time they'd bring rain.

For the space of a long breath he stood watching the sky. Then, with a last glance at Laura's dark window, he turned and walked slowly back toward the shed.

The night wind whipped through the big cottonwood tree. Moonlight shone through its tossing branches to flicker on the wall of the bedroom where Laura lay, lost in fitful sleep.

The lace curtains twisted and turned as a long shadow fell across the coverlet. Hovering on the edge of sleep, Laura sensed a powerful presence at her bedside. A fingertip brushed her cheek, caressing the path of the scar as if it were a thing of beauty.

A moan of awakening pleasure uncoiled in her throat. She opened her eyes to find him leaning over the bed, his coppery black eyes gazing down at her with a hunger no woman could mistake. His lean bronze body was clad in nothing but a leather loincloth. The shaft that strained beneath it left no doubt about the power of his arousal. Moonlight cast the contours of his muscles into stark relief. He looked every inch the savage he was—fierce, proud, untamed and utterly beautiful.

His callused fingers flowed from the scar to her mouth. They stroked across the sensitive flesh of her lower lip, awakening every nerve ending in her body. She stirred and whimpered, feverish with need.

Her tongue stole out to lick the salty tip of his finger. She drew it into her mouth, sucking and nibbling in a sly pantomime of what both of them had in mind. The color deepened in his face. His hooded eyes were hot and hungry.

Laura had gone to bed wearing her nightgown, but now she was unashamedly naked. He leaned over her. His mouth skimmed a searing line of kisses from her throat, along the hollow between her breasts and down her belly to brush the nest of hair between her thighs. His breath was a warm caress on the sensitive folds.

Her loins clenched, triggering a gush of slickness between her thighs. He had barely touched her, but she was already aching for him. She had wanted him from that first day, when she'd glimpsed him washing at the pump, and her heart had stopped at the sight of him. Now he was here, breathtakingly close, touching her in ways she'd dreamed of being touched by him.

His hand moved downward to take possession of her breast, stroking the nipple lightly with his thumb. She gasped as her flesh puckered in response, rising hard to his touch. She whispered his name, loving the sound of it, wanting to say it over and over.

"Caleb..."

He bent and kissed her, his hand sliding under her back to bring her up to him. His mouth was familiar, the shape and feel of it, the little catch of his breath as his rough tongue met hers. She met each exploring thrust, blood racing, heart pounding, the smoky-sweet taste of him swimming in her senses. Her hands found his naked shoulders, fingers working his flesh in a frenzy of need.

With a mutter of impatience he flung the covers aside and lowered himself to lie beside her. His mouth found her nipple. She arched against him as he fondled and sucked her. Her hands tangled in his hair, pressing him close, cradling him in her softness.

The hunger between her thighs was more than she could stand. Wild to ease the throbbing, she found his hand and moved it down her body to her crotch. With a little groan, he began to stroke her, his fingers gliding over the silky wetness of folds and hollows to find the sensitive nub that lay at their center. Sensation exploded through her body, so intense that she cried out. Wild with wanting him, she clawed at the thong that anchored his loincloth, breaking the knot in her urgency.

Her head fell back. Her eyes closed as he moved between her legs...

"Just hold still, girlie, while I get a hand under them petticoats."

The voice sent a sickly jolt through Laura's body. Her stomach convulsed as she raised her head to stare into a pair of leering, bloodshot yellow eyes...

"Behave yourself, now, and you'll be fine. Hell, you might even enjoy it."

She screamed herself awake.

Caleb spent the morning riding fence around Laura's ranch. Animals and weather had taken their toll. The barbed wire was rusted and sagging and many of the wooden posts were knocked off-kilter where wild mustangs and stray cattle had tried to push through. Caleb fixed the worst of the damage, grateful that Mark Shafton had bought quality materials and done a decent job of putting up the fences. The pastures were in good condition as well. The grass was thick and rich, needing only the gift of rain to green it up.

Laura had the makings of a fine ranch here. And with the army buying so much beef, ranching could be a profitable business these days—he'd told her that much last night. If she got her calves on the land in the next few weeks there'd still be plenty of time to fatten them up and sell them next spring at a profit. The best animals could be kept for breeding. Before too many years she'd have herself a herd and a promising future for her son.

Maybe she'd have a new family as well, with a husband and more babies to love. But that was something he wouldn't be here to see.

As he worked, shoring up posts and fastening loose wire, Caleb struggled to keep himself from sinking into despair. Laura had looked strained and tired at breakfast. Bad dreams—they happened sometimes, she'd explained with an edgy little laugh. Caleb hadn't pressed her for more. He knew the sort of bogeymen who prowled those dreams of hers. He was one of them, and he'd been there when her nightmares were born.

For him, the afternoon would be bittersweet. He'd be spending a few precious hours with the only two people in the world who felt like family. But the fact that he was leaving would cast a shadow over their time together. And the temptation to stay longer would be a constant battle—one he'd lost too many times and couldn't risk losing again.

A glance at the angle of the sun told him it was well past noon, time to be getting back to the house. Robbie would be waiting for him, probably pestering his mother to distraction. The thought of the boy's excitement tugged Caleb's mouth into a fleeting smile.

His eyes swept the horizon as he mounted his horse and swung toward the ranch. The sky was clear, with just a few wispy clouds drifting over the mountains. Good fishing weather, at least, and he'd already scouted out some easy fishing holes. Caleb nudged the horse to a trot. This afternoon he would put his gloom aside and make the most of the time that remained. The memory would be his parting gift to Robbie, to Laura and to himself.

* * *

Laura filled a picnic basket with bacon sandwiches, fresh carrots, raisin-filled cookies and a small jug of cider. While she fussed over the food, Robbie flitted around her, his eyes sparkling.

"Will Mr. Caleb be here soon?" he asked for perhaps the thirteenth time.

"He'll be here as soon as he gets the fences mended." Laura polished three precious apples and added them to the feast. "He wants to finish the job before we go."

"What time will he be done?"

Laura sighed. "He said he'd try to be here by one o'clock. But don't get too anxious. It might take longer. Go play with your puppy. That'll make the time go faster."

"Can't we take Buster with us? Please?"

"I already told you no, Robbie. We'll be going way up along the creek. Buster's too little to walk that far."

"We could carry him."

Laura shot her son a stern glance. "You'll be too busy fishing to look after a puppy. Use your old nightshirt to make him a nice, soft bed in the toolshed, and leave him a bowl of water. He'll be just fine."

"But won't he be lonesome?"

"Maybe for a little while. But then he'll just curl up and take a nap. When he wakes up, you'll be there to let him out. Think how happy he'll be to see you!"

Robbie furrowed his brow. His lower lip crept outward, making him look so much like his father that it almost broke her heart. Without a word he marched into his room. A moment later he came out holding a threadbare flannel nightshirt that he'd long since outgrown.

"This one?" he asked.

"Yes, that one. You're a good boy, Robbie, and I love you."

He looked up at her, still pouting. Then he walked out the back door, closing it carefully behind him.

Laura watched him out the window as he dragged his feet all the way to the toolshed, with Buster licking at his heels. At last, with a sigh of relief, she turned away and began tidying up the kitchen.

The house seemed strangely quiet now. Robbie had been badgering the life out of her all morning, so that she'd yearned for a little peace and quiet. Only now did she realize that his questions had kept her thoughts from wandering onto dangerous paths.

Last night's dream had disturbed and terrified her. The lovemaking part was no surprise—even awake, she'd wondered what being loved by Caleb might be like. But hearing that nasal voice, looking into those devilish yellow eyes at the very moment Caleb was about to make her his… How could her slumbering mind have made such a horrible leap?

But why torment herself when the answer was right in front of her? Last night she'd talked with Caleb about the awful thing that had happened in the springhouse. In the devious way of dreams, her thoughts had been broken, twisted and reconnected to create the nightmare. None of it had been real. It was time she shrugged it off and put the whole thing behind her.

And that included Caleb.

Wringing out a rag, she flung her energy into scrubbing the tabletop. She'd done far too much talking last night, she chastised herself. Caleb would be leaving today, almost certainly for good. So what had she been thinking, unburdening herself to a virtual stranger who didn't give a hang about her? Oh, yes, Caleb had been kind and helpful. He'd even stolen a few kisses—simply because he could, Laura suspected. But that didn't mean he really cared for her. Likely as not, he wouldn't even remember her name in a few weeks' time. The sooner she buried those intoxicating memories of being in his arms, the better.

From outside the window she could hear Robbie shouting. The elation in his voice told her that he must have spotted Caleb.

Leaning outward she could see the tall rider moving down along the fence, headed toward the house. Despite the lecture she'd just given herself, Laura's heart leaped at the sight of him.

Instinctively her hands went to her hair, arranging the rumpled wings to frame her face. Pleasing Caleb would be a wasted effort, she knew. But there was still a part of her that wanted to look nice for him.

Fumbling behind her waist, she untied her damp

apron, flung it onto the nail behind the door and smoothed her skirt. She knew there was no hurry—Caleb would need time to unsaddle his horse and put the tools away. All the same, her feet flew as she seized the picnic basket and darted outside. This afternoon was the last the three of them would have together. She would hoard the minutes, each one like a precious bead on a string, so that when he was gone and her life faded back to shades of drab, she would remember light and color and happy laughter.

By the time she'd closed the house, he was in the yard, swinging off his horse with an easy grace that tightened Laura's throat. Robbie was beside himself with excitement. The pup raced in circles, chasing his tail.

"I've got the pole from last time, and Mama helped me dig the worms," Robbie announced. "Hurry, Mr. Caleb. Let's go catch some fish!"

"Don't forget to put Buster in the shed," Laura reminded him. "We don't want him trying to follow us."

"Can't he *please* come?" Robbie's eyes would have moved Attila the Hun.

"You heard your mother, Robbie," Caleb warned. "Do as she says."

While Caleb unsaddled his horse, Robbie carried his pet to the toolshed. Buster seemed to know he was about to be left behind. No sooner had Robbie closed the door and fastened the simple swing latch than the pup began to whine, then to yelp.

"He's crying, Mama!"

"That's what puppies do. He'll be fine." Laura was determined not to spoil the afternoon. "Come on, Robbie, you take the pole, and we'll start hiking along the creek. Caleb can catch up with us when he finishes here."

Caleb hefted the saddle onto the corral fence. "Leave the basket, I'll bring it," he said. "And don't worry about your pup, Robbie. He can go with you when he's older. For now, he needs to learn to stay put."

Laura picked up the worm can, took her son's free hand and set off for the trail that wound upward through the willows. Buster's yelps had become heartrending howls. Before long he'd get tired of howling and settle down. Meanwhile, she needed to get Robbie out of earshot and get his mind on something else—like fishing.

Glancing back over her shoulder, she saw Caleb coming up the path with the picnic basket. A fresh breeze blew down the slope, deliciously cool on her damp face. The air smelled faintly of moisture. But that was just her imagination, Laura told herself. These dry thunderstorms were like the boy who cried wolf, all noise and flash with nothing to show for it.

Caleb caught up with them on an open rise, crested by an outcropping of rock. From where they stood, they had a clear view of the ranch—the house and outbuildings, the corral and the edge of the pastureland. "I can see our animals down there!" Robbie exclaimed. "Hello, horses!" he shouted. "Hello, Bessie! Hello, chickens! Hello, Buster!" He glanced back at Caleb. "I can't see Buster, but maybe he can hear me."

"Maybe he can. Dogs have good ears." Caleb patted the boy's shoulder. "Let's get moving. There's a grassy spot by the first hole where we can have our picnic."

They trooped up the game trail into the aspens, Robbie scampering ahead, Laura following him and Caleb bringing up the rear. He took simple pleasure in her strong, confident stride and the graceful sway of her hips. She had arranged her hair in a loose braid that hung down her back. The colors of it were like shades of pulled taffy. He'd seen some pretty women in his life, and he'd doubtless see more. But Laura's proud, warm, soul-deep beauty would be the measure of all the others.

Clouds were moving in above the mountains, boiling like porridge on a hot stove. Caleb frowned as he studied them. Were they darker than the empty clouds of the past few days? Were they heavier, more turbulent? Was that really rain he smelled on the breeze? There were no sure answers to those questions, but a hillside wasn't a good place to be in a storm.

He checked the impulse to turn the little party back toward home. Robbie would be heartbroken if he didn't get a chance to fish. It would end the whole day on a sour note. And judging from the look of the sky, they had plenty of time. The cloud bank's dark edge had barely cleared the peaks. Even if the threat of rain was real, they should be fine for the next hour or two.

They spread a cloth on the grass and enjoyed the food Laura had packed in the basket. Caleb was grateful for Robbie's constant chatter. It made small talk with Laura unnecessary. When he rode away he'd be leaving many things unsaid. He could only hope she'd understand and realize that it was for the best.

Every few minutes he caught himself glancing at the sky. Laura, he noticed, was doing the same. The clouds were darkening and spreading slowly outward above the peaks, but the sky was still bright and blue overhead.

Reaching for the pole Caleb scrambled to his feet. "Come on, Robbie, let's catch some fish!"

The creek was low, the shadowed pockets teeming with hungry trout. For a young boy just learning to fish it was heaven. Robbie caught four fair-sized cutthroat trout in the first fifteen minutes. At that point Caleb insisted on moving upstream. Thinning out the population of each crowded hole would do more for the surviving fish than emptying just one spot.

By the time Robbie had caught seven fish, he was ready to let Laura try her hand. Caleb stood behind her and guided her arm, showing her how to let the bait drift with the current. After watching her boy, she'd likely learned the skill herself. But the instruction gave him an excuse to be close to her. He was pleased that she didn't protest.

"I've got a bite!" She squealed as the willow pole bent nearly double. "It feels like a big one!"

"Back up!" Caleb coached her, wishing they'd had a store-bought pole with a reel and a net. "Slow and easy now. If you jerk, you could lose him!"

He stepped back to give her more room. In the water they could see the silver flash of the fish—for a creek of this size it was a monster. Robbie was jumping up and down, jabbering with excitement.

"Careful..." Caleb urged her as she played the fish. "Give him a little slack. Let him get tired. That's it."

She was leaning back, pulling against the strength of the fish when, without warning, the line snapped. Laura stumbled backward, crashing into Caleb. Together they tumbled into the long, soft grass.

There was a beat of stunned silence. Then Laura began to giggle. Lying beneath her, Caleb felt the laughter go through her body to burst out in peals of hilarity. Before he knew it he was laughing with her. Then Robbie flung himself on top of them dog-pile fashion and they toppled over in a tangle of arms and legs, all of them shrieking with laughter.

Caleb would remember it as one of the perfect moments of his life.

The growl of thunder from above the peaks ended the silliness at once. It was time to go home. Caleb hastily cleaned the fish, hooked their gills over a sharpened willow twig and laid them on some leaves in the picnic basket. The sky above them was still blue, but over the mountains the clouds churned and tumbled, spreading outward and growing darker by the minute.

Lightning shattered the sky as they hurried down the trail. Thunder cracked across the foothills with a deafening boom. The first drops of rain spattered into the dust. There wouldn't be time to get off the hillside before the storm struck. The safest place for shelter would be just below the rocky outcrop, where they'd stood looking down on the ranch.

Gathering Robbie under one arm and catching Laura's hand with the other, Caleb broke into a run. They scrambled down the slope, half falling, as the clouds burst open above them. Soaked and out of breath they reached the line of rocks and clambered down to their base. An overhang jutted outward, just far enough to protect the three of them from the rain. They crawled into the tight, dry space beneath it, huddling together with Robbie in the middle.

Laura was still clutching the picnic basket under one arm. Dripping tendrils of hair framed her face. Robbie's eyes were huge in the shadows.

"Are you all right?" Caleb asked above the clatter of the raindrops.

Robbie nodded. "Is this an adventure?"

"I should say it is!"

"Wow!" Robbie breathed, his eyes growing even wider.

Caleb chuckled and dropped his arm around the boy's shoulders in a hearty hug. He ached to draw Laura close as well, but he sensed an invisible line between friendship and intimacy—a line he'd already crossed too many times and shouldn't cross again.

Clouds raced in an inky flood across the sky. As lightning crackled and boomed, the rain swept down in sheets, flattening the grass and streaming down the hillside. Caleb was grateful for the protection of the rocky overhang. Until the storm ended, it was the safest place they could be.

Robbie leaned forward. "Hey, I can see the rain falling on our place down there! The chickens have gone in the coop, but Bessie and the horses are just standing outside, getting wet!"

"Cows and horses don't seem to mind rain," Caleb said. "Maybe it even feels good to them."

Robbie didn't seem to hear. He was straining forward, staring down the hill at the yard far below. Suddenly, with an anguished cry, he pointed. "Oh, no! Look down there, by the tree! It's Buster!"

Chapter Twelve

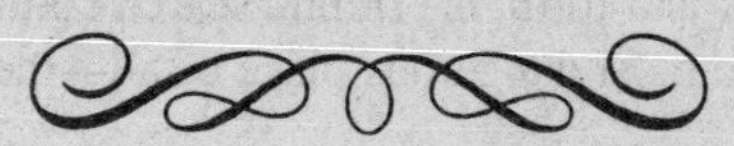

Caleb swore under his breath as he spotted the tan speck between the cottonwood tree and the house. How had that blasted dog gotten out of the shed? Maybe he'd chewed his way through the splintery wood, or the flimsy latch had given way. Or maybe Robbie had left it unfastened on purpose. Whatever the cause, Buster was cowering in the deluge, alone, terrified and probably crying his little puppy heart out.

"He'll drown! I've gotta get him!" Robbie sprang up and stumbled out into the rain.

"No!" Laura cried, but by then Caleb's hand had already darted out and seized the back of the boy's overalls. Thrashing, kicking and sobbing, Robbie was hauled back under the overhang and into his mother's arms.

"Let me go! Buster mustn't stay out there! It isn't safe! Please!" Tears streamed down his cheeks, streaking the splatters of rain-splashed mud.

"Stay with your mother, Robbie. I'll go." Caleb ducked out from under the rocks and plunged into the blinding rain. The hillside was slimy with water and flowing mud. Even when he tried to zigzag, gouging into the slope with the sides of his boots, he slid more than he ran. Raindrops pelted his face in a solid stream. His blurred vision could barely make out the moving figure of the pup far below. Buster was darting back and forth, his frantic search taking him toward the most dangerous place of all—the swelling creek.

Caleb swore as he twisted his ankle and went down. He slid a good ten feet before he could right himself. "Buster!" he shouted. "Come up here, damn you! Come on, boy!" But the pup paid no attention. Either he couldn't hear above the rain or he didn't know enough to mind.

Lightning cracked across the sky, painting the world a ghastly bluish white. Thunder exploded, causing the pup to shrink against the mud, a quivering, rain-soaked ball of misery. The air shook with sound—the echo of thunder, the drumroll staccato of the rain and a subtle, watery roar that seemed to swallow everything. Caleb knew that sound. It chilled his bones to the marrow.

By now he'd hit the bottom of the slope and was on more or less level ground. Wild with urgency he lunged toward the little dog. The terrified Buster yelped and darted away, straight for the raging creek. Cursing, Caleb charged ahead at an angle, hoping to head the pup off.

Once, as a boy in Texas, he'd won a greased pig contest at the county fair. The same timing came into play now as he raced on a course meant to intercept the pup at the water's edge. His muscles tensed—he made a clutching dive. For an instant he thought he'd succeeded. Then the muddy dog slipped through his fingers and tumbled into the rushing torrent.

From far up the slope, Caleb could hear Robbie's scream. He plunged into the muddy water, grabbing frantically. His fingers brushed wet fur, then clenched around the squirming body. Moments later he lurched onto the bank with the exhausted Buster clasped against his chest.

Lightning crashed across the sky again, so close that the boom seemed to shatter Caleb's eardrums. Through the ringing aftermath, the watery roar echoed down the mountainside.

Flash flood. It was already pounding down the creek bed, a murderous wall of water, rocks and debris. On the steeper slopes, its momentum would keep it within the high banks. But where the land eased off toward the flats the water would burst outward, hurling limbs and boulders like giant cannonballs. And Mark Shafton's dam, if it didn't break, would channel the whole hellish mess right toward Laura's house.

As long as they stayed put, Laura and Robbie should be safe. The animals in the sheds and corral, which lay beyond the house and on slightly higher ground, might get their feet wet, but they'd likely survive as well. Right now it was Caleb and the dog who were in the worst possible spot. They had seconds, if that, to scramble out of the way.

The roar of oncoming water told him there'd be no time to outrun the flood. Only the sturdy cottonwood, standing a dozen yards from the creek, promised any chance of safety.

Thrusting the pup inside his shirt, Caleb sprinted toward the tree and caught a lower branch. As he swung upward, the flood burst down the creek bed and exploded outward. He felt the massive tree quiver as the water struck. If the roots didn't hold there'd be nothing he could do but swim and pray.

The brunt of the flood fanned out. Water swirled around the roots of the tree, carrying away the woodpile and drowning Laura's precious vegetable garden. The rain was falling harder than ever. Muddy water roared down the creek's narrow funnel and streamed across the yard, scraping away layers of earth. If it continued, it would undermine the springhouse, then the house itself.

Clasping the pup under his arm, Caleb surveyed the yard. Mark Shafton's accursed dam was still holding. Breach that dam, and the water might return to its original course, flooding out onto the lower pastures. Somehow, Caleb knew, he had to make that happen.

Ripping off his shirt, he fashioned a makeshift sling to keep the pup in the tree. Buster yelped in protest as Caleb hung the sling from a limb. It held securely, with little chance of escape. As long as the cottonwood lasted, the dog should be all right.

"Hang on, boy," Caleb muttered, giving the soggy head a pat. Then he swung out of the tree and dropped into the churning, thigh-deep water.

"What's he doing, Mama?"

"I don't know." Laura's arm tightened around her son's shivering shoulders. Their place under the lip of the overhang was cramped and cold, but at least the rocks around them broke the flow of the runoff and kept them from getting washed down the hill. The spot also gave them a rain-blurred view of the disaster below.

Laura bit her lip to keep from crying out as Caleb floundered through the flood. The water was only about three feet deep, but the debris it carried was a constant danger. Jagged limbs and tree roots swirled and swung with the current. It would be all too easy for one to strike him and drag him under. And there could be snakes in the water as well, rattlers swept down by the flood, biting at anything they could reach.

She bit back a groan as he stumbled over something under the water, then managed to right himself. Oh, why hadn't he stayed in the big cottonwood, where there was at least a chance of safety? What in heaven's name was he trying to do?

Robbie leaned outward, straining against his mother's grip. "I can see Buster! He's trying to get out of the shirt! What if he falls?"

"Just pray that he doesn't." Laura seized her son's overalls and dragged him backward. Her instincts screamed at her to take action, to race down the hill and help Caleb, or at least to rescue the puppy. But she didn't dare leave Robbie alone and unprotected.

Her eyes followed Caleb's path through the churning flood. His attention seemed to be fixed on something near the surface of the water. Only as he pulled and swung it upward did Laura realize what it was. He had seized the handle of the large ax he'd used earlier that day to chop wood. The massive stump that served as a chopping block had trapped the buried blade, keeping the handle upright. Now, with the ax in his grip, Caleb was pushing toward the dam that channeled the water through the spring-house.

Laura's heart dropped as she realized what he was about to do.

The floodwaters had swamped the springhouse and were battering the foundation of the house itself. Before long the foundation would wash through and the house would collapse. Breaking through the dam would divert the water and save the house. But Mark had built that dam to last for generations. Beneath its outer layer of earth and sod was a core of logs, each one as thick as a man's leg. Not only would cutting through such a mass be difficult, it would be dangerous. If the dam gave way suddenly, those heavy, rolling logs could crush Caleb to death or drag him under.

She held her breath as he mounted the dam, spread his legs for balance and began pounding with the ax. His hair and clothes were soaked with muddy water. His long johns were torn at the shoulder where something, likely a sharp limb, had gashed through the fabric. Blood made a blossoming red stain that flowed down his sleeve. He paid no heed to the injury as he raised the ax again and again. The water that spilled over the top of the dam swirled around his feet, washing away the layer of earth and exposing the logs. The dam began to shudder beneath him as he drove the blade into the wood. Rain poured down his body, mingling with blood.

Suddenly, without warning, the whole structure gave way. Logs rolled and tumbled as the water burst through, into its old channel.

"No!" The scream ripped from Laura's throat as Caleb lost his footing. Like a slow-motion scene from a nightmare she saw him teeter, his feet and arms flailing for a desperate moment. Then the dam dissolved and he vanished into the smashing melee of logs, mud and water.

Snatching up Robbie, Laura plunged down the hill in the rain. With the boy's weight keeping her off balance, their progress was slow and slippery. An eternity seemed to pass before they reached the yard, but the break in the dam had done its work. The water was draining out into its overgrown channel, leaving a mess of mud and debris behind. And somewhere in that nightmarish tangle was the man who'd sacrificed himself to save her home.

Buster still dangled in his makeshift sling, whimpering but safe. Laura left Robbie under the cottonwood to keep an eye on him while she searched for

Caleb. Would she find him alive? But she already sensed the answer to that question. Caleb was a powerful man, but how could anyone survive that explosive rush of water and the crushing force of those logs?

Heartsick, she splashed through the mud toward the broken dam where she'd seen him go down. She would start looking there and work her way downstream. Somewhere, somehow she would find him.

How long had it been since the three of them had been fishing on the mountainside, laughing like fools as they tumbled onto their backs in the grass. Such a precious, perfect moment, and she'd simply let it pass. If she'd known what was going to happen, she would have wrapped her arms around him and held on with all her strength. She would never have let him go.

By the time she reached the broken dam the mud was over her boot tops. Stranded fish thrashed in the shallows. A pair of ravens perched in a scraggly pine tree, waiting.

Something glided against Laura's leg. She glanced down to see a rattlesnake slither under a flattened chokecherry bush. A shudder passed through her body, but she forced herself to keep moving.

Below the dam, where the water had piled logs like so many jackstraws, she saw a booted leg sticking out from under a pile of rubble. Sick with dread, Laura dropped to her knees. Her fingers clawed away the mass of sticks, grass, mud and leaves until she could see into the space between two large logs. Caleb was sprawled facedown, his head and body coated with mud. The logs had come to rest in a position that shielded him from being crushed, but their weight had likely held him under long enough to drown. He was lying absolutely still.

The thickest log lay on top. With strength she hadn't known she possessed, Laura seized one end, lifted it and rolled it out of the way. Now she could reach Caleb and, perhaps, pull him clear.

With a silent prayer, she seized his mud-soaked long johns in one hand and his belt in the other. Gasping with effort, she pulled him free of the logs and rolled him over onto his back. Rain drizzled down her cheeks, blending with tears as she stared down at him. His face was a lifeless mask of mud, the eyes closed, the lips lightly parted. Fresh blood trickled from a gash on his temple.

Dizzy with fear, Laura laid her hand along the base of his neck. Her fingertips groped, fumbled and suddenly found it—the thready flutter of a pulse. He was alive—barely. But he needed help, and she was no doctor. She could only rely on her own instincts to save him.

First she cleansed his face, using the wet rain and a wad of her skirt to clear the mud from his eyes and mouth. Then she wrapped his wounded head and shoulder with strips torn off her petticoat. Caleb's only response to her ministrations was an incoherent whisper.

Clasping his hands in hers, she wiped the mud

from his palms and his long, sinewy fingers. She rubbed them, kissed them, whispering his name and begging him to live.

His skin was like ice. More than anything, he needed warmth. Somehow she'd have to move him into the house.

"Mama! Where are you?" Even at a distance, Laura could sense the fear in her son's voice. With snakes and heaven knows what else slinking around the place, she couldn't delay getting him to safety. Tearing herself away from Caleb, she took a few frantic moments to rush back to the cottonwood tree, untie Buster and carry the boy and his pup into the house.

"Is Caleb going to die?" Robbie asked her as she thrust more kindling into the stove and set a kettle of water on the burner.

"Not if I can help it." She rummaged in a chest and found a sturdy blanket. She could roll Caleb onto it and drag him across the mud as far as the porch. Then she'd have to figure out a way to get him up the steps and into the house. Even with her best efforts Caleb could die. He might even be dead already.

Robbie tugged at her skirt. "I said a prayer for him, Mama."

"Well, say another, my little love," she murmured, racing for the door. "Our friend Caleb is going to need all the prayers he can get!"

Caleb drifted in and out of awareness. There were rare moments when, as if through a distant fog, he sensed voices and movement. At other times the darkness enfolded him like a shroud and he was sure that he must be dead. For the most part he saw, felt and heard nothing. There was only a vague sense of black silence and weightless floating, devoid of coherent thought.

Later on there would be pain and flashing visions of his mother's old gods with their painted faces, chanting mouths and drumming hands. There would be the fevered heat of bonfires and the bitter taste of willow bark tea, forced between his lips. Then, at long last, there would be the touch of angel hands and the sweetness of two gray eyes gazing down at him from a place of warmth and sunlight—eyes that had been there along, watching over his wandering spirit and calling him home.

But that was still to come. For now he could only rest his battered body in mindless sleep, cradled by softness and bathed in the scent of clean flannel sheets. His spirit struggled to awaken, but his body lacked the strength to move.

It was all he could do to keep breathing.

Laura stood in the yard taking stock of the damage to her property. Three days of New Mexico sun had dried the mud to a layer of flaking grit that coated everything the floodwaters had touched. Her garden was buried in mud, and she was still looking for the clothesline. But at least the sheds and corrals, along with the animals in them, had been spared as had, by some miracle, the privy.

The springhouse had not fared so well.

She turned now to stare at the place that had held her nightmares for five long years. The brunt of the flood had struck the log foundation, lifting and twisting the entire structure. As the water drained away through the broken dam, the springhouse had settled back to earth with one collapsed wall and a roof that sagged nearly to the ground. The wood might be salvageable, but the building was useless. She would have a new, smaller springhouse built on the creek, where it belonged. Until then, she would just have to manage with the cool box.

And that was all right, Laura mused as she watched Robbie darting among the sheds with his puppy. The springhouse had bound her to years of grief and terror. Now it was gone, and she could move ahead with her new life. She was free to be happy again.

A meadowlark trilled from the hillside as she turned back toward the house. Her steps were light, her spirits high. Caleb was recovering. He still slept a great deal, and she was concerned about the slight fever he'd developed that morning. But he'd taken some oatmeal porridge for breakfast and murmured a word of thanks. Then he'd taken her hand and held it until he drifted back into sleep. Her heart had soared.

She entered the house and tiptoed through the kitchen to the open doorway of her bedroom, where Caleb lay sleeping in her bed. A tender smile played around her lips as she studied him—such a beautiful man, with his savagely chiseled features, his raven hair like tousled silk and his skin a rich golden copper against the white pillows. He was far from well. There were purple bruises under his eyes, and he still wore the blood-speckled bandage around his head. But his color was good, his breathing deep and even. The worst, Laura told herself, was over.

Getting him this far had taken all her strength of will. After the flood she'd dragged his unconscious body into the house. Abandoning all pretense of modesty, she'd stripped off his mud-soaked clothes and sponged him clean with rags dipped in warm water. Then she'd re-dressed his wounds, maneuvered him into her bed and covered him with thick flannel blankets she'd warmed above the stove.

As life returned to his flesh, he'd begun to shiver. That first night, Laura had lain beside him on top of the quilt, wrapping her arms and legs around his covered body. Every hour or so she'd gotten up to exchange his cooled blankets with the ones she'd left in the warming oven. When even that failed to stop the shivering, she'd slipped between the sheets in her nightgown and gathered him close, cradling him like a child. All night she'd held him, overcome by a tenderness so deep that it brought tears to her eyes. At some point during the black hours before dawn, she had come to realize that she loved him.

Soon Caleb would be well and strong, Laura told herself. And this time he wasn't going to ride off into the sunset. Not if she had anything to say about it.

As soon as he was able to listen, she would make it clear that she wanted him to stay.

For the space of a breath she allowed her eyes to linger on his battered face. Then she turned away and went back outside to check on Robbie. She had scoured the yard for snakes and other vermin washed down by the flood. Still she worried. It would be all too easy for a curious boy and his puppy to run afoul of danger.

She found her son playing on the swing, with Buster snoozing in the hollow of the tree root he'd chosen as a favorite spot. Laura took up her search for the missing clothesline. She had just found it, half buried in mud, when a movement along the wagon road caught her eye. She groaned as she recognized the big pinto horse and its tall rider. The last person she wanted to deal with right now was Tom Haskins.

Catching sight of her, he waved his Stetson and spurred his horse to a canter. Moments later he came thundering through the gate and reined up by the corral. The grin on his face faded to a look of shock as he surveyed the yard. "Holy hell, Laura, what happened here?" he gasped.

"Flash flood. It could've been worse." Laura curbed the sharp answer that had nearly leapt off her tongue. Tom's ranch was on the flatland, well out of the water's path. He wouldn't have known about her own disaster until now.

"And you here alone with your boy!" He swung off his horse and took a step toward her. "Lordy, girl, forgive me for not being here. I'd have ridden this horse to death if I'd known you were in danger!"

"We were all right." Robbie scampered across the yard to stand next to his mother. "Mr. Caleb saved Buster and the house. Then he almost drowned. Mama had to put him in her bed."

Laura could see the red heat creeping up Tom's neck to flood his face. "That damned drifter's still hanging around? I thought I ran him off the last time I was here."

"It's not your place to say who stays or goes on my property," Laura said coldly. "Caleb nearly gave his life for us. Without him, the house could have been swept away. Robbie and I could've been hurt, or even killed. You should thank him, not curse him."

Tom muttered something under his breath as he hitched his horse to the corral fence. "I'll bring a crew of my boys over here tomorrow to get things shipshape for you," he said. "You won't need that saddle tramp hanging around here anymore—especially not in your bed!" He swung away from her and strode toward the house.

"Where do you think you're going?" She raced after him, catching his arm on the front porch.

"I'm going to have it out with that half-breed bastard once and for all," he growled. "He's got you and your boy thinking he's some kind of hero. But he's nothing but a thieving liar—I know because I did some checking with the marshal. Caleb McCurdy did time in Yuma for bank robbery. He just got out a couple of months ago. Chew on that, Laura, if you think he's so damned wonderful!"

"I don't have to chew on it. I've known all along. I also know that he's gone straight."

"Straight, my foot!" Tom spat out the words as he pushed past Laura, into the house. "I'll give that jail-bird a piece of my—"

The words died on his lips as he reached the bed-room door. Caleb lay back against the pillows, his eyes bloodshot beneath drooping lids. His lips were crusted, his skin flushed. Laura's heart crept into her throat. He'd felt a bit feverish after breakfast, but she'd dismissed her worries, telling herself how much better he looked. Now it appeared that he'd de-veloped a raging infection, maybe from the flood-water getting into his wounds.

Laura knew little about medical matters, but she sensed that Caleb was beyond her help. He needed medicine and a doctor. Otherwise he could die.

She checked the impulse to fling herself down at his side and take him in her arms. To show her true emotions in front of Tom would be a mistake. Tom Haskins was her only hope of getting Caleb the help he needed. She would have to play her cards very carefully.

She stood beside Tom at the foot of the bed. Caleb's eyes watched them cautiously, but he made no effort to speak. Perhaps he couldn't.

"As you see, Tom, Mr. McCurdy is in no condi-tion to leave just yet," she murmured. "Right now I need you to ride into town and fetch the doctor. Tell him I'll pay anything he asks if he'll get here right away. Would you do that?"

When he hesitated, she added, "Please, Tom. I'll be in your debt forever. I'll do anything to repay you."

"Anything?" His eyes narrowed.

"Anything. Just hurry. Please."

Still, he hesitated, and Laura held her breath. At last, slowly, he exhaled. Then, with a deliberate glance at Caleb, he turned toward Laura, swept her into his arms and planted a passionate, lingering kiss on her mouth.

Chapter Thirteen

Caleb closed his eyes as Tom Haskins released Laura from his embrace. He'd seen enough—more than enough to know where things stood. If he had the strength, he'd get up and leave right now. But he couldn't seem to move his legs. In fact, he couldn't remember a time in his life when he'd felt so damnably rotten.

He clenched his teeth as a wave of dizziness swept over him. It was as if his heart was pumping poison through his veins and some devil with a brace and bit was boring into his skull. What little he could see, he saw through shimmering curtains of pain.

Earlier that morning he'd hoped he might be on the mend; then this new sockdolager had struck without warning. He didn't know what dying felt like, but maybe he was about to learn.

With his eyes closed, he could hear Tom Haskins's footsteps walking out of the bedroom, across the parlor and out the front door, with Laura pattering after him. Then the front door closed, leaving the house cloaked in stillness. Maybe Haskins was kissing her again on the front porch. She'd seemed to like it well enough the last time. He shoved the surge of jealousy out of his mind. He'd wanted Laura to find happiness. Now, it appeared she had.

But that didn't mean he was ready to die in her bed. Battling pain, Caleb fought to keep his mind clear. If he could figure out what was wrong with him, maybe he'd have some idea what to do.

He'd been in the flood with open wounds, and he'd likely swallowed water when he went under. Lord knows what was in that water, probably any one of a dozen things that could make a man deathly ill. If his wounds had festered, he could have blood poisoning. Caleb had seen a man die from that, and it wasn't pretty. But he'd be damned if he was just going to lie here and let it happen.

He was struggling to get out of bed when Laura came back into the house. She ran to him and pushed him back onto the pillows. "No! You're burning up with fever! You're too sick to get out of bed, Caleb!"

He was too weak to resist. Even speaking was almost too much for him. "Gotta do something..." he muttered.

Her beautiful eyes swam in front of his face. "Tom's on his way into town to get Dr. Trimble. Even if the doctor can come right away it's going to take hours." She clasped his hands, her fingers cool against his burning flesh. "A woman in town told me that willow bark tea is good for fevers. I can get some willow bark outside and boil it. Tell me what else I can do. What would your mother's people have used?"

Caleb searched his sluggish mind. "Skunk cabbage…some out in that swampy spot behind the cow shed. You mash the root…mash it raw. Goes on wounds. And cedar bark, if you can find it. Maybe some sage…" His thick tongue could barely form the words. "Clean water…boil it, even for you and Robbie…" He sank into the pillows and closed his eyes. Her fingers felt so good, so cool, but he knew he had to let her go. Let her go to Tom Haskins, if that was what she wanted.

She squeezed his hands and moved away. "I'll hurry," she said. "Don't try to get up."

Caleb's response emerged as a groan. He could feel his reason slipping. He clung to the sound of her retreating footsteps until they faded away. Then the red mist crept over him and he sank into a slow whirlpool of fever, nightmares and oblivion.

Seizing a shovel, Laura raced behind the sheds to the patch of sunken ground where the skunk cabbage grew. She'd always thought it an ugly weed with its huge leaves and oddly sheathed flowers that drew swarms of flies in springtime. But if its roots had the power to help Caleb heal, she would bless it forever.

Jamming the shovel blade into the damp earth, she raised clumps of thick, white roots and tossed them into a pile. The skunk-like stench that arose from the broken plants made her gasp, but she kept digging until she had enough to bundle into the skirt of her apron and carry back to the house.

Tom had kissed her again before he mounted up and galloped away. Laura had willed herself not to resist, even though she'd felt like a traitor to her own heart. Tom was a decent man who deserved a woman's honest love. But with Caleb's life at stake, there was nothing she wouldn't do to save him.

How long would they have to wait before the doctor arrived? Desperation gnawed at Laura as she calculated the time. Without a change of horse, it would take Tom at least four hours to ride to Benbow, and at least five hours for Dr. Trimble to make the return trip in his buggy. If the doctor had a sick patient or other pressing business, he might not be able to come at all.

And what if Tom decided that Caleb's life wasn't worth saving, even to win her gratitude? The thought that he might simply turn aside and go home almost made her ill. She'd always believed Tom Haskins to be a good man, but what if she were wrong?

She could have asked him to help her get Caleb to town. But Caleb was far too weak to stand the rough trip. It would be up to her to do whatever she could for him. The rest was beyond her control.

Wrapping the washed cabbage roots in a clean flour sack, she laid them on the porch and began crushing them with a hammer. The odor was so strong that it made her eyes water—or was she simply weeping? Dear heaven, what if she couldn't save him? What if any chance they might have had at happiness was already over?

She took a few precious seconds to make sure Robbie was all right. Then she gathered up the smelly mess and hurried into the house.

The willow bark tea was simmering on the stove. But was it strong enough yet? And how would she know? Laura cursed her own helplessness as she scraped the cabbage root into a bowl and cut some fresh wrappings from her old nightgown. She would let the tea boil while she re-dressed Caleb's wounds with the poultices made from the roots. Maybe by the time she finished, the brew would be strong enough to bring his fever down.

Caleb's eyes were closed when she walked into the bedroom. Lost in some nightmare, he rolled his head back and forth on the pillow, muttering broken phrases that meant nothing to her.

"...No...let her go, Zeke...don't...I won't let you kill her, Noah...she's going to have a..."

His body struggled and strained beneath the quilts. Alarmed, she seized his hand, holding it, pressing the fingers to her lips. His flesh was on fire.

When she touched his face, his eyelids fluttered open. "You were dreaming, Caleb," she whispered. "Lie still now. I've brought the cabbage root for your wounds."

He seemed to understand. Quieter now, he lay back on the pillow while she peeled the blood-soaked dressing from his head. The wound on his temple appeared to be healing cleanly, but she fashioned a small poultice all the same, plastered the smelly paste over his lacerated flesh and covered it with clean wrappings. That was when she noticed something strange. The mashed cabbage root was warm to the touch. It was generating its own heat. This was powerful medicine. She could only pray that it would be strong enough to help Caleb.

Laura's stomach clenched when she uncovered the shoulder wound. It had been an awful sight to begin with, looking as if a jagged limb had caught him in the flood and torn a long, deep gash, almost to the bone. Laura had cleaned it as best she could, but now she saw that the flesh around it was swollen and the wound itself was swimming in pus.

Caleb's eyes were open. He was gazing up at her, his helplessness tearing at her heart. "I'll have to clean it again," she said. "It'll hurt—"

"No." His hand reached out to clasp her wrist. "Just the root—put it on, work it in."

"But—"

"Do it, Laura."

Tears welled in her eyes as she packed all that was left of the cabbage root into the suppurating wound. She could feel the strange heat of it, sense it sinking into his flesh as she applied clean wrappings.

"Ugh! What's that smell?" Robbie was standing in the bedroom doorway with Buster peering around his legs.

"It's Indian medicine," Laura said. "When you say your prayers, pray that it will help."

"Is Mr. Caleb going to die? I don't want him to

die. And I don't want him to go. I want him to stay here with us."

Laura tiptoed to the doorway and kissed her son's rumpled golden head. "So do I, Robbie," she whispered. "So do I."

Caleb lost track of time as he moved in and out of the dark. In moments of clarity he lay watching Laura as she changed his dressings and spooned her teas into his mouth. She never seemed to sleep. Any time he awoke she was there, bending over him, her hair mussed and tumbled, her dove-colored eyes sunk into violet shadows. Sometimes she held his hands, kissing his fingers, pressing them to her cheeks. Sometimes she laid her head on his chest, resting against his heart.

The fact that he'd seen this woman kissing another man was lost in the depths of his need for her. She was his lifeline, his angel. Whatever the future held, even if he never saw her again, he would never stop loving her.

Now and again he was aware of the parlor clock striking the hour. But he'd long since lost track of how long he'd been lying here, in her bed. He remembered her saying something about the doctor, but no doctor had come. Sometimes Robbie had stood by the bed, staring at him with solemn eyes. Once he'd even held the puppy up to lick Caleb's face with its wet pink tongue before he scampered off to play.

But always there was Laura. She sat on the edge

of the bed now, cradling his head with one arm while she tipped yet another cup of tea to his lips. The fever still burned, but the fog in his mind was clearing a little.

"Get some rest," he muttered. "We can't have you getting sick, too."

"I'll be all right." Her voice was hoarse with strain. The window was dark and there was no sign of Robbie. Caleb guessed the boy had gone to sleep.

"Here—" He summoned the strength to point to an empty spot on the far side of the bed. "Lie down on top of the covers, next to me. I'll wake you if I need anything." He attempted a feeble joke. "Believe me, ma'am, your virtue will be safe tonight."

"What a disappointment." A whimsical smile flickered across her face. Without another word she blew out the lamp and stretched out in the narrow space, cradling her head against his good shoulder. It was heaven, having her so near. He pulled her closer, so that he could feel her hair against his cheek. She sighed contentedly and they drifted off together.

"Laura! Are you all right? Wake up!"

The deep male voice startled Laura into sudden awareness. Morning light gleamed through the bedroom window, silhouetting a familiar stocky figure at the foot of the bed.

"Dr. Trimble?" She sat up, rubbing her blurry eyes. "How did you get—?"

"Robbie let me in." The doctor's unshaven face

was lined with weariness. "I came as soon as I could. Becky Keeler was in labor with a breech birth. Couldn't leave her till the baby came. How's your…uh, hired man?"

Laura flushed as she realized what his eyes had taken in. But then, as a doctor, he'd likely seen more scandalous sights than a woman lying next to a man with her clothes on. She glanced down at Caleb, who was beginning to stir.

"I've been doctoring him with Indian remedies—bark tea and skunk cabbage. He told me what to do—at least when he was able to talk."

"Skunk cabbage?" The doctor shook his head. "So that's what I've been smelling in here. Probably as good as anything else you might've used. Now, let me have a look at him."

He moved toward the bed and Laura realized he wanted her out of the way. "I'll make you some breakfast," she said, slipping past him toward the kitchen.

"Coffee will be fine for now. Awful shame what that flood did to your place." He set his black satchel onto the foot of the bed. "Oh—Tom Haskins asked me to give you this." He reached into his pocket and drew out a folded, crumpled sheet of paper.

Laura took it from him and slid it into her apron pocket. Still dazed, she measured ground Arbuckle coffee and water into the enamel pot and thrust some fresh kindling onto the coals in the stove. She found Robbie on the front porch playing with his pup. He'd dressed himself and done a fair job of it, except that his shoes were on the wrong feet and the laces were untied. Merciful heaven, she was usually up before dawn. How could she have slept so late?

She washed Robbie's hands and gave him a jam sandwich to tide him over until she could fix a real breakfast.

"How's Mr. Caleb, Mama? I said a prayer for him last night."

"It must've helped. He slept well." She bent down and squeezed her son's shoulders. "We'll know more after the doctor's finished with him."

She splashed her face with water and smoothed back her hair. Outside there were chores waiting to be done, but she would wait for the doctor first. While the coffee simmered on the stove, she sat down at the kitchen table to read the note Tom had written.

"My dearest Laura,
Forgive me for not coming back to your place. You see, I'm not quite the fool you take me for. When I held you in my arms and kissed you, I realized that your heart belonged to another. I know you would have promised me anything to save your friend McCurdy. But the one thing I want is the one thing you could never give me—your sincere love.

Be happy, my dear. I wish you the best and hope you will always consider me a friend.
Tom"

Laura stared at the crumpled page, feeling as if a heavy weight had been lifted from her shoulders.

Had Tom really understood her that well? Or had he visited the land office and looked up the deed to her ranch while he was in town? It didn't matter. To her great relief, he was no longer her suitor.

She wanted to laugh, to sing—but that would have to wait for other news. She stared at the closed bedroom door, holding her breath, silently praying as the knob turned. The door swung open and Dr. Trimble stepped out into the kitchen.

His face wore a tired smile. "The fever's broken and the infection's clearing up," he declared. "I'll take that coffee now, and maybe some breakfast to go with it."

With the fever down, Caleb's condition improved rapidly. By midday he was able to sit up in bed and eat some of Laura's tasty rabbit stew, feeding himself with a spoon. He was gritty and sweaty and still too weak to walk. But for the first time since the flood his body felt alive. It felt damned good.

The skunk cabbage had done its work on his infected shoulder wound. The swelling was down, the flesh healing to a healthy pink. He stank to high heaven, and so did Laura's bedroom, but that could be remedied in time.

Now, if only he could find a remedy for his heart.

His gaze followed Laura as she flitted in and out of the room. Lines of weariness were etched beneath her eyes. But her smile was radiant, her step so light that she seemed to float. As she fussed over him, Caleb filled his senses with the sight of her face and the sound of her voice. He loved her to the depths of his battered, bleeding soul, but she could never be his. These memories would have to last him for life.

He could only hope Tom Haskins would love her the way she deserved to be loved.

"You'll wear yourself out," he lectured her gently as she cleared away his lunch tray. "Get some rest, Laura."

"I did." She flashed him a radiant smile. "I slept so late, it nearly caused a scandal when the doctor walked in on us."

"I'd wager it wouldn't have been much of a scandal. I told you your virtue was safe with me." He met her eyes, forcing himself to ask the question. "So, have you and Haskins made wedding plans yet?"

"What?" The tray slipped from her hands and clattered back onto the quilt as she stared at him. "Whatever gave you the idea I was going to marry Tom?"

"I'm not blind, Laura. I saw him kissing you—he made sure I saw it. And I saw you kissing him back. That had to mean something."

She picked up the tray, her hands shaking. "It wasn't what you think. I kissed Tom because I was desperate to have him ride into town for the doctor. He did what I asked, but he saw through me. He didn't come back here, and he won't. We'll likely remain friends, but we certainly won't marry."

Caleb felt something clench beneath his ribs. Lord, no, it couldn't be what he suspected. This calamity was the last thing Laura deserved. "What do you mean, he saw through you?" he asked cautiously.

The color deepened in her cheeks. "Tom could tell I was only pretending to care for him," she murmured. "He knew I'd do anything, promise anything, to save your life."

"Laura—" He groaned her name.

"I don't love Tom," she said. "I love you, Caleb, and I want you to stay."

Stunned into silence, he gazed at her across the rumpled bed. Lord, if only he could reach out, take her in his arms and tell her all the things she wanted to hear. But the past was etched in stone, and a hundred loving truths would not be enough to wipe out one monstrous lie.

He cleared his throat and began what needed to be said. "I can't stay, Laura. Lord knows, it has nothing to do with the way I feel about you. It's just that I have secrets—dangerous secrets that you're better off not knowing. These days spent here on this ranch with the two of you have been the happiest of my life. I'd give anything if they could last forever. But some things can't be changed. I'm sorry."

She stood as if she'd been turned to ice, her lips pressed tightly together. She had offered him her heart, and he had turned and crushed it. Caleb yearned to take back everything he'd said—to throw caution to the winds, fall on his knees and beg her to be his. But it was already too late for that. Laura, he knew, would never open herself to trust again.

Lifting her head, she spoke. "You can stay on

until you're strong enough to ride. After that, I'll plan on getting by without your help."

Caleb felt the icy sting of her words and the wounded pride beneath. "That flood must've done a lot of damage," he said gently. "I'll be happy to stay a few extra days and help you get the place back into shape."

She turned away without a word and walked out of the room.

Gripping the hoe, Laura dug into the ruins of her vegetable garden. If there was anything alive and growing beneath the mud, by heaven, she would find it and bring it back to light and air. Nothing could be allowed to die and go to waste.

Nothing except love.

Next to the clothesline, her bedsheets simmered in the big copper wash boiler. The essence of skunk cabbage drifted on the steamy air. Twenty-four hours had passed since the doctor's visit, and Caleb had continued to improve. Last night Laura had slept in the parlor, insisting that he stay in her bed one more night. But this morning he'd risen, dressed himself in the clean clothes she'd washed and declared that he'd be sleeping in the toolshed for the rest of his stay.

From the direction of the creek came the sound of sawing. Caleb was using lumber from the old springhouse to build her a new one. It would be smaller and not so handy to the back door but it was all she needed.

Caleb had started hauling lumber right after breakfast. Laura had argued that he should rest, but Caleb was a stubborn man. As if to defy her, he had flung himself into the work. Through the trees, she could see that the frame was already rising.

With a sigh, she set the hoe against the cottonwood, picked up a broom handle and used it to stir the boiling wash. Much as it stung her pride, it was just as well that Caleb had insisted on staying a few more days. Tom, practical soul, had reneged on his promise to send his men over. Without Caleb she'd be faced with doing everything on her own.

What would it be like when he left? Laura wondered. Would he go in the night to avoid telling her goodbye? Would he shake her hand and wish her luck, or would he just mount up and ride off in silence?

The only thing she could be sure of was that he wouldn't look back.

For now an uneasy truce lay between them. After making such a fool of herself, Laura was too humiliated to meet his eyes. Caleb treated her with a gentle courtesy that bordered on pity. He probably couldn't wait to mount up and leave. Oh, why hadn't she kept her silly mouth shut? Why had she blurted out that she was in love with him?

She should have known he wouldn't return her feelings.

How could any man love her, as unsure and frightened and scarred as she was?

Robbie came running from the direction of the

creek with Buster tagging at his heels. "Mr. Caleb needs some nails, Mama!" he shouted.

"There's a keg of nails in the toolshed. I'll get you some to take back." Putting down her stick, she strode toward the shed. Robbie, it seemed, had become a messenger between herself and Caleb. Talking to the boy had become a substitute for their talking to each other.

She reached the toolshed a minute before Robbie did. The floodwaters had stopped short of the door so it was dry inside. Caleb's bedroll lay in the corner he'd cleared out. It was little more than a scratchy woolen blanket doubled in half, its edges thick with trail dust. It wasn't much of a bed for a man who'd recently been at death's door. She would hang the blanket over the clothesline and give it a good beating, Laura resolved. Then she'd bring a pillow and some quilts from the house to make things more comfortable.

Robbie came inside the shed, reminding her of her original errand. The small keg, half-full of nails, was sitting on the workbench. "How many nails does he need?" she asked.

"A lot! Maybe a hundred!"

"In that case, we'll just take him the whole keg."

Robbie reached up and tried to lift the keg with his good arm. "Oof! It's heavy!"

Laura smoothed his hair. "Then I'll have to come with you and carry it, won't I? Come on, let's go."

They trooped back down the gentle slope toward the creek. As they passed the windmill, Buster caught the scent of some small animal and went bounding uphill into the grass.

"Buster! Come!" Robbie called to him, but the pup had more compelling things on his mind. "Buster! You dad-blamed varmint!" Robbie took off after him. He caught his pet scratching furiously at a small hole in the hillside. Laura had to smile as he picked up the pup and began scolding him. "I'm going to put you in the shed!" he said sternly. "You can't play outside if you can't learn to mind!"

While Robbie took care of the dog, Laura went on down toward the creek. She could see where the frame for one wall jutted above the willows. Wherever he could, Caleb was using assembled sections of the old springhouse. The work involved a lot of cutting and fitting. Laura came into the clearing to see him struggling to brace the wall upright while he hammered it onto the square base he'd built.

He looked hot and frustrated with his straight black hair tumbling into his face, but he grinned when he saw her. "Just when I needed an extra pair of hands. Hold up this wall, will you?"

Lowering the nail keg to the ground, Laura grasped a pair of timbers and steadied the wall frame. Caleb maneuvered around her as he checked the alignment and straightened the corners. When he reached past her for the hammer, his arm brushed her breast, awakening sensations she never wanted to feel again.

"Sorry about the smell," he said, standing so close that she could feel the warm, pungent aura of his body. "Between the skunk cabbage and the hot day, I'm afraid I'm in sore need of a bath."

"I've become well accustomed to that smell." Laura made a move to step away, but the wall swayed and she realized she was trapped holding it. His nearness made her knees go watery. "You're welcome to use the washtub after dark," she said. "You can set it by the pump—it'll be a warm night. I'll bring you some soap and a towel."

"Will you wash my back?"

The heat that rushed to Laura's face left her dizzy.

"It wouldn't be the first time you know."

"That was different, you were unconscious." Confused and flustered, she lashed out at him. "What do you want, Caleb? What kind of game are you playing with me?"

"I'm trying to get a rise out of you, Laura. Maybe then you'll listen to me instead of turning away when I want to talk to you."

"Why should I listen?" she retorted. "I've already made a complete fool of myself. And I already know how you feel about me. What's left for you to say?"

"This—" His hand caught the back of her head, twisting her toward him. His mouth captured hers in a crushing kiss that went through her with the heat and force of a lightning bolt. She went molten against him and would have sent the wall crashing if he hadn't caught it with his free hand.

"Damn it, Laura, I'd give twenty years of my life to stay with you!" he muttered, holding her fiercely. "I want to be your husband and Robbie's father. I want to build up this ranch and give you all the babies your arms can hold. I love you more than words can say! But sometimes a man can't have what he wants. I have to go—I have no choice!"

"But *why?*" She tried to pull away, but his grip held her fast. "For the love of heaven, Caleb, can't you at least give me a reason? After you ride away and leave me alone, am I going to spend the rest of my life wondering if I was the cause?"

He released her, and when he spoke his voice was gentle. "You're not the cause of anything except my loving you. But there are other things... If I were to stay, you'd curse me when you learned the truth. You'd damn me to hell. And that's all I'll say. Don't ask me any more."

"Caleb—"

"No, my love. That's the end of it." He dropped to a crouch and picked up his hammer. "Now be a good girl and steady this wall for me. I hear Robbie. Let's make sure he sees us smiling."

Chapter Fourteen

Supper was a quiet affair, eaten by lamplight after a long day's work. Caleb was physically and emotionally spent, and so, he suspected, was Laura. Robbie yawned over his dessert of apple cobbler with fresh cream.

Caleb studied Laura as they finished the meal. She took tiny bites, keeping her eyes on her plate. Whatever the reason, she looked exceptionally pretty tonight. There were tired shadows under her eyes but her color was high, her skin glowing. He suppressed the urge to reach across the table and touch her hand. She was as much his as she would ever be, he reminded himself. He would have to be content with that.

Had he done the right thing, confessing that he loved her? It wasn't something he'd planned—not until he'd seen the hurt in those beautiful gray eyes. Then some instinct had whispered that if he rode away without letting her know, she might never have the courage to love again.

He could only hope he hadn't made things worse.

Pushing her chair away from the table, she rose. "Say good-night to Mr. Caleb, Robbie. It's time to get you ready for bed."

"G'night, Mr. Caleb." The boy stumbled drowsily to his feet. "Thanks for letting me help you."

"Thank *you,* Robbie." Caleb resisted the urge to hug him. "If we keep working together, we should have that new springhouse done in the next day or two."

Robbie grinned. Buster uncurled himself from under the chair and followed along as Laura led her son off to bed.

She paused at the bedroom door. "Oh—if you want that bath, the tub's next to the kitchen door. I'll get you some soap and a towel as soon as Robbie's tucked in."

"Fine." Caleb rose wearily to his feet. "In the meantime, I'll start cleaning up in here." He began gathering up the dishes, scraping the leftover bits into the battered pie tin that served as Buster's bowl. He was bone tired but it had felt good to be up and working today. He could feel his strength coming back. Tomorrow, after a night's rest, he should be as good as ever.

But what was he supposed to say to Laura? The understanding between them was like thin-blown glass, so fragile that a look, a word or a touch could shatter it. He'd already told her too much about his reasons for leaving. What if she demanded to know more? Caleb felt pinpricks of nervous sweat break out between his shoulder blades. If she backed him into a corner, he'd have no choice except to leave at once. Anything, even the most cloddish behavior, would be better than telling her the truth.

For now, the only solution was to avoid being alone with her. As long as Robbie was with them he'd be safe from her questions. At other times, like tonight...

Hastily he filled the dishpan, added a sliver of soap and some hot water from the kettle on the stove. Leaving the dishes to soak, he slipped out the kitchen door and found the washtub propped against the house. His shoulder twinged as he carried it over to the pump. He felt lower than a snake as he slunk back toward the toolshed, but the alternatives would be even worse. A curious woman could be as relentless as a weasel. No thanks to his big mouth, he'd roused Laura's curiosity to a fever pitch.

If he had any sense he'd leave right now. But with Tom Haskins out of the picture, Laura would be left alone with the springhouse to finish and the flood damage to repair.

Caleb thrust his hands into his pockets and stared up at the rising moon. From the day he'd arrived here on Laura's ranch, he'd come up with one reason after another to put off leaving. Maybe it was time he faced the truth—it was Laura he couldn't stand to leave. He was so damnfool crazy in love with the woman that he'd risk all the fires of hell just to spend more time with her.

It felt good to be honest with himself. But it didn't change the fact that he had to leave. And it didn't change the fact that when he rode away, the misery in his soul would be its own kind of hell.

As he stood in the shadows he saw her come out the house. She paused by the pump, as graceful as a white heron. Peering into the darkness, she spoke his name. When he didn't answer, she laid the soap and towel on a log next to the tub and went back into the house.

Caleb stood looking after her, watching the flicker of lamplight as she moved past the kitchen window. Then he turned and went inside the shed.

At once he noticed how she'd added a pillow and several quilts to his sleeping place. That small gesture almost undid him. He imagined her work-worn hands folding each quilt to the right size, carefully smoothing away the wrinkles. Damn her, she was tearing him apart! He wanted *her* on that bed, pinned to the quilts by his body, her slim white legs wrapping around his hips, binding him inside her as he drove harder and deeper…

Even now, he felt his body responding to his thoughts. Swearing under his breath, he rummaged for his clean long johns and prepared to take his bath. The cold water would be just what he needed.

Laura finished the dishes and wiped her hands on the towel. The lamp wick had burned down to a glowing stub but the risen moon bathed the house and yard in liquid silver. Through the window she could hear faint splashing as Caleb pumped water into the tub. In her mind she pictured him standing naked in the night, beads of water gleaming like jewels on his lean, muscular body. She was sorely tempted to blow out the lamp and steal a forbidden glance. But what excuse would she make if he saw her?

Will you wash my back? The memory of his words mocked her. She had washed him while he was unconscious, and there was no part of him her eyes hadn't seen. But now things were different. He was awake and aware.

She loved him.

And he had said he loved her.

Did anything else really matter?

Emotions churning, Laura carried the lamp into her bedroom. Caleb had told her he was hiding a terrible secret, one that would drive her to curse him if she knew the truth. But what difference would the truth make, now that she'd abandoned all hope of his staying?

They had a few days left at most. Did she love him enough to put the secret aside for that time? Could she live with never knowing what had driven him away?

Sweet heaven, what should she do?

The guttering lamplight gleamed on the face in the silver frame. Setting the lamp on the nightstand, Laura picked up Mark's photograph and gazed tenderly at the familiar, almost too perfect features. She had loved him with all her girlish heart. But now he was gone and she was a woman, with a woman's needs.

Bowing her head, she pressed her lips to the cool glass. "It's time, my dearest," she whispered. Then she opened a drawer and slipped the portrait face-down under her clean stockings. Her hands trembled as she twisted the thin gold wedding band off her finger, laid it beside the picture and closed the drawer.

Hastily she undressed, pulled her white nightgown over her head and unpinned her hair. Then, feeling naked, vulnerable and strangely alive, Laura walked into the kitchen and picked up a kettle of hot water from the stove. Trembling, she stepped out the back door, into the night.

Caleb had stripped off his dirty clothes and was just stepping into the cold water when he heard her come outside. Startled, he grabbed for the towel and clutched it in front of him. "Laura?"

She stepped into the moonlight, a fairy-tale creature in simple white with her glorious hair floating loose around her face. Caleb's breath stopped for an instant at the sight of her. Then his natural caution reared its head. What was she doing here? As if he couldn't guess. He cursed under his breath, knowing he'd been outmaneuvered. Unless he wanted to make a naked run for the shed, he was trapped.

"I thought the water might be cold," Laura murmured, holding up the kettle. "Move over a little and I'll warm it for you. Look out, this is hot."

Still clasping the towel, Caleb edged his chilled

feet to one side. Carefully she poured the steaming water into the tub. The diffusing warmth was heaven.

"Now, about that offer to wash your back..." she murmured, setting down the kettle and picking up the soap.

He groaned, realizing he was already aroused beneath the towel. "Laura, it's not going to do any good. I can't stay, and I can't tell you any more than I already have."

"I'm not asking you to." Her voice caught the edge of a tear. "Whatever demons are troubling you, Caleb, I don't want to know about them—not if my knowing would cause you hurt. And I can't keep you here if you're set on leaving. But why not make the most of the time we have left?"

Caleb felt the pain swell and burst inside him. Lord, what good had he ever done in his miserable life? How could he deserve to be loved like this, so sweetly and unconditionally, by this beautiful woman?

He gulped back the rising lump in his throat. "Laura—"

"Hush," she whispered, dipping the soap in the water. "Just be still and let me wash you."

She lathered her hands and slid them lightly up his back. Caleb braced himself for the rough sting of the homemade lye soap she kept by the pump for laundry and hand washing. But this soap was different—rich and creamy, its scent the familiar wildflower fragrance of Laura's own skin and hair. Caleb gasped, then sighed as her hands kneaded his aching shoulders, relaxing the taut muscles. The aroma stole through his senses, almost drowning him in pleasure.

Her careful fingers unwrapped the sweat-soaked bandage and peeled the rank-smelling poultice off his shoulder wound. "Better," she murmured, dabbing the skin gently. "We can let it air till morning."

Dipping water onto his head she worked the soap through his hair. Caleb stood transfixed as her nimble fingers worked their way over his scalp, down the back of his neck and along his spine. The towel had long since fallen from his hand and onto the rim of the tub. Without its concealing cover, his arousal jutted upward and outward like a blasted flagpole. He could only hope it wouldn't send her running when she got around to the front of him.

His heart convulsed as her lathered hands slid over his buttocks. A moan escaped his lips. Never in his wildest fantasies had he imagined being bathed by a loving woman. The sensations that pounded through his body were so intense they left him dizzy. He resisted the urge to turn, seize her in his arms and slake his lust on the spot. Better that this slow, exquisite torture continue until she was fully ready for him.

With the long-handled tin dipper, Laura drizzled warm water over his head, shoulders and down his spine, rinsing away the soap. By the time she was finished, her heart was pounding and her breath was raw in her throat.

Washing Caleb's back had been safe enough as

long as she went no further. Even now, it wasn't too late to make a joke of it and flee back to the sanctuary of the house. But her blood was racing and her senses were on fire. The sinewy smoothness of Caleb's skin beneath her hands was like a drug in her system. She couldn't get enough of touching him.

Her nightgown was damp against her skin. She trembled in the warm breeze as she moved around the edge of the tub to face him. Still half-shy, she kept her gaze above his shoulders. His smile flashed in the darkness.

"Well, you're not going to stop, are you?" he teased. "The front of me is just as dirty as the back."

She hesitated, her lips parting. Reaching out, he drew her into his arms and cradled her head in the hollow of his throat. "Lord, girl, I want you so much it hurts," he whispered against her hair. "But if you're afraid, it's all right. Only you'd better go now if you're going, because I don't know how much longer I can control myself."

In answer she caught the back of his neck with her hand, stretched upward and kissed him full on the mouth. His lips tasted of sweat and earth. Cool and damp and hungry, they captured her and swept her away. His probing tongue answered hers, thrusting hard and deep. His arms molded her against him. With nothing between them but her thin muslin nightgown, she could feel his erection jutting against her belly. She was wild with wanting him, wanting his body on her, around her, inside her, filling her emptiness and warming her with his heat. She pressed her hips close and heard him groan.

"Maybe we'd better finish the bath, Laura…"

Her damp nightgown clung to him as she pulled away. Somehow she found the soap and lathered her hands again. His chest was like polished copper—someone had told her once that Indians had little body hair. Caleb had the barest sheen of it, making a shadow trail down the midline from chest to navel to—

He chuckled as her eyes flashed upward. "I fear that's one secret I can't keep from you, my love. I think it's asking to be washed like the rest of me."

Trembling, Laura soaped her hands. Mark's love-making had been so proper and discreet—he would never have asked her to do anything so outlandish. But the thought of sliding her hands along Caleb's rigid shaft weakened her knees and triggered freshets of moisture between her thighs. Desire was a hot, wet fountain of need inside her. She ached with wanting him.

Her heart lurched as she wrapped her soap-slicked fingers around him. Sweet heaven, how could anything so hard be so silky soft? She loved the feel of him!

He made a little animal sound as she began to work the soap up and down, pulling back the fore-skin as she had with Robbie when he was a baby and splashing it clean. His grip tightened on her shoulder.

"Laura—" he rasped. "Unless you want to end this here and now—"

Understanding, she moved her hands lower, soaping the insides of his muscular thighs and working upward. When her hand touched him again he seized her shoulders, jerking her upward against him. His mouth ground hungrily onto hers. "I think I'm damn well clean enough!" he growled, stepping out of the tub and sweeping her up in his arms.

There was a beat of hesitation as he turned toward the house. "No," she whispered. "We might wake Robbie—"

He swung toward the shed and strode across the moonlit yard. Her thin white gown fluttered around him as he carried her. The warm night wind dried the wetness on his skin. Laura's head lay against his chest. She could hear his heartbeat throbbing in counterpoint with her own. She closed her eyes, savoring the feel of his arms around her. When he was gone and the years loomed bleak and lonely she would have this night to keep and remember.

As for the secret that was too awful to share, she would let it go, like a paper boat set loose on a stream. After he rode away it wouldn't make any difference, so why should it matter now? Caleb was with her. She loved him. Tonight that was her whole world.

He carried her inside and lowered her to the thick pile of blankets. She lay with her hair fanning over the pillow, her eyes gazing up at him in the darkness. His fingers fumbled with the tie at the neck of her gown and she realized he was trembling. Loving his vulnerability, she helped him with the tangled knot.

He pulled the wispy garment down to her hips, kneeling above her where she lay in a shaft of moonlight.

"You're so beautiful, Laura," he whispered. "So help me, you're the most beautiful thing I've ever seen in my life."

To her own amazement, Laura believed him.

He touched her breasts, tracing the shape of them, cupping them with his hand. Only when she thought she would die from wanting it did he bend down and kiss them. She gave a little gasp as her nipple slid into his mouth, hardening to a taut nub as he sucked and nipped it, tracing the sensitive aureole with his tongue. Something tightened in the core of her body, a pulsing, throbbing hunger that begged to be satisfied. She whimpered with need.

Hurriedly now, he slid the nightgown down her body and pulled it off her feet. She heard his breath quicken as he looked down at her. "I want you so much, girl," he murmured. "I've wanted you since the first time I saw you. But I never thought—a man like me—"

Pulling him down to her, she stopped his words with a long, deep kiss. Her fingers guided his hand down between her thighs to the place where her hunger burned. His fingertips found the moist folds, the tiny swollen center. Their stroking touch triggered spasms of release through her body. But even that wasn't enough. Her legs parted. Her hips arched upward in a silent plea for what only he could give her.

He mounted and entered her, filling her in one

long, gliding stroke. Laura moaned as her flesh closed around him. Her frenzied hands clasped his buttocks, holding him, drawing him deeper, meeting each thrust with her own.

She felt him in every shimmering cell of her body as he carried her with him, spiraling upward until they burst like two comets into shattering starlight.

The new springhouse, with its thick log walls, jutted over the creek on stout pilings. The cool box was in place, as were the shelves and the hooks for meat. Only the roof remained to be finished, and that would be done by the end of the day. It was a fine structure, every bit as functional and solid as the old springhouse had been.

Laura wanted nothing more than to seize the ax and tear it apart, log by log, nail by nail, so that Caleb would have to stay and rebuild it.

He would be leaving tomorrow morning, and Laura had promised herself she wouldn't try to change his mind. But as the hours flew by and the time grew closer she sank into despair. When she was with Caleb and Robbie she did her best to hide it. But when she was alone it came and perched on her shoulders, pecking at her resolve like a hideous black bird.

Whatever Caleb had done, it was so vile in his eyes that he'd rather leave than tell about it. But what if he'd judged himself too harshly? What if he'd underestimated her capacity to forgive?

Why shouldn't he tell her the truth and let her judge for herself?

Questions tore at her as she scrubbed his work pants on the washboard, rinsed them and hung them on the line. Should she risk everything and confront him one more time? Or should she let him go in peace, leaving nothing behind but good memories?

The memories *had* been good. They'd been wonderful. By day she and Caleb had kept their behavior circumspect for Robbie's sake. But for the last two nights she'd gone to Caleb in the shed and they'd made sweet, wild, passionate love. It was understood that they wouldn't talk about the future. Laura had broken that rule only for a brief time last night, when they lay resting in each other's arms.

"Will you write to me?" she'd asked him.

"I don't know if I should," he'd murmured, brushing a kiss along her hairline.

"Just once or twice, to let me know you're all right?"

"Maybe. But you won't be able to write to me."

"What if I have your child?"

He'd sighed, his arms tightening around her. "Would that make you happy, Laura?"

"Happier than you can imagine. I'd have a part of you, and Robbie would have a little brother or sister. Oh, there'd be gossip at first. But it would die down over time. It would be all right—I'd make it all right."

"What would you tell Robbie?"

"That we loved each other."

His throat had moved in the darkness but he'd made no reply. He'd simply held her close. She had clung to him until it was time for her to go, memorizing the contours and textures of his body, the scent of him, the warmth of him, the taste of him…

Tonight they would make love again. She would lie in his arms for the last time.

She could hear the sounds of tools and voices from beyond the willows, where Caleb and Robbie were finishing work on the springhouse. Her own heart wasn't the only one hanging in balance, Laura reminded herself. Robbie worshipped Caleb, and the boy needed a hero to emulate. Caleb would make a wonderful father. But if the awful secret, whatever it was, became known, Robbie could be shattered. The boy's whole life could be changed. An absent Caleb, at least, would never lose his shining image.

Laura thought of her precious, fragile son. She thought of the empty years ahead without the man she loved. She thought about the risks involved in keeping him with her.

What in heaven's name was she going to do?

Caleb prowled the moonlit yard, checking the gates and fences to make sure everything was secure. His senses were prickling tonight. But he was probably just concerned about leaving Laura alone tomorrow. She'd managed on her own for the past five years and she was a tough little woman. Still, he would wonder and worry about her every day.

Lord, could he do it? Could he just ride away and leave her and the boy, knowing he'd never see them again? If they cried it would kill him. Hellfire, it would kill him anyway. He couldn't even imagine how much it was going to hurt.

The night seemed peaceful enough. The air was warm with just a breath of wind. A waning teardrop of a moon hung low above the trees, veiled now and then by drifting clouds. A small animal, likely a pack rat, scurried along the edge of the granary.

Lantern light gleamed faintly in Laura's kitchen window. When it went out he would know she was ready to come to him. But she wouldn't leave the house until her son was deep in slumber. If the boy was having a bad night, he could be restless for hours. Caleb knew that Robbie was upset over his leaving. It stood to reason that tonight might be one of those nights.

Thrusting his hands into his pockets, Caleb walked slowly back toward the shed. He would try to get some rest; sleep would be asking too much. Laura would come when she could. They would make bittersweet love and lie in each other's arms for the last time.

Caleb swore under his breath. He'd never loved anyone or anything the way he loved Laura. But the unchangeable past they shared could destroy them both. And there wasn't a damned thing he could do about it. He wanted to scream at the sky, to rail at whatever gods might be listening. Why did life have to be such a hellish mess?

Closing the door of the shed he kicked off his boots and stretched out on the quilts. For a long time he lay there, listening to small night sounds. He didn't realize he'd fallen asleep until he was startled awake by a light rap on the door.

He sat bolt upright. "Laura?"

There was no reply.

Still sleep-dazed he rolled off the quilts and staggered to his feet. The darkness around him was absolutely still. Even the crickets had fallen silent.

Stumbling slightly in his stocking feet, he reached the door and slipped the simple wooden latch. The door creaked outward to reveal two lanky figures. Caleb's throat jerked tight, as if he'd just been dropped from a gallows.

"Well, howdy, little brother!" Zeke's lopsided grin flashed in the moonlight. "Noah and me, we come a long way lookin' for you, boy. So where's your manners? Ain't you goin' to invite us in?"

Chapter Fifteen

Thunderstruck, Caleb stepped back and allowed his half brothers to enter. They swaggered into the shed, their holstered Colt revolvers in plain sight. Caleb had hidden his own gun in the rafters, away from Robbie's curious little hands. There was no way he could get to it and little he could do to warn Laura. He tried leaving the shed door open in the hope that she'd hear voices and recognize the danger. But Noah pulled it shut behind him.

"We heard you got out of Yuma." Noah settled himself on a wooden crate and fished his tobacco pouch out of his vest. "We been trailin' you from town to town, askin' questions. Finally figured out you'd been fool enough to head here."

He rolled a cigarette and thrust it between his lips. A match flared briefly as Zeke lit it for him. The rank aroma of burning tobacco hung in the air.

"We been hidin' in them hills up there watchin'

you for a couple of days now." Zeke's grin chilled Caleb's blood. "You got yourself a nice setup here, with that sweet little filly. Only thing I can't figure out is why you're still sleepin' in the shed!" He guffawed and slapped his leg.

Caleb cursed silently. He'd worried about the chance that Laura would remember him, and he'd worried about the law. But it hadn't even occurred to him that his brothers might show up. What now? How was he going to protect Laura and Robbie?

"What do you want?" he demanded. "You didn't trail me all this way to make a social call."

Noah raised one grizzled eyebrow. "Hell, boy, you're our brother, our blood kin. We want you back with us like the old days."

"I remember the old days," Caleb snapped. "You staked me out in front of that bank for law-bait while you two got away with the loot! I did five years in purgatory for it!"

Noah blew a stream of smoke into the darkness. "Now, that's not quite how it was. In the first place we left you outside so you wouldn't get blasted by some trigger-happy bank clerk. We figured you might not have the nerve to shoot him first. In the second place, we didn't get the loot. We left that damned bank as poor as we went in. We been livin' poor ever since, just waitin' for you to get out so we can pull that big job we planned on."

Caleb groaned silently. Zeke and Noah never changed. Why hadn't he seen them for the dangerous fools they were and cleared out before they got him arrested?

"Trains—that's where the money is," Zeke said. "One good hit and we're set for life. Only the two of us ain't enough. We need three men, at least. That's where you come in, little brother. We figure prison taught you a trick or two, so you'd be good enough for the job. Besides, ain't nobody we can trust like our own flesh and blood."

"Get somebody else," Caleb said. "I'm not interested. I've gone straight."

Zeke guffawed. "Straight? Hell, yes! I bet you go straight as a poker every time you get near that little honey. I got half a mind to go down to that house and finish what I started five years ago."

"No!" Caleb's pulse slammed. He stepped in front of the door. "You touch her, either of you, and so help me, I'll kill you myself. That's a promise!" He turned to Noah. "You want me to go with you? Fine. But only if we leave now—right this minute. Laura's not to see you or know you were here. Agreed?"

"Sounds fair to me." Noah's cigarette glowed bloodred as he unfolded his lanky frame. "Our horses are up the hill in that stand of junipers. Let's get out of here."

Caleb unlatched the door, hoping to warn Laura and get her to safety if he could. "Go on, I'll saddle up and meet you."

His brother's abrupt silence told Caleb he'd said the wrong thing. Noah's cold eyes narrowed dangerously. "You listen, boy, and you listen good," he growled. "We're not takin' our eyes off you till we're out of here. Cross us, and I'll turn Zeke loose on your woman. You don't want to see what he can do. By the time he's finished, you won't even know her!"

Dressed in her nightgown, Laura sagged against the doorframe of Robbie's bedroom. Her son was asleep at last, or so she hoped. He'd had a rough night of it so far. So had she.

"But why does Mr. Caleb have to go?" he'd argued over and over. "I want him to stay. Doesn't he like us?"

"He likes us fine, Robbie," she'd soothed him even as her own heart threatened to shatter. "It's just that Mr. Caleb needs to be someplace else. He's already stayed longer than he planned to."

"But I want him to stay! Buster does, too!" he'd argued as only a stubborn four-year-old could. His lower lip had thrust outward. Tears had welled in his eyes and he'd broken into wrenching sobs. He had cried himself to sleep, only to open his eyes a few minutes later and start the whole litany again. Now, after the second time, he seemed to have worn himself out. Laura was worn out, too, and anxious to be with Caleb. But the last thing she wanted was to have her son wake up again and find her gone.

Now Robbie lay with his arm around the sleeping pup. His wet-lashed eyes were closed, his cheeks blotched with tears. His breathing had been deep and even for the past ten minutes or so. Maybe he was finally down for the night.

Still, Laura hesitated. The boy usually fell into a sound, peaceful sleep. But he'd had such a miserable time. What if he had a nightmare and woke up in terror? How could she leave him, even for one last time in Caleb's arms?

With a sigh, she turned away from the bedroom. There was only one thing to do. She would go out and invite Caleb into the house. They would need to be quiet and careful, but it was less worrisome than leaving Robbie alone tonight.

Opening the kitchen door, she walked out into the warm darkness. Her muslin nightgown floated around her like a fairy robe as she crossed the moonlit yard. How quiet the night seemed, as if all the small, wild creatures had fallen silent. Only the horses were restless, snorting and shifting in the corral.

She had just passed the woodpile when her nostrils caught a faint whiff of tobacco smoke. It struck her as odd. She'd never known Caleb to smoke—but then, there was a whole world of things she didn't know about him and likely never would. She only knew that when she was with him she felt alive and glowing, almost beautiful.

Somehow she would learn to live without him. But the years ahead loomed bleak and lonely. If only she could pout and rage and weep like Robbie. Maybe that would ease the feeling that her heart was being ripped into pieces.

But she'd made this choice, Laura reminded herself. She'd made it with her eyes open, knowing that

Caleb's secrets would compel him to leave her. She had accepted him for who and what he was, wanting only his love. For the rest of her life she would live with that choice. But for all the hurt of it, she would have no regrets.

She didn't see Caleb outside. But then it was so late, he'd probably gone to bed. She hoped he wouldn't mind coming back to the house with her. Surely he'd understand her wanting to be near Robbie.

Her pulse quickened as she hurried toward the shed. The thought of Caleb's arms around her, his warm golden skin gliding against hers as their bodies thrust and mated, made her blood race. She wanted him…needed him…

She reached the shed just as the door swung open.

The first thing she saw was the smoldering tip of a cigarette. In its hellish glow three faces emerged from the darkness—three faces she knew.

Time seemed to stop as she stared at them. The murderer, grizzled, unshaven and cold; the leering monster with yellow eyes and swollen red lips; and the shadow, the dark, quiet boy…

Caleb.

No! Oh, Lord in heaven, no! She reeled backward, stumbling blindly. That was when she heard his voice.

"Run, Laura! Get out of here!"

She wheeled in terror, but it was already too late. The man she'd thought of as the monster for the past five years had already seized her wrists. She fought frantically as he jerked her around and spun her against him. He grinned, showing a mouthful of tobacco-stained teeth. His breath drowned her senses in a miasma of whiskey and rotting meat.

"Let her go, Zeke! Don't hurt her, or so help me, I'll kill you!" Caleb lunged toward her but the older man drew his gun and jammed the muzzle with bruising force against Caleb's belly.

Caleb strained forward as if impaled on the pistol. "For the love of God, Noah, tell him to let her go!" he rasped. "She's not part of this! She hasn't done anything to hurt you!"

"She's had a look at us," the man named Noah growled. "You know what that means. And you'd be smart to watch yourself, brother. It'd pain my conscience to shoot my own kin, but I'd plug the little lady in a twitch. Hellfire, I should've done it five years ago and saved myself the trouble." He holstered his pistol as if daring Caleb to defy him. "Let's get down to the house. There's bound to be some grub there. We can chaw on what to do next while we fill our bellies."

No—not the house! Laura began to struggle again. Let them beat her, rape her or murder her, but they mustn't get to Robbie. Maybe if she could get loose, if she could make them chase her—

With a sudden twist of her body she drove her knee hard into Zeke's groin. He grunted like a bull, doubled over and swore the vilest oath Laura had ever heard. His grip loosened and she tore herself away. For an instant she thought she was free; but then her foot struck a rock. She stumbled. He caught a fistful of her nightgown and slammed her back against him.

"Bitch!" He spat the word in her face. "Try that again and I'll cut your eyes out! I should've screwed you to death when I had the chance!"

Laura sagged against his arm as he half dragged her toward the house. Fighting these men physically would only get her killed. She would have to find some other way to protect her son.

In the past, she'd trained Robbie to be wary of strangers. If that training had sunk deep enough he might remember to hide. But that wasn't likely now. So many things had changed since the day she'd met Caleb McCurdy at the door with the shotgun.

Heaven help her, she should have pulled the trigger.

She could see Caleb out of the corner of her eye, walking next to Noah, avoiding her gaze. How could she not have recognized him after the horror of that day? How could she have allowed herself to love him? He had put her and Robbie in danger by coming here. Worse, he'd lied to her and betrayed a young boy's trust.

Had Caleb contacted his brothers while he was in town, or had they simply followed him? The answer made no difference, Laura realized. Noah had told her all she needed to know. She had seen their faces and could identify them.

She and Robbie would both be killed.

* * *

Sick with dread, Caleb kept his eyes on the ground in front of him. He didn't dare exchange glances with Laura. Not while Noah was watching them both. He needed to keep things calm until he could come up with some kind of plan to save her and Robbie.

Laura would hate him. That was a given. He'd lied to her, shattered her trust and abused her love. His betrayal would break her son's tender heart. But the past was beyond changing. All that mattered now was saving their lives, even if it meant losing his own.

But he would need to be excruciatingly careful. Noah didn't make idle threats. One suspicious move on his part, and Zeke would be unleashed on Laura. After they'd filled their eyes with the horror, both he and Robbie would likely die.

The house was dark, but moonlight flooded the windows. As Noah opened the kitchen door, the desperate hope flashed through Caleb's mind that Robbie might hear strange voices and hide. But he hadn't counted on the dog.

Barking wildly, Buster charged out of Robbie's room and into the kitchen. With a menacing puppy growl, he sank his teeth into Noah's trouser leg.

Noah cursed, shook the pup loose and planted a solid kick in the dog's plump midsection. Buster yelped, whimpered and crept back into Robbie's bedroom.

"You hurt my dog, you dirty, low-down varmint!"

Robbie exploded out of the room, his good arm flailing. Sobbing with fury, he punched and kicked at Noah's leg.

Noah grabbed him by the collar of his nightshirt. "Feisty little bastard," he muttered. "I'll teach you some manners!" He raised his hand to strike.

"No!" Laura's cry tore at Caleb's heart. "Leave him alone! I won't make trouble! I'll do anything you say!"

"Fine." Keeping an iron grip on Robbie, Noah pulled a chair out from the table and sat down. "Light a lamp and fix us some grub. Any tricks, and you'll see what a knife can do to this boy."

He shot a glance at Zeke and nodded his head. Zeke released his hold on Laura who stumbled free, her hair hanging in her face. She brushed it back, lifting her head in a small gesture of defiance. Caleb could sense her terror, sense her silent rage. Lord, how she must hate him.

Her unsteady hand lifted the lantern from its hook above the table, opened the glass side and struck a match. Moving carefully, she touched the flame to the wick. The yellow light flickered and filled the room.

Caleb had been standing in the shadow. Now Robbie noticed him for the first time. "Do something, Mr. Caleb!" he cried. "Get your gun and shoot these bad men!"

"Be quiet, Robbie," Caleb said in a low voice. "Don't do anything that will make these men hurt you or your mother. Understand?"

The boy's mouth tightened. Caleb could see the sparkle of childish faith dying in his eyes.

Laura reached up to replace the lantern on its hook. Its light outlined her bare breasts and lovely, uncorseted body beneath the thin nightgown. Zeke and Noah ogled her, their jaws sagging with lust.

Caleb clenched his teeth in silent fury. He was unarmed, with two beloved hostages to save. He would die for them. He would kill his own flesh and blood for them. But none of that would do any good unless he could get them out of harm's way.

The only weapon he had to use against his brothers was his mind. Somehow that would have to be enough.

Laura lifted her apron from the hook on the door, slipped the neck strap over her head and tied the strings in back. Noah's eyes watched her every move. His chilly gaze raised gooseflesh on her skin. Decently covered now, she turned back to face him.

"I can make coffee," she said. "There's bread and some leftover beans on the stove. For anything else, I'll have to go out to the springhouse."

"What's here will be fine. Just make it fast." Noah's left arm tightened its chest lock around Robbie, who was braced against the side of the wooden chair. The boy hadn't spoken since Caleb's warning to be still. He sagged listlessly, his eyes on the floor, looking as if all the people he'd ever counted on had let him down. Laura ached for him.

Almost afraid to breathe, she took four sticks of kindling from the wood box and thrust them into the stove. Her mind churned frantically as she measured coffee and water into the tall metal pot. Maybe she could get the coffee boiling and fling it into Noah's face, giving her a few seconds to snatch Robbie and run. But then there'd be Zeke to deal with. And there'd be Caleb, who had become a shadow once more, silent and unreadable.

She could see him now, standing against the far wall, out of the light. Could she count on his help, or would he side with his brothers? Once he'd told her that he wanted nothing to do with them. But why should she believe him, after so many lies? What a fool she'd been, letting herself be taken in by the man. She'd been so vulnerable, so hungry for love. She should have known better.

Zeke, restless and twitchy, had wandered into the parlor. Now he came back into the kitchen, grinning. In his hands was the loaded shotgun Laura kept on its rack above the front door.

"Say, look at this new toy I found!" He strode to the table, thumbed back the twin hammers and pointed the double-barrel right at Robbie's head. His finger tightened slowly on the trigger.

Laura sprang for him with a little cry. Caleb lunged, but before either of them could reach him, Zeke laughed, released the trigger and raised the gun. "Got a rise out of you with that one, didn't I?"

Caleb sagged back against the wall. Laura steadied herself against the counter as her knees threatened to give way. Robbie had begun to cry, little hiccupping sobs.

"Unload that gun and give me the shells, you crazy fool," Noah growled. "Hell, you could've shot me instead of the boy." He glanced at Robbie. "Stop your sniveling, you little brat, or I'll give you something to bawl about!"

Zeke ejected the two shells and tossed them onto the table. Then, still grinning, he propped the empty shotgun in the corner. "Not a bad piece. Maybe I'll take it with me when we ride out of here."

"Sit down," Noah snapped. "You, too, little brother. You're making me nervous, standing around like that."

Zeke pulled out a chair and sat down. Caleb, after a moment's hesitation, did the same. In the lamplight his expression was an unreadable mask. Laura unwrapped a loaf of bread and began cutting it into thick slices. On the stove, the coffeepot was begging to hiss.

"Now that's more like it." Noah used his free hand to fish his tobacco pouch out of his pocket and toss it across the table. "Roll me a cigarette, Zeke. Then we can tell little brother here about the job we got planned."

Obediently, Zeke took out a cigarette paper, moistened the edge with his tongue and filled it with a line of loose tobacco.

"You always do just what Noah tells you, don't you, Zeke?" Caleb spoke for the first time in several minutes. "Hell, you might as well be his dog. Stand up. Sit down. Light my cigarette. I'll bet he even does most of your thinking for you, doesn't he?"

"Watch your mouth, boy," Noah snarled.

Caleb ignored him. "I'd lay down money that you don't even take a piss without his say-so. Isn't that right?"

"No, it ain't," Zeke sputtered. "I piss where an' when I want to."

Caleb leaned back in his chair, focusing his attention on Zeke. "When we were growing up, Noah always claimed he was smarter than you. He bossed you around and treated you like a baby. As I see it, he still does, and you let him."

"That ain't so." Zeke's fingers crushed the cigarette he'd just rolled. "I'm bigger an' tougher an' meaner than Noah ever was. He wouldn't be nobody without me!"

Laura's heart crept into her throat as she realized what was happening. Caleb was goading his volatile brothers, trying to ignite a clash that would distract them long enough for her to grab Robbie and get away. If and when he succeeded, she would have to be ready. Her fingers closed around the handle of the coffeepot. Her pulse was racing; her muscles were coiled springs. Silently and wordlessly, she prayed.

"Shut up, both of you!" Noah's fist crashed down on the table. "Zeke, you were never right in the head. And you, little brother, you were nothin' but a snot-nosed half-breed brat. Pa told me to look after you both, and I did. I'm still lookin' after you, for all the thanks I get."

Caleb didn't stir. He was playing a dangerous

game, and Laura knew he was playing it for her and Robbie. Whatever had happened in the past, he was trying to save them now.

"Listen to him, Zeke. He says you aren't right in the head? Do you believe him? Is that why you follow him around like a hound on a leash, licking the crap off his boots? Is that why, when he wants dirty work done, all he has to do is turn you loose?"

Laura risked a glance at Caleb's brothers. Zeke's yellow eyes bulged in the lamplight. Noah's ears had darkened. His neck muscles bulged against his collar. But his left arm remained firmly locked around Robbie.

"You're a fine one to talk, little brother," he snapped. "I shot a man right here to save your stinkin' hides! If I hadn't done it, you'd both be dead! And if I'd shot the woman, too, we wouldn't be havin' this conversation. That bitch has poisoned you against your own kin! I must've been weak in the head when I let you talk me out of killin' her! Well, I don't make the same mistake twice." He reached down, slid his gun out of its holster and thumbed back the hammer. "Coffee's hot. Might as well get this over with now, before—"

The rest of his words were lost in the deafening boom of Zeke's pistol. Noah's body jerked. Then he slumped over the table in a spreading pool of blood.

Chapter Sixteen

Robbie was screaming. Laura snatched him up in her arms. He was wild with terror and splattered with Noah's blood but he didn't appear to be hurt.

"Run, Laura!" Caleb was on his feet. "Take Robbie and get to a horse!"

Not without you! Laura wanted to shout back at him. But she knew better. Her son's safety had to come first. She spun toward the kitchen door, but before she could open it another bullet from Zeke's gun slammed into the wooden door frame, inches from her head.

"Not so fast, little lady." Zeke was standing at the far end of the kitchen, the cocked pistol in his hand and an expression of utter madness on his face. Caleb's strategy had backfired. Noah, while he lived, had kept his brother under control. Without that control, Zeke was a rabid dog, capable of anything.

"I'm callin' the shots now, y' hear? An' you're not

goin' nowhere, little honey, 'less I say so. Now put that boy down nice and slow. Set him on that chair in the corner where I can keep an eye on him. Be nice and sweet to me, and I might let him live." He glanced at Caleb. "You try any tricks, either of you, and the little brat gets a bullet right between the eyes."

Robbie had settled into a fragile silence. Laura lowered his feet to the floor. "Be brave," she whispered, squeezing his shoulders. Without looking at her, he tottered over to the chair and sat. The four of them faced each other in the small kitchen, Laura standing between the foot of the table and the back door, her son in the corner, Zeke standing at the head of the table and Caleb to one side. Noah's body lay slumped in the lamplight, his right arm dangling over the table's edge. A big green horsefly, trapped in the house, buzzed around his head.

"Let them go, Zeke," Caleb said. "I'll do anything you want as long as you don't hurt them."

Zeke's laugh curdled Laura's stomach. "Let 'em go? Hell, I been havin' wet dreams about this little honey for five years. I woulda had her back then if you hadn't come bustin' into that springhouse like Deadeye Dick to the rescue. Served you right, gettin' your shoulder broke like you done. If you'd minded your own business, I'd have showed the lady a good time and rode off, and everything would've been just dandy!"

Laura felt the sudden shock, like a burst of light as her memory cleared. Caleb hadn't rushed into the springhouse to join his brother. He'd been trying to save her! He'd hurt himself, she remembered now, and Zeke had kicked him away. That was when she'd bitten Zeke's arm. And later—yes, it was just as Noah had said. Caleb had talked his brother out of shooting her, thrusting himself in the way to protect her. And when he'd insisted on staying, Noah had knocked him unconscious and dragged him outside. She owed Caleb her life and Robbie's.

"Tell you what, little brother." Zeke was swaggering now, relishing his power. "You haul ol' Noah outside and bury him someplace where he won't stink too bad. I'll stay in here and have me some fun with this little lady. She's gonna treat me real nice, 'cause she knows what'll happen to her boy if she don't."

"You don't want to do that, Zeke." Caleb spoke in a flat, gritty tone that Laura had never heard before.

"The hell I don't. I can do whatever I want." Zeke hesitated, then asked, "Why not?"

"Because there are things I learned from my mother that I never told you about. The Comanches, they've got ways of slow-killing a man that can put him through a hundred living hells. I know them all, Zeke, and I swear on her grave that if you touch this woman or her boy, I'll track you down and make you wish you'd never been born!"

The lamp wick sputtered in the silence that filled the kitchen. Laura glanced back at the chair where Zeke had told Robbie to stay.

The chair was empty.

Her heart leaped. Maybe her son had gotten away and was hiding somewhere safe. But no sooner had that thought crossed Laura's mind than she felt a furtive movement next to her leg. Something cold and heavy slid upward to press against her fingers.

The lamplight cast looming shadows as Caleb faced his half brother over the table. Zeke's eyes were wild in his sallow, unshaven face. A thread of tobacco-stained drool glimmered at one corner of his mouth.

"You don't scare me none, little brother," he said. "I killed Noah. I can sure as hell kill you. All I have to do is pull this trigger."

"Do that, Zeke, and you'll be all alone," Caleb said softly. "The woman won't last. The way you're bound to treat her, she'll die or run off the first chance she gets. I'm your only blood kin. Ride out of here now and I'll stay with you. We can go to Mexico, get some land. The whiskey's cheaper than water down there and the women are hot and willing. Come on, what do you say?"

Zeke hesitated, scowling. Then his mouth spread in an evil grin as he aimed the gun squarely at Caleb. "Mexico can wait. Right now I got a hankerin' for what's between your little sweetheart's legs. An' since I don't trust you any farther than I can spit, little brother, we might as well get this over with..." His finger tightened on the trigger.

Caleb dived for his brother, but he wasn't fast enough to stop the gun from firing. Two shots rang out. One grazed his shoulder. The other slammed into Zeke's chest and sent him staggering backward. He struck the wall and slid slowly to the floor, leaving a long crimson streak down the clean whitewash.

By the time Caleb reached him, Zeke was dead.

Shaken, Caleb straightened and turned around.

Laura stood pale and trembling at the edge of the lamplight. Noah's smoking pistol dangled from her hand.

Caleb loosened the gun from Laura's trembling fingers and laid it on the table. She stood with Robbie clinging to her legs, her face a mask of shock.

Pulling a small quilt from Robbie's bed, Caleb wrapped it around her shoulders. He wanted nothing more than to gather Laura and her son into his arms and hold them close. But that couldn't happen now. He'd betrayed their trust. She would want nothing to do with him.

"Let's get your mother outside, Robbie," he murmured, guiding the two of them toward the back door. "She can rest on the bed in the toolshed for now." He glanced down at the boy. "Can you stay with her and make sure she's all right?"

Robbie nodded, his eyes huge in the lamplight. Sooner or later the boy would have his own fears to deal with. But tonight he'd behaved like a hero. The thought of what he'd done raised a lump in Caleb's throat.

As they neared the door a small movement caught Caleb's eye. Buster had crept into the kitchen to follow his master outside. Scooping him up, Caleb placed the pup in Robbie's arms. Robbie pressed his face against the warm little body. "Good dog," he crooned. "Don't cry, Buster. You're safe now. We're all safe."

Laura had not spoken. She moved like a sleepwalker through the shadows, one hand on Robbie's shoulder, the other clasping the edges of the quilt around her body. Caleb walked beside her with the lamp. He ached to reach out to her and tell her how sorry he was, but it was too late for that now. His terrible secret was out. There was nothing he could do but clean up the horror and move on.

The door to the shed was open. Caleb set the lamp on the tool bench and stepped aside so she could enter. "Stay here," he said. "Try to get some rest. I'll take care of everything."

Laura sank onto the bedroll, drawing Robbie down beside her. She had just killed a man—a crazy, remorseless monster of a man. Her courage had been astounding. Even so, Caleb knew she would need time to get over the shock of what she'd done.

For now, the best thing he could do was leave her alone.

Closing the shed door behind him he walked back toward the house. First he would drag Zeke and Noah's bodies outside, somewhere out of sight. Then he would come back to the house, get a bucket, a brush and some soap, and scrub every trace of blood from Laura's kitchen. When everything was clean and in order he would load the bodies onto his horse, ride up a hidden canyon and dig a grave for his brothers to share.

And after that? Caleb steeled himself as he stepped back over the threshold. Staying here was out of the question. He would do what had to be done. Then he would take Zeke and Noah's horses, maybe sell them somewhere, and keep riding all the way to Mexico. Laura would never have to see his lying face again.

Hellfire, he wouldn't have blamed her if she'd shot him, too.

Robbie had fallen asleep in Laura's arms. For a long time she'd simply held him, soothed by his warm little body and the childish cadence of his breath. But by the time the lamp flickered out, her nerves had stopped screaming and she'd begun to worry.

Where was Caleb?

Lowering Robbie's head to the pillow she tucked the quilt around him and settled Buster against his side. Then she rose, walked to the shed door and eased it open.

The air was warm and still, without so much as a breath of wind. In the east, a streak of dawn silvered the horizon casting its faint light over the silent house and yard. A ragged sob escaped Laura's throat. Her little world was safe at last. But the nightmare would haunt her for a long time to come.

Only one good thing had come out of the ordeal. She knew Caleb's secret and she knew he was blameless. As a boy, he'd done his best to save her. As a man, he'd come back here with nothing but good intentions in his heart.

Heaven help her, she needed him. She needed to feel the strength of his arms keeping her warm and safe. She needed to tell him all was forgiven, to beg him to stay. Why hadn't he come back to her?

I'll take care of everything, he'd told her when he'd left her in the shed. Too drained to speak, Laura had let him. Later there would be time to talk, she'd reasoned. Later they could sort things out and come to some kind of understanding. But that had been hours ago. Had something gone wrong?

Dark shapes shifted in the corral. She could make out the forms of the milk cow and her own two horses. Her heart dropped as she noticed that Caleb's mount was missing.

Laura bit back a cry as she realized what had happened. Believing she would never forgive him, Caleb had put things in order and left.

Frantic, she darted outside. Why hadn't she spoken up at once? Why hadn't she made it clear that she no longer blamed him?

"Caleb!" her voice echoed in the stillness. "Caleb, where are you?" *Please,* she prayed silently. *Please let him hear me!*

Weary in every bone, Caleb was bringing the horses off the mountain. Burying his brothers had left him physically and emotionally exhausted. It had taken hours to dig the grave in the rocky bed of the canyon where Laura would never come across it. It had taken another hour to find the spot where Zeke and Noah had tethered their horses and to dispose of the things in the saddlebags. Bleak and bitter realities had weighed on him the whole time. He had no family. He had no home. And the woman he loved to the depths of his soul would never forgive the wrong he'd done her.

He would ride back by way of Laura's ranch, return the shovel he'd borrowed and take one last look around to make sure everything was all right, Caleb decided. It was early yet. With luck, Laura and Robbie would still be asleep. By the time they awakened he would be long gone.

He was rounding the last bend in the trail when he heard Laura calling his name. A moment later, he saw her standing outside the shed in her white nightgown.

Catching sight of him, she flew up the hillside. By the time he was out of the saddle, she had reached him. With a little sob she flung herself into his arms.

Dizzy with wonder, he held her close. Had a miracle happened? Could it be that she'd forgiven him?

"I thought you'd left us," she whispered. "I was afraid I'd never see you again."

"I thought that was what you wanted—never to see me again." Caleb kissed her tangled hair, her damp eyelids. "Lord, girl, I wasn't even gone and I was already dying of loneliness. I don't know how I could've lived without you."

He held her for a long, silent moment, both of them trembling. "You buried them?" she asked softly.

Caleb nodded, his chin brushing her temple. "The grave's where you won't find it. They were my brothers. I asked God to have mercy on their souls." He exhaled slowly. "You can tell the marshal about them if you want. You can even tell them about me. I just want to put things right once and for all. No more secrets."

Laura shook her head. "What's done is done. I'm through looking back. We have the rest of our lives to build something good here. That's what's important."

"The rest of our lives…" He cradled her in the circle of his arms. Along the desert horizon, clouds glimmered with the first light of a new day. "Can you handle being married to a half-breed and an ex-convict?" he asked cautiously. "It may not be easy at first, getting the town to accept me as your husband."

Laura's only reply was a long, heartfelt kiss.

Epilogue

July 1886

Laura sat with Caleb on the steps of their stone and log house, their two children squeezed comfortably between them. Nine-year-old Robbie and four-year-old Kate were in their night clothes. It was long past their bedtime, but the moonless sky was as clear and dark as obsidian. It was a perfect night for stargazing.

Laura listened contentedly as Caleb pointed out his mother's constellations—the elk, the drum, the seven brothers and so many more. By now the children knew all their names and stories, both Indian and Greek. Caleb was teaching them everything he knew.

Robbie sat with Buster curled at his feet. The bright, gentle boy was growing up to be the image of his father. As for the little tan pup, he had matured into a sturdy, protective dog who followed his master all over the ranch.

Young Kate was also her father's child. Quick and dark and fearless, with a curiosity that matched Caleb's, she was the constant companion of his days.

Laura smiled as she felt the stirring below her ribs. Maybe this new child would be like her, fair and gray-eyed, a lover of peace and beauty.

Caleb had built the new house with his own hands, on a piece of land he'd added to the original ranch. Since then he'd bought more land with the profits from their cattle herd, so that the ranch was more than three times its original size. The first five hundred acres would be Robbie's. The rest would go to their other children, however many they might have.

They rarely spoke of that horrible night when Caleb's half brothers had returned to the ranch. Even Robbie's nightmares had long since ceased. Now they lived for the present and for the future of their family.

"Time for bed!" Caleb declared, pulling the children to their feet. "Run along now. You've already said your prayers."

Kissing their mother good-night, the two of them scampered across the broad porch and into the house. Caleb settled himself behind Laura and pulled her back against him, making a nest for her between his long legs. His hand rested on the growing mound of her belly.

"Tired?" he asked her.

"A little." She twisted her head and grinned up at him. "But not too tired for you."

He chuckled, running his thumb along the curve of her breast. Laura felt his touch as a warm tingle that rippled deliciously through her body. "Let's give those two a little time to settle down before we go inside. Meanwhile, we can watch the show."

Laura leaned back against his chest. Her eyes gazed up at the glittering panorama of the sky, where every falling star was like a wish come true. "Heaven," she whispered.

"So it is." He brushed a kiss along her hairline. "And so it will be."

* * * * *

Every Life Has More
Than One Chapter™

Award-winning author Stevi Mittman delivers another hysterical mystery, featuring Teddi Bayer, an irrepressible heroine, and her to-die-for hero, Detective Drew Scoones. After all, life on Long Island can be murder!

Turn the page for a sneak peek at the warm and funny fourth book,
WHOSE NUMBER IS UP, ANYWAY?,
in the Teddi Bayer series,
by STEVI MITTMAN.
On sale August 7

CHAPTER 1

Before redecorating a room, I always advise my clients to empty it of everything but one chair. Then I suggest they move that chair from place to place, sitting in it, until the placement feels right. Trust your instincts when deciding on furniture placement. Your room should "feel right."

—TipsFromTeddi.com

Gut feelings. You know, that gnawing in the pit of your stomach that warns you that you are about to do the absolute stupidest thing you could do? Something that will ruin life as you know it?

I've got one now, standing at the butcher counter in King Kullen, the grocery store in the same strip mall as L.I. Lanes, the bowling alley cum billiard parlor I'm in the process of redecorating for its "Grand Opening."

I realize being in the wrong supermarket probably doesn't sound exactly dire to you, but you aren't the one buying your father a brisket at a store your mother will somehow know isn't Waldbaum's.

And then, June Bayer isn't your mother.

The woman behind the counter has agreed to go into the freezer to find a brisket for me, since there aren't any in the case. There are packages of pork tenderloin, piles of spare ribs and rolls of sausage, but no briskets.

Warning Number Two, right? I should be so out of here.

But no, I'm still in the same spot when she comes back out, brisketless, her face ashen. She opens her mouth as if she is going to scream, but only a gurgle comes out.

And then she pinballs out from behind the counter, knocking bottles of Peter Luger Steak Sauce to the floor on her way, now hitting the tower of cans at the end of the prepared foods aisle and sending them sprawling, now making her way down the aisle, careening from side to side as she goes.

Finally, from a distance, I hear her shout, "He's deeeeeeaaaad! Joey's deeeeeaaaad."

My first thought is *You should always trust your gut.*

My second thought is that now, somehow, my mother will know I was in King Kullen. For weeks I will have to hear "What did you expect?" as though whenever you go to King Kullen someone turns up dead. And if the detective investigating the case turns out to be Detective Drew Scoones…well, I'll never hear the end of that from her, either.

She still suspects I murdered the guy who was found dead on my doorstep last Halloween just to get Drew back into my life.

Several people head for the butcher's freezer and I position myself to block them. If there's one thing I've learned from finding people dead—and the guy on my doorstep wasn't the first one—it's that the police get very testy when you mess with their murder scenes.

"You can't go in there until the police get here," I say, stationing myself at the end of the butcher's counter and in front of the Employees Only door, acting as if I'm some sort of authority. "You'll contaminate the evidence if it turns out to be murder."

Shouts and chaos. You'd think I'd know better than to throw the word *murder* around. Cell phones are flipping open and tongues are wagging.

I amend my statement quickly. "Which, of course, it probably isn't. Murder, I mean. People die all the time, and it's not always in hospitals or their own beds, or…" I babble when I'm nervous, and the idea of someone dead on the other side of the freezer door makes me very nervous.

So does the idea of seeing Drew Scoones again. Drew and I have this on-again, off-again sort of thing…that I kind of turned off.

Who knew he'd take it so personally when he tried to get serious and I responded by saying we could talk about *us* tomorrow—and then caught a plane to my parents' condo in Boca the next day? In July. In the middle of a job.

For some crazy reason, he took that to mean that I was avoiding him and the subject of *us*.

That was three months ago. I haven't seen him since.

The manager, who identifies himself and points to his nameplate in case I don't believe him, says he has to go into *his cooler*. "Maybe Joey's not dead," he says. "Maybe he can be saved, and you're letting him die in there. Did you ever think of that?"

In fact, I hadn't. But I had thought that the murderer might try to go back in to make sure his tracks were covered, so I say that I will go in and check.

Which means that the manager and I couple up and go in together while everyone pushes against the doorway to peer in, erasing any chance of finding clean prints on that Employee Only door.

I expect to find carcasses of dead animals hanging from hooks, and maybe Joey hanging from one, too. I think it's going to be very creepy and I steel myself, only to find a rather benign series of shelves with large slabs of meat laid out carefully on them, along with boxes and boxes marked simply Chicken.

Nothing scary here, unless you count the body of a middle-aged man with graying hair sprawled faceup on the floor. His eyes are wide open and unblinking. His shirt is stiff. His pants are stiff. His body is stiff. And his expression, you should forgive the pun—is frozen. Bill-the-manager crosses himself and stands mute while I pronounce the guy dead in a sort of *happy now?* tone.

"We should not be in here," I say, and he nods his head emphatically and helps me push people out of the doorway just in time to hear the police sirens and see the cop cars pull up outside the big store windows.

Bobbie Lyons, my partner in Teddi Bayer Interior Designs (and also my neighbor, my best friend and my private fashion police), and Mark, our carpenter (and my dogsitter, confidant and ego booster), rush in from next door. They beat the cops by a half step and shout out my name. People point in my direction.

After all the publicity that followed the unfortunate incident during which I shot my ex-husband, Rio Gallo, and then the subsequent murder of my first client—which I solved, I might add—it seems like the whole world, or at least all of Long Island, knows who I am.

Mark asks if I'm all right. (Did I remember to mention that the man is drop-dead-gorgeous-but-a-decade-too-young-for-me-yet-too-old-for-my-daughter-thank-god?) I don't get a chance to answer him because the police are quickly closing in on the store manager and me.

"The woman—" I begin telling the police. Then I have to pause for the manager to fill in her name, which he does: *Fran.*

I continue. "Right. Fran. Fran went into the freezer to get a brisket. A moment later she came out and screamed that Joey was dead. So I'd say she was the one who discovered the body."

"And you are...?" the cop asks me. It comes out a bit like who do I *think* I am, rather than who am I really?

"An innocent bystander," Bobbie, hair perfect, makeup just right, says, carefully placing her body between the cop and me.

"And she was just leaving," Mark adds. They each take one of my arms.

Fran comes into the inner circle surrounding the cops. In case it isn't obvious from the hairnet and bloodstained white apron with Fran embroidered on it, I explain that she was the butcher who was going for the brisket. Mark and Bobbie take that as a signal that I've done my job and they can now get me out of there. They twist around, with me in the middle, as if we're a Rockettes line, until we are facing away from the butcher counter. They've managed to propel me a few steps toward the exit when disaster—in the form of a Mazda RX7 pulling up at the loading curb—strikes.

Mark's grip on my arm tightens like a vise. "Too late," he says.

Bobbie's expletive is unprintable. "Maybe there's a back door," she suggests, but Mark is right. It's too late.

I've laid my eyes on Detective Scoones. And while my gut is trying to warn me that my heart shouldn't go there, regions farther south are melting at just the sight of him.

"Walk," Bobbie orders me.

And I try to. Really.

Walk, I tell my feet. *Just put one foot in front of the other.*

I can do this because I know, in my heart of hearts, that if Drew Scoones was still interested in me, he'd have gotten in touch with me after I returned from Boca. And he didn't.

Since he's a detective, Drew doesn't have to wear one of those dark blue Nassau County Police uniforms. Instead, he's got on jeans, a tight-fitting T-shirt and a tweedy sports jacket. If you think that sounds good, you should see him. Chiseled features, cleft chin, brown hair that's naturally a little sandy in the front, a smile that...well, that doesn't matter. He isn't smiling now.

He walks up to me, tucks his sunglasses into his breast pocket and looks me over from head to toe.

"Well, if it isn't Miss Cut and Run," he says. "Aren't you supposed to be somewhere in Florida or something?" He looks at Mark accusingly, as if he was covering for me when he told Drew I was gone.

"Detective Scoones?" one of the uniforms says. "The stiff's in the cooler and the woman who found him is over there." He jerks his head in Fran's direction.

Drew continues to stare at me.

You know how when you were young, your mother always told you to wear clean underwear in case you were in an accident? And how, a little farther on, she told you not to go out in hair rollers because you never knew who you might see—or who might see you? And how now your best friend says she wouldn't be caught dead without makeup and suggests you shouldn't either?

Okay, today, *finally,* in my overalls and Converse sneakers, I get it.

I brush my hair out of my eyes. "Well, I'm back," I say. As if he hasn't known my exact whereabouts. The man is a detective, for heaven's sake. "Been back awhile."

Bobbie has watched the exchange and apparently decided she's given Drew all the time he deserves. "And we've got work to do, so…" she says, grabbing my arm and giving Drew a little two-fingered wave goodbye.

As I back up a foot or two, the store manager sees his chance and places himself in front of Drew, trying to get his attention. Maybe what makes Drew such a good detective is his ability to focus.

Only what he's focusing on is me.

"Phone broken? Carrier pigeon died?" he asks me, taking in Fran, the manager, the meat counter and that Employees Only door, all without taking his eyes off me.

Mark tries to break the spell. "We've got work to do there, you've got work to do here, Scoones," Mark says to him, gesturing toward next door. "So it's back to the alley for us."

Drew's lip twitches. "You working the alley now?" he says.

"If you'd like to follow me," Bill-the-manager, clearly exasperated, says to Drew—who doesn't respond. It's as if waiting for my answer is all he has to do.

So, fine. "You knew I was back," I say.

The man has known my whereabouts every hour of the day for as long as I've known him. And my mother's not the only one who won't buy that he "just happened" to answer this particular call. In fact, I'm willing to bet my children's lunch money that he's taken every call within ten miles of my home since the day I got back.

And now he's gotten lucky.

"*You* could have called *me,*" I say.

"You're the one who said *tomorrow* for our talk and then flew the coop, chickie," he says. "I figured the ball was in your court."

"Detective?" the uniform says. "There's something you ought to see in here."

Drew gives me a look that amounts to *in or out?* He could be talking about the investigation, or about our relationship.

Bobbie tries to steer me away. Mark's fists are balled. Drew waits me out, knowing I won't be able to resist what might be a murder investigation.

Finally he turns and heads for the cooler.

And, like a puppy dog, I follow.

Bobbie grabs the back of my shirt and pulls me to a halt.

"I'm just going to show him something," I say, yanking away.

"Yeah," Bobbie says, pointedly looking at the buttons on my blouse. The two at breast level have popped. "That's what I'm afraid of."

HARLEQUIN

COMING NEXT MONTH FROM

HARLEQUIN® HISTORICAL

- **WHIRLWIND BABY**
  by **Debra Cowan**
  (Western)
  When rancher Jake Ross finds a baby on his doorstep, he has to hire a nanny—and fast! All he needs is someone to take care of the child, so why can't he get Emma York out of his mind?

- **DISHONOR AND DESIRE**
  by **Juliet Landon**
  (Regency)
  Caterina Chester has kept her passionate nature tightly confined. After she is forced into marriage, it seems that her most improper husband may be the only man who can free her!

- **A NOTORIOUS WOMAN**
  by **Amanda McCabe**
  (European)
  Venice is a city filled with passion, mystery and danger. Especially for a beautiful perfumer suspected of murder, when the only man who can save her has been ordered to kill her.

- **AN UNLADYLIKE OFFER**
  by **Christine Merrill**
  (Regency)
  St. John is intent on mending his rakish ways. He won't seduce an innocent virgin. But Esme is determined and beautiful, and her offer is very, very tempting....

HHCNM0707